A WICKED...

VALERIE SAXON

CHIMERA

A Wicked Conquest first published in 2006 by
Chimera Publishing Ltd
PO Box 152
Waterlooville
Hants
PO8 9FS

Printed and bound in Great Britain by
Cox & Wyman, Reading.

This book is sold subject to the condition that it shall not, by way of trade or otherwise, be lent, resold, hired out or otherwise circulated without the publisher's prior written consent in any form of binding or cover other than that in which it is published, and without a similar condition being imposed on the subsequent purchaser.

The characters and situations in this book are entirely imaginary and bear no relation to any real person or actual happening.

Copyright © Valerie Saxon

The right of Valerie Saxon to be identified as author of this book has been asserted in accordance with section 77 and 78 of the Copyrights Designs and Patents Act 1988.

A WICKED CONQUEST

Valerie Saxon

This novel is fiction – in real life practice safe sex

The lanky one leered down at her, his cock engorged with excitement. 'Watch and learn, my friend,' he taunted the fat one. 'Watch and learn. Mayhap women would be more willing to open their legs if you had something more exciting to offer.'

Rowena's eyes glazed over purposefully. If she thought of other things he would not be able to touch her, not the part of her that mattered, anyway. But to her dismay his cock had steel and he knew how to wield it to pleasure them both.

'Come,' he said, panting into her ear, 'let's have a good fuck, you and I.'

Chapter One

Rowena spread her arms wide, glad to be free of the burh. It was beautiful in the forest and so far removed from all the evil that was fast winging its way towards them. She had spent the entire morning in earnest prayer with her mother. Then, feeling the need for some respite, she had gone for a walk, slipping away foolishly despite Grainne's warnings. It had not been easy; she was forced to bribe one of the guards on the ramparts in order to exit the stronghold. Now she must make haste to return before her absence was noticed.

She touched her breasts uneasily. Eadred had been stubborn, refusing to allow her through the gate. She had sighed with disappointment, her bosom rising with her intake of breath. Eadred's eyes almost popped out of his head, giving her an idea.

She sighed deeply again and watched with satisfaction when his gaze settled longingly on her womanly shape. 'Of course,' she said hesitantly, fluttering her eyelashes at him, 'I would reward you well if you please me.'

'How well?'

His eyes had not risen once above the swell of her bosom, and she leaned into him with a sly smile. 'I shall leave that to your imagination.' Despite her virginal state the thought of Eadred, a fine looking man, touching her breasts, taking the nipples in his mouth and sucking them as she had seen him do to her cousin Gilda, made the roseate tips blush and swell. The tender bud that lay between her legs began to throb and she dropped her head with shame. What was she thinking?

But the seed was sown. Eadred's mouth dropped open and he nodded quickly, as though the gift of speech had deserted him, and casting a keen eye around them allowed her through the gate to freedom.

A loud noise startled her, and she cast her eyes nervously around for any sign of danger, for there was plenty in the forest. Bands of thieves roamed there and a body was not safe in such territory.

Satisfied that the noise had been that of an animal, or a branch falling from a tree, she let out a relieved sigh. But her relief was not to last; a thunderclap rent the air, followed by a fork of lightning. Clouds cloaked the sun and it felt as if the very ground she stood on was charged with danger. It was as though the land was possessed, aware of the peril that awaited her father and brothers, all of them if the men were not successful this day.

Her green eyes widened in fear, the balmy afternoon had been transformed into a raging tempest, the sky so overcast it was like night descending. Trees that had previously shaded her from the glare of sunshine took on an avenging profile as they swayed against the storm. Her clothes flapped around her, but gritting her teeth she clutched the hood of her mantle and made her way through the forest heading for the burh.

The wind took her breath away, forcing her to gasp for air. A few yards hence she shuddered to a halt as a large, dark shape took form out of the shadows of the trees. The strangest uttering poured forth from its inhuman face and Rowena dug her nails into the brooch that held her mantle, as though its solidity would give her courage, rid the forest of the monstrous being. Rain began to fall heavy as stones and in moments she was soaked through. But still she could not will her limbs to move, motivate herself away from the apparition of evil, as evil it must surely be.

The flapping of wings distracted her, as part of the apparition appeared to change itself into a bird. She closed her eyes against the spectre, trying to persuade herself it was a figment of her imagination brought about by the stress of the day. She prayed silently. Why hadn't she listened to her mother, who warned her against the terrors of the forest often enough?

Her ears strained for sounds above that of the thundering wind, the pounding rain, the nearby stream, already turned into a rushing torrent. There was a strange gurgle. She forced herself to look, and as lightning forked the sky she saw blood and feathers mix with the water of the stream, a toothless smile as the old hag held out her arms in supplication to ancient deities.

Rowena was overcome with relief and felt suddenly foolish. 'Cwendritha, 'tis you. You almost frightened me out of my skin!'

The old crone looked down at her crude shrine before facing Rowena warily. She had been found out! Picking up the wooden idol she thrust it beneath her mantle. 'I did not think to see anyone here.'

Rowena shook her head and scolded, 'You know it's wicked to practice the old ways, Cwendritha. Father Edwin has already warned you about such things.'

Cwendritha wiped the chicken blood from her knife on the leaves and moss at her feet, and had the grace to look mildly ashamed. She was fond of the thane's daughter with the sweet oval face. The girl was so beautiful it puzzled her that she could remain so completely unaware of her attributes. She suppressed a smirk. She had seen many a man ogle her with hot eyes, wishing their aching members could be eased in the secret garden that lay between her sweet thighs.

Rowena was waiting for an answer. Cwendritha shrugged her shoulders. ''Tis my duty to offer up a sacrifice for protection,' she explained defensively, tucking the knife away safely.

'We shall all need protection if the northmen are not defeated,' Rowena replied soberly. 'And you would be better served offering your prayers in the church than to some pagan god.'

The old hag sniffed disdainfully. 'I can't see the harm in honouring both. I'm sure the situation warrants as much help as possible.'

Rowena saw the stubborn set of Cwendritha's mouth

and knew it was pointless arguing with her. If Father Edwin could not reason with the old woman, what chance did she have?

'I must get back to the burh,' she said with a sigh, turning away. 'Mother will need me. And you should return too, Cwendritha.'

The woman followed in Rowena's wake, her shoes squelching in the mud, her claw-like fingers held determinedly on to her headrail as the wind threatened to steal it away. 'The poor lady has more reasons than most to be afeared this day.'

Rowena nodded her agreement, her head down against the driving rain as she managed to avoid some foraging pigs that were guzzling acorns. Her mother, Grainne, an Irish princess, had been stolen away from her land by the Norse as a young woman. Luckily, she escaped when they continued their plunder along the English coast.

Rowena's father, Athelwine, had found the lovely young girl and promptly fallen in love with her. He had taken her to his home and made her his wife. She served him faithfully and gave him two more children, Rowena and Athelstan.

Cwendritha's thoughts ran along the same path as Rowena's, for she knew more about it than most. The Irish princess confided in the old woman. It had seemed like yesterday when Grainne came to her hut, her eyes brimming with tears.

'What troubles you, mistress?' she had asked worriedly.

'I am so ashamed, Cwendritha.' Her beautiful hair was a dark cloud around her white face. 'And I don't know where else to turn. You seem to brew much magic and you have healing powers.'

'What can I do?'

She wrung her hands. 'When I was taken by the heathens their leader touched me between my legs.' Her tears ran faster. 'I tried to protest, tried to stop him, but he would not listen. His massive head came down to my level and he kissed me.' She shuddered. 'It was horrible. His hands grabbed my breasts and the more I struggled the more forceful he became.'

She had been quite overcome and Cwendritha encouraged her. 'Go on. If you will not confide in me I cannot help you.'

'He bore me to his bed and forced me to remove my clothes.' She wiped her wet cheeks with the back of her hand. 'As I stood there naked and trembling he kissed my breasts. I was repulsed by him, and... and yet I felt my body thrill to his touch. I was so confused that when he lifted me and lay me down I only half struggled because part of me, that wicked part deep inside, wanted him.'

Cwendritha nodded. 'Was he handsome?'

'He had the finest pair of shoulders I have ever seen, and the reddest beard and the bluest eyes,' she said dreamily, before hanging her head in shame.

''Tis only natural to feel so when an exciting man touches you.'

'Is it natural to want him to fondle me in all my private places? I pushed my breasts towards his mouth and almost swooned with ecstasy when he sucked the nipples. His hands made whorls on my stomach, his fingers so rough and yet so tender.' She shivered with the memory. 'When he covered my mound I opened my thighs to him, my pulses racing and the private place between my legs weeping with need.'

'And then?'

'He stroked me, down there,' she said, inclining her head, blushing profusely. 'I had never believed anything could be so wonderful. By this time I'd have given all I possessed as long as he did not stop. Then he disrobed and I was amazed to see he had a massive staff between his legs, and a great sack that he said contained his seed. He bade me touch his staff and when I did it grew even bigger.' She bit her lip. 'I am ashamed to say that I was thrilled to feel the wonderful power of this rod, to see the tiny droplets that came from its eye. My red-bearded heathen bid me slide it up inside my private tunnel. I did and it was the most lovely feeling I had ever experienced. Although I'd thought it far too big, it fit me well and I sighed as he drove in and out of me like a bull.' She dropped her head once more. 'We did it many times in the weeks I was with him and he was most kind to me.'

'So why did you run away?'

'I escaped because I was ashamed of what I was doing. I was enjoying a man without wedlock, a man who worshipped false gods.'

'What's the trouble now?'

She began to cry again, distressed sobs that rent Cwendritha's heart. 'I am about to wed Athelwine and he believes me to be untouched. When he realises I have lain with another he will cast me out.'

Cwendritha smiled. 'There is an easy way out of this dilemma. ''Tis a trick women have used time and time again. I will give you a pig's bladder filled with blood. You must secrete it somewhere on your person. When your husband takes you pierce the pig's bladder and when he sees the stain he will believe he deflowered you himself.'

Grainne had been radiant with gratitude and relief, and Cwendritha kept her secret well – although the princess never returned for the pig's bladder, leaving her to wonder what she told her husband on their wedding night.

Cwendritha realised she had been lost in the past and quickly resumed her conversation. 'I thought the king had sent all the heathens off with fleas in their ears,' she complained.

Rowena was intent on keeping her footing on the slippery ground. 'Father says there will always be the odd band of northmen coming from over the seas to try their luck.'

It was the same ilk that was a danger to them now.

They had threatened to attack if a price was not paid for peace. Athelwine had declared that he would not be dictated to by vermin and immediately set off, heading the militia, to fight off the invaders.

Rowena shuddered violently and shrugged deeper into her mantle but, no matter what, she could not dispel the mixture of excitement and terror that warred in her belly. For if the militia failed the vermin would plunder the burh, taking many slaves when they left.

'No doubt father has made contact with them by now,' she remarked, with more conviction than she felt, wiping the water from her face with the hem of her mantle. 'And taught them a lesson they will not forget.'

'Would that you were right,' Cwendritha replied, panting heavily from her exertions. 'If not...' She shrugged her shoulders; there was no need for her to go on. They were like a disease striking when least expected, leaving death and deprivation in their wake.

Rowena stopped for the old woman to catch her breath, wiping mud from her new leather shoes with a stick. She smiled bravely. 'If father is outnumbered I am sure he will agree to pay their price.' She crossed her fingers as she spoke, for although Athelwine was a wealthy thane with much land, he had sworn to fight to the death before handing over any of his silver.

When the earthworks of the sturdy timber enclosure came into view, Rowena regarded it sadly. The previous day it had been a hive of industry, now all was quiet. Many were in the church, and others went about their business silently.

Parting from Cwendritha she spied Eadred, the warrior she had bribed earlier. He was guarding the ramparts and watching for her anxiously. He laid his shield aside and patted his sword meaningfully. 'You'll be the death of me, my lady. If your father finds out what I've done he'll feed me to the dogs.'

Rowena laughed. 'Have no fear, I'm hear now.' She had brought him wild flowers from the forest, considering them payment enough for his service. 'These are for you.'

Emboldened by her gesture Eadred edged close, pushing his ridged cap back from his forehead. He wanted nothing to come between him and the lovely vision of the thane's daughter. 'Can we meet up later?'

His hand was shaking as he reached out to touch her shoulder and Rowena shook her head. 'I think not, Eadred. 'Tis not a day for assignations.'

Recalling the reward he had been promised the young man licked his bottom lip. 'I can make you forget the troubles. Just stick your fingers on me breeches and feel how hard my dick is for you. One suck o' that and you'll want no other.'

His breeches were stretched over his large erection and Rowena stiffened. She had seen her younger brother naked but had never seen anything like that which Eadred was pointing to. She gave a small sniff. 'You'd better pay attention to your duty. If my father finds you lacking he will do more than feed you to the dogs.'

Rowena turned on her heel and his hot eyes followed her as she skirted the wattle and daub huts of the militia. He watched as she waved to Alfred the moneyer, who worked in the mint producing coinage, her dainty womanly figure making him ache for her. Then unable to stand any more he faced the timber fence and taking his penis from his breeches masturbated, thinking longingly of the soft flesh that had been so close to his own. He was so worked up that he spurted his seed within seconds and surreptitiously fed his cock back into his breeches.

Rowena sought her mother in the church but Grainne had already left, so she said a prayer with Father Edwin before continuing on to her mother's bower.

The burh was cluttered with animals that had been brought in for safety, and she was obliged to push her way through some cross-looking goats and bedraggled geese who honked at her with disdain. The hens clucked disagreeably at being disturbed and waddled away with a flapping of wings and a flurry of feathers, causing Rowena to laugh.

Passing the weaving sheds and kitchen, she shed her mantle and shook it in the doorway before entering Grainne's bower. Her mother was busy at her needlework, surrounded by her ladies. Her gentle smile warmed Rowena's heart and she marvelled at her composure, for she knew that behind that calm façade Grainne was deeply worried.

She gave a gasp at her daughter's disarray. 'Rowena, where have you have been? You've been missing a goodly time and are soaked through.'

'With Cwendritha,' she replied quickly, hoping Grainne would assume she had merely been passing the time of day with the old woman. She did not wish to cause her mother distress by telling her she'd been wandering in the forest with the heathens at large.

'You will catch your death, child!' Aunt Elfrida clucked, horrified at her niece's bedraggled state.

Rowena smiled and dried her hair with the towel her mother handed her. 'I should have stayed and worked my needle,' she said contritely.

'You should have a lusty husband to tend.' Elfrida giggled. 'A few inches of hard meat between those virginal thighs would soon put a twinkle in your eyes. You're well passed the age of marrying. I can't imagine what your father's thinking. At your age I already had three children and was soon abed with my fourth.' She nudged the knee of her friend. 'My Alfred liked a good tumble, God rest his soul.'

Grainne gave her sister-in-law a disapproving glare. 'Athelwine is waiting to find a suitable match for his daughter.'

Rowena blushed. 'I am in no hurry to wed,' she said shyly.

She watched her mother work. It was obvious why Athelwine had fallen for the dark-haired Irish princess, and she wondered why she had not inherited any of her charms; a fact her father often remarked upon. He was sorely disappointed in his daughter in every way.

Grainne wielded her needle gracefully. 'Athelwine has had a lot on his mind. I'm sure he will defer to the matter in time.' She smiled up at Rowena. 'Hurry and change out of your clothes, child, or you will surely catch your death.'

The green eyes so like her own dwelt on her kindly, and Rowena's heart went out to her, she was so brave. She fluffed out her red-gold curls until they were like a halo around her head and shoulders, quite unaware of the lovely picture she made. 'Let me sit here a while and feel the warmth of the fire.' She was loath to admit that her limbs were still shaking; the experience in the forest had upset her more than she'd thought.

The ladies' fingers worked industriously. It was cosy in the bower. She stretched and yawned, but the languor was not to last. The sound of horses brought them to their feet and the colour drained from Grainne's face.

They rushed to the door, terrified of what awaited them on the outside. When it was flung open her father, Athelwine of Wessex, came riding towards them, his colours flying free, side by side with the banner of another.

As the other ladies squeezed into the small space behind Grainne and Rowena, their voices broke into an excited babble. There for all the world to see was the standard of the raven, the symbol of the Vikings!

All talking ceased as quickly as it had begun, the awesome sight stunned them. The men dismounted and made for the great hall before anyone moved. Rowena felt her mother go limp and put her arms out to cushion her fall. Gilda and Everild helped her inside and eased her to a seat.

Luckily the faint did not last long. Rowena was busy rubbing her hands when she came around. Grainne, though white of face, was appalled by her weakness, and after just a few moments in which to compose herself,

The stranger removed his helmet and his blue eyes seemed to sear her like a flame.

She trembled uncontrollably beneath his regard. Her mantle had been blown aside in her haste to reach the hall, and her kirtle and tunic still being damp, clung to her body like a second skin. Her full breasts, tiny waist and curving hips brought a gleam of admiration to those eyes. Only then did she know why he was staring at her so intently.

Her breasts tingled beneath his regard, and to her shame the small nub sited between her thighs pulsed with need. She adjusted her clothing, blushing furiously. She was wanton! How was it possible for her body to act in such a way? Had he met her in the woods he would have thought nothing of defiling her. As it was, he was guest of her father and as such must be treated with courtesy. She dropped her eyes as a maiden should and her father appeared to be pleased with her demeanour.

With a satisfied grin Sigurd Thorkelsson turned away, exposing the left side of his face, and it was her turn to stare, for there partially covered by his beard was a deep scar. But instead of marring his looks it seemed to add something to the lean, piratical face.

Athelwine introduced him to the other ladies, and although they were all shocked at having heathens in their midst, their inbred manners came to the fore. Grainne immediately ordered refreshments to be brought. Towels were swiftly supplied and warm water from the heavy cauldron that hung from the rafters over the fire. The men sat wearily at trestle tables that had been set up and greedily fell upon the food and drink before them.

Elfrida shook her head in disbelief. 'I never thought to see such a thing, Norse and Saxon warriors breaking bread together.'

Grainne swallowed nervously, trying to still her trembling hands. 'I am grateful we have ample supplies. The rest of the heathen army is camped outside the burh and Athelwine has ordered that food and ale be taken out rose and commanded they all repair to the hall. The Irish princess was made of sterner stuff than any of them had ever realised. With sinking hearts they retrieved their mantles and followed in her wake.

The gabled entrance hall was cluttered with weapons of all description, for they were banned from the hall itself. But when they followed Grainne in to the interior of the building some of the ladies gasped. 'The northmen still have their weapons. We are doomed.'

Rowena bit her lip worriedly; the situation was indeed volatile.

The hall thronged with people, and everyone seemed to be talking at once. Athelwine held up his hand for silence. 'Our guests are here to strike a bargain, not to war with us.'

'How is that possible?' Rowena whispered to her aunt, who was the closest to her. 'How are we able to feel safe under the circumstances?'

Elfrida shook her head. 'I know not, niece.' Her hands were shaking; Rowena patted them gently.

Grainne rushed to her husband's side, relieved that none of her family seemed to have sustained serious injury. Rowena turned curious eyes on the strangers in their midst. They were all huge, and the largest of all sat at Athelwine's side, clad in mail and helmet like her father – his nose shield making him appear even more formidable. Scorning the many beads, rings and other decorations worn by his men, his only gilding was the brooch that held his mantle, and a single armband, the sign of a chieftain.

'Sigurd Thorkelsson, great chieftain of the Norse, meet Grainne, my wife,' Athelwine said with pride,' patting the ornate arms of the Yppe, the chair in which he sat – the high seat of the lord. 'And this is my daughter, Rowena, a rare jewel in any man's language.'

Rowena was unable to hide her surprise; her dour father gushing about her looks! It was unheard of. Something was not right here.

to them.'

Elfrida made a moue with her mouth. 'I wonder what is in the wind, sister. Nothing good, I'll be bound.'

Athelwine ordered Rowena to sit on the raised dais at the end of the hall, between Sigurd Thorkelsson and himself, which both worried and surprised her. It was not like her father to show her so much favour.

All through the meal she felt the Norse pirate's icy-blue eyes assess her unblinkingly. Her ire began to rise. He is looking at me as though he is about to purchase me, she thought angrily, and abruptly turned away from him. But the cold eyes did not leave her and her own gaze returned unerringly to the man. It was as though she had no will of her own where the stranger was concerned.

'You are not happy with our presence in your hall, Rowena, daughter of Athelwine,' he remarked dryly.

His English was good, but she wondered why the words 'daughter of Athelwine' seemed to be laced with irony. She forced herself to view him calmly, blatantly matching his steady gaze. 'You are my father's guest; my opinion is of no consequence.'

'I am curious.'

She was annoyed at having been put in this position, and something deep inside her rebelled. 'Then your observation is correct,' she snapped rudely.

Sigurd laughed long and loud, causing curious glances around the hall. Rowena bristled; she'd said nothing amusing. How dare he laugh at her?

'You are not afraid of me, Rowena?' he asked, when his mirth had died down.

'Should I be?' She tried to appear unconcerned. She would not waver before him.

'It would be prudent.' For a moment the blue chips of ice brought chills to her spine, but then he laughed. 'You have pleased me. I like a woman with spirit.'

Rowena pursed her lips. She did not want to please him! He was a ruthless fiend, yet she was unable to shake off the attraction that festered inside her like a fever. Her throat was dry; she raised her goblet to her mouth and drank deeply of the mead, and as she did so her sleeve fell back to reveal the sinuous birthmark on her wrist.

Sigurd grasped her arm firmly. 'What mark is this?'

Startled by his action she paled, and Grainne, who had just joined them on the raised dais, shook visibly. ''Tis a birthmark,' she explained, trying to shake off his strong grip. He released her thoughtfully. Was she wrong or was there a gleam of satisfaction in his eyes?

'What is your age?' he asked boldly.

She wanted to slap his inquisitive face, tell him it was none of his business, but she knew she could not besmirch her father's hospitality in such a way. 'Eighteen summers,' she snapped angrily.

'Your information is grudging, lady. Am I right in thinking you are disappointed that my Nordic blood is not replenishing the earth of Wessex this day?'

It was her turn to smile. If he were trying to shock her he would be disappointed. 'I cannot deny it,' she said sweetly.

Athelwine, who had been busy placating her mother, overheard Rowena's remark, gasped and angrily swept his hand across her mouth in a stinging slap. 'You are here to honour our guests. Apologise immediately.'

Rowena's fingers lifted to her painful mouth. She had gone too far this time. Grainne had always said her impetuous tongue would be the death of them all. 'Forgive me, sire,' she said, hiding her face, blushing with embarrassment.

Sigurd studied her closely for a few moments that seemed like an eternity. She wriggled nervously beneath his all-encompassing stare, and she noticed that Athelwine's face had turned deathly pale. She waited for an explosion of anger that did not come. Instead Sigurd turned to her father.

'I will have no trouble in accepting your terms, Athelwine of Wessex. The wench has appeal. I look forward to taming her. A few strokes of the whip will soon show her who is master.'

Grainne gave a small cry and looked as though she were about to faint again. Athelwine expelled his breath loudly and his mouth broke into a broad grin. 'That is good, my friend.' He clapped Sigurd on the back. 'The bargain is struck.'

Rowena looked to her mother to see huge tears coursing down her face. She was too stunned to feel anything but confusion, but that soon passed to leave a deep, cold fear. All the while her body was betraying her he was looking her over like a piece of meat.

She was not cowardly, and she was well used to being punished. Even Father Edwin had been given cause to chastise her more than once for her bad behaviour. Her bottom still stung when she recalled the times he'd found her dreaming in the church, when she should have been attending to her devotions.

She knew she'd deserved being put over his knee. But she did hate it when he lifted her skirts and slapped her hard on her bare cheeks. And even when he finished he wouldn't let her up. He made her lie there, half-naked with her skirts in the air, while she contemplated her sins.

The men rose to toast one another and her stupefied mind studied the man to whom she had been betrothed. Although they were heathens the Norse were not filthy, unkempt beings as she had surmised. Apart from the obvious soiling on his clothes from the fray, this particular individual was neat and clean.

He stood tall and proud in his red mantle that hung almost to the floor front and back, a gold brooch pinning it on his right shoulder. His hair, which was cut off at the neck, not long like that of the Saxons, was as golden as the summer sun. His neat beard and moustache were of the same colour. She had to admit he was striking, taller and broader by far than any other man in the hall, and beneath the handsome façade was a devil who had promised to master her!

Grainne tried to talk with her husband, but was waved

away. Athelwine had made his bargain and was not to be thwarted. 'What think you of the mead, my friend?' he enquired cordially, when the fine speeches were at an end.

Sigurd nodded contentedly. 'Very pleasant.'

Athelwine smirked slyly. 'Rowena gathers the honey with her own fair hands and helps in the making of the mead.'

Sigurd accredited her with a smile that did not fool her for a moment. He was every bit as formidable as the golden eagle that decorated the back of his mantle.

'You have many talents. That is good.'

Rowena bit back an oath she'd heard her brothers mutter many times. She hated the heathen with his glib tongue that spoke her language like a native.

'Do you not fear being stung, lady?"

His face was far too close for comfort as he lifted his piercing eyes to hers again, his breath disturbingly fresh despite the mead. He was testing her and she bristled with anger. His lips lifted a little and she flashed her eyes. If he were sneering at her he would sorely regret his actions. 'I fear nothing that flies, northman,' she spat. ''Tis the beast that crawls in the slime that makes me shudder.'

As soon as the words were out she knew she'd made a mistake. She was grateful her father had not heard her. Sigurd's face was like granite and a pulse beat at the side of his mouth. 'Can't you wait for your punishment, lady? If that is the case I can accommodate you. It would not disturb me to leave my mark on your tender skin. In fact, the thought appeals to me.'

His eyes flashed a warning and she knew he would show her little mercy. She had momentarily amused him, but that was over and he was showing his true colours. She said nothing lest she was exposed in front of the whole hall and beaten half-naked for all to see.

Sigurd turned his head away, dismissing her far more efficiently than words ever could. She was annoyed but she smouldered silently. He spent a goodly time talking to Father Edwin. Rowena caught snatches of conversation and was surprised at the knowledge the warrior had of their faith. Soon Father Edwin was smiling and conversing with him easily.

Rowena slanted her eyes at Sigurd; he had wrought a miracle! She had underestimated him; his charm was far more potent than she'd realised. He would bear watching. Bored and upset, she slid from her seat wishing the hall were not so noisy. Even the warriors, who just a short while ago had been opposed in battle, were now amiable. She supposed she should be pleased, but it irked her.

She felt as though invisible chains already joined her to the Viking. But she should not think this way. It was a ruse. Her father may have treated her coldly in the past, but she knew he would not see her carted off to a foreign land by such scum. She tried to read his face, but Athelwine was playing his part well. She sighed; she would speak to him later and they would laugh at the game he'd dared play with their enemy. No doubt he had lured them into the burh and sent for reinforcements. The thought cheered her. It was the only answer.

Looking more relaxed, she found the new pups in the corner of the hall. They were silky smooth; mewing softly, their teeth needle sharp. Their mother, Ede, guarded them anxiously, although she knew Rowena would not harm them. She held a wriggling pup in her gentle hands, laughing as it licked her face. It was the smallest of the lot and Rowena had a soft spot for the tiny scrap.

'The runt of the litter,' a deep voice remarked behind her.

She glared at Sigurd indignantly. 'He's adorable.'

His thick eyebrows rose in surprise. 'You should always choose the strongest, the ones more likely to survive. A large cock is not only more likely to satisfy,' he smirked, 'but it also gives forth the best seed. Isn't that why your loins heat when you gaze upon your betrothed?'

Her face flamed. 'You flatter yourself! Besides, I dislike violence and all those who perpetrate it.'

His answer was to drag her head back by her hair so that she had no choice but to look up at him, her scalp raw with pain. He searched her face with his cold eyes. 'You test me sorely, bitch. I think it's time you tasted my sting.'

So saying, he dropped his head and took her mouth with his own. There was no gentleness in the kiss; he was branding her with his own special mark. She tried to break free but it inflamed him all the more. He reacted by tugging her hair harder and pressing his lips more fiercely to hers. She tried to cry out but was unable to do anything but suffer his cruel advances.

When he released her she fell back to the dirt floor. He smirked down at her. 'So, my great lady, how do you fare now? Shall I take you away with me to the forest while all are feasting and divest you of your maidenhead? Or will I wait and have you as a bride first?'

Rowena jerked herself into a sitting position, brushing dust and straw from her clothes, touching her bruised lips with shaking fingers. The force of the man had left her breathless, weak. He was like a shaft of lightning, a thunderbolt striking in her uneventful life, rendering it spoilt and changing her forever.

'You will do as you wish whatever I say,' she breathed, trying to rub his repulsive kiss from her sore mouth. 'But remember, I will not come to you willingly. I despise you and all you stand for.'

His grin did nothing to lighten the lean features. 'No man could resist such a challenge.' He made a step towards her and she shrunk away from him. With an amused glint in his eye he hauled her to her feet, dragging her to him. 'Make no mistake, madam, when I take you you'll beg for more. There's not been a woman born who did not faint with ecstasy after I've bedded them. And as you have decided to do it the hard way, it will be all the more enjoyable for me also.'

Rowena tried not to cower in the face of her enemy. She was daughter of Athelwine, child of an Irish princess. She held her proud head higher. 'Do what you wish. But you will never take my heart or destroy my spirit.'

His reply was to whip out a huge hand and catch her by one slender wrist. 'You have a lot to learn, Saxon bitch. But this night I will leave you to mull over your fate. I have the urge to make merry, to slake my thirst and drive away the dust of battle from my throat. As for my other needs, I have seen interest aplenty in the maidens that adorn your hall; maidens who have warm blood in their veins as apposed to the ice that runs through yours. Your time will come soon enough, Rowena.' He tossed her aside once more and strode away.

If only he knew, she thought helplessly. For even as he mistreated her so a great fire burned in her belly and her private place longed for him to touch her there. She brushed away a tear of shame; how was it possible for her body to betray her so? She hated the man with a vengeance! Besides, she knew not what to expect in the marriage bed. Apart from the rutting of animals, and a few bawdy comments from some of the older women, she had been left to sit and wonder about the complexities that surrounded the mating of a man and a woman.

A great weariness descended on her. She rubbed her sore hand, found a clump of hair in the dirt that the Viking had torn from her head, and blinked back her tears. At least no one noticed her shame, for everyone was far too drunk to care what had gone on at the back of the hall.

The men drank far into the night. Rowena went to bed with their talk ringing in her ears and the memory of Sigurd's taunting gaze locked fast on hers as she left the hall, promising everything he had threatened earlier. Her feet dragged along the floor and she slept little that night.

The following morning Mildred, Rowena's handmaiden, began to help her dress as usual. 'Your father bade me tell you to dress with care, my lady. Then he would talk with you.'

Rowena seethed, there was but one reason her father would demand such a thing – to impress Sigurd. She shook her head defiantly. She would wear her everyday clothes. 'I will not wear any finery for the dog of the north!'

Mildred looked uncomfortable; she knew it was not wise to thwart Athelwine. She opened Rowena's wooden chest and brought out her best kirtle and tunic. 'Think how annoyed your father will be if you defy him.'

Rowena absently felt the fine thread of her new kirtle before throwing it aside angrily. 'I shall not wear it.'

Mildred could not hide her fear. 'What will become of you, my lady? 'Tis the worst day ever.' She sought for words that would cheer. ''Tis said Sigurd is a fine warrior. I swear all the women secretly envy you your prize.'

'They are welcome to him,' Rowena seethed. 'Besides, I do not believe my father has really sold me to the northern pig. He has something up his sleeve, I'm sure.'

'In that case would it not be judicious to do as he asks?'

Rowena thought about this, and giggled. 'Mayhap you are right. I shall strive to be alluring and when my father tells Sigurd Thorkelsson the truth he will mourn his pithy attitude.'

Encouraged by her mistress's lighter mood Mildred smiled, and shaking out Rowena's smock and kirtle, helped her dress. 'You must admit he's all man. If he were not from across the seas I would be panting for him myself.'

Rowena bit her lip. She had known Mildred for as long as she could remember and they shared many a secret. 'What would you be panting for, Mildred?' she asked hesitantly.

The woman stared at the floor in front of her, then at her mistress. 'I have lain with a few lusty lads, none as handsome as your betrothed, mind you. And I can tell you that they cannot live without the bounty that lies in the sacred place between your legs. Men have murdered for it. When you touch yourself there it is soft and warm, it is this softness they crave. When they pierce your maidenhead it leads them into your virginal passageway. This is where they spend their seed, where paradise is opened up to them.'

Rowena blushed. 'I… I see. Thank you, Mildred. I don't think I need fret. My father will soon clear up this unfortunate business.'

Mildred nodded. 'I pray that you are right.'

Rowena straightened the gold circlet in her hair, as Mildred tied the girdle on her elaborately embroidered kirtle of her favourite blue from the woad plant. She awaited him patiently, and when he came he sat down beside her, his usually stern face expressionless. It was strange to see him in her bower. His attention was reserved for his sons who were far more use to him than a mere daughter.

'You look well, Rowena,' he said, gazing at the sweet face, ignoring the dark smudges beneath her eyes from lack of sleep.

'Thank you, father,' she murmured, feeling relieved that he had come.

Mildred was dismissed and Athelwine cast his eyes around the bower, admiring the furs his sons had hunted that covered the walls. A weak sun slanted through the round window. After a few moments he turned his attention back to Rowena.

'We went in search of our enemies with high hopes. But we soon found we were outnumbered and outclassed. They caught our spears in mid-flight and returned them without pause.'

His words held repressed anger. She knew how difficult it was for him to admit defeat. She was flooded with pity. 'If King Edward's favourite and most prized warrior could not conquer Sigurd Thorkelsson, then he cannot be conquered without a larger army,' she said with conviction.

He did not appear to be listening; his eyes were on the pelts that furnished the floor. He shook his head as if in confusion. 'I expected a small band of northern pirates, but Sigurd's army is vast.'

A sharp breeze blew through the room, dimming the flame in the bright pottery lamp in a niche in the wall. Rowena recalled the chieftain's corded muscles, his fearless but cruel eyes, and a strange tremor ran down her spine. 'Aye, I can imagine he would be an intimidating adversary.'

'He strikes when you least expect him. He's cunning and deadly and stronger than most. His men call him the Eagle, a fitting name for such a man.'

'The Eagle,' she repeated slowly, thinking how apt it sounded.

'Not wanting to risk lives I had to stand the militia down.'

'How were you able to dissuade him from killing and pillaging, father?'

'You know how,' he said coldly. 'Your hand, along with a large dowry.' He smirked. 'He is wise enough to realise that I do not keep my silver in a chest for all and sundry to find.'

'Why?' she asked, the cold hand of fear clutching her. 'Why would you bargain with me?'

'Out of necessity.'

'But… but marriage to a heathen,' she stammered.

'It was a sensible decision. You are of marriageable age and of little use otherwise.'

She could hardly believe her ears. She was aware he had little regard for her, but Athelwine had always hated the northern vermin; why would he see her wed to one? Her lips trembled. 'You are joshing, father. You have sent for reinforcements, have you not? It is a ploy, to hold him here until the rest of the militia return to rid us of the cur.'

Athelwine viewed her sourly. 'You talk foolishly.

There is no ploy.'

Rowena reeled with shock. 'No, you cannot be serious.' The colour drained from her face. How could her father possibly consider handing her over to a barbarian? Her mouth was dry; she ran her tongue over her lips. 'I cannot, father. I cannot do it.'

Athelwine's lips pursed impatiently. 'There is no question of you refusing.'

Rowena got to her feet and trod angrily around the room. 'Do not ask this of me, please.' Her face crumpled as she begged his mercy, but he remained hardened to her pleas.

'I will not listen to this whining! Sigurd has agreed to a Christian ceremony to please your mother. It will take place later this day.'

She swiped distractedly at her tears. 'So soon?' She shook her head. 'Christian or pagan, it makes no difference. I will not be bride to the Eagle or any of his ilk!'

Athelwine's jaw tightened. 'You have no more say in this, Rowena,' he roared. 'The matter is settled.'

'What of mother? Surely she does not approve.' She wanted to scream, to throw herself at his feet, but she knew nothing would sway him. She had always tried to please him, but he was asking far too much of her.

Athelwine got to his feet, his face stony. 'Do not look to your mother for help; she will abide by my wishes. You will remain in your quarters until you are sent for.' He glanced disdainfully at her tearstained face. 'Compose yourself in readiness; otherwise you will be responsible for many lives. Think on what I have said.' He paused meaningfully. 'And if that does not sway you perhaps a hearty beating will set you right.'

Rowena spent the time of her incarceration deep in thought. While she was thus tortured the memory of the icy blue orbs came to haunt her. So that was what his look had promised, she thought numbly, ownership. In one simple ceremony he would own her body and soul.

To her shame the thought brought the ache alive deep inside her. She lifted her kirtle and slipped her fingers into the damp warmth of her secret place. When she slid a finger over the small nub the most wonderful sensation swept through her. She delved deeper, for here lay the entrance to the valley that all men, according to Mildred, strove to cultivate. She stroked it gently, imagining her future husband with his hands on her. Suddenly a feeling of complete abandonment overwhelmed her.

She continued to rub the swollen flesh, slumping weakly on her bed, thinking of the handsome Norse pirate touching her so. It was such a turn on every nerve in her body seemed to tingle. Her mouth opened and her breath whispered through her teeth, as with one last rub the tension within her exploded, causing her to shudder with the force of her climax. She gazed dazedly at her finger. If only she had known what bounties lay in her own body she would have explored them before.

Then bad thoughts spoilt the good and she turned onto her stomach, wondering what would become of her, trying to wipe the pictures of the proud Norwegian from her mind. She no longer wanted to dwell on the overpowering male she was being forced to wed. A beating did not frighten her. She had suffered many at Athelwine's hand for the slightest misdemeanour in the past. It was the fate of the people that must concern her now. If an alliance would save them she would do her duty.

Chapter Two

When Athelwine came she was ready for him. She took the arm he offered. 'Then you are determined to see me thrown to the rabble, father,' she said bitterly. 'So be it. Lead on.'

She held her head high. The heathen, Sigurd, would not see her downed this day. None would know of the writhing emotions that burned so close to the surface.

When Sigurd followed Rowena to his place at the high table after their wedding he was accosted by Rig, his general. Rig gave him a wry smile. 'Me thinks you have met your match, dear friend.'

As the feasting began and everyone made merry, the chieftain switched his gaze from Rig to Rowena's stiff-backed person. 'Someone else thought so too, Rig,' he said darkly, fingering the scar on his cheek. 'And he is soon to learn how wrong he was. My Saxon wife does not know how important this alliance is to me.'

Rig's brow furrowed. 'But she is such a beauty I thought mayhap you would have changed your mind.'

'It will be a pleasure to deflower the little virgin. To teach her how much a man likes to use her sweet mouth to fuck in. But you do not know me as well as you think, Rig, if you believe I am to be swayed from my task by a pretty face.'

'Would it not be foolish to throw away such perfection in search of revenge?'

Sigurd laughed bitterly. 'You forget the advice Odin gave Loddfafnir, Rig,' he said, referring to one of the stories that are told around their fire to while way the winter evenings.' Did he not say, "Never succumb to a witch's sweet words and soft snaring embraces"?'

Rig nodded. 'But your bride does not look like a witch to me, Sigurd. Is there no other way you can gain retribution?'

'You are growing soft in your old age, Rig. What better way to ensnare a beast than to use its young?'

Rig shook his head, despairingly this time. 'Loddfafnir was also told not to despise the grey-haired singer, for the old are often wise. And this old man advises you to reconsider your plan. Rowena is young and sweet. You cannot think of using her so.'

Sigurd viewed his bride with narrowed eyes. 'A wolf is young and sweet as a cub, but it soon grows sharp teeth. Save your voice, Rig. The first phase of my mission is complete. I cannot be halted now.'

'I hope you do not live to regret it.' Rig quaffed his ale sorrowfully.

Sigurd smiled. 'Never. The Serpent rests quietly in his hole. Let him have his respite for it will soon be at an end.'

'Whatever you say.' Rig sighed and moved on.

Rowena saw the smile and her already pale skin blanched milk-white, her hair a red-gold mist falling to her shoulders. She was numb, she spoke, she moved, but nothing seemed real except for the man she had just wed. He was real enough – too real.

The wassail cup was handed round and Saxons and Norwegians alike toasted the couple. Shortly after Gilda sidled up to her, her face flushed with excitement. 'How lucky you are, Rowena. I would give all I own to wed such a man. I vow this hall has never seen the like. He is by far the handsomest man here.'

Rowena stiffened. 'Would it not trouble you that he is a northern barbarian?'

Gilda giggled. 'No, cousin, I would think only of the strong arms that would reach for me in the night. I swear no Saxon would pound into you with as much ferocity as Sigurd. Look at your husband, Rowena. He is huge. Just imagine how large his manhood will be. I swear your little cunny will be stretched to its limit to accommodate him.' Gilda rolled her eyes. 'Oh, what bliss!' She made a face at her disgruntled cousin. 'If you are not willing to take a tumble with him I will act as substitute any time you like.'

Gilda's fertile mind envisioned herself in Rowena's place, with her plump thighs wrapped tightly around the Norseman. Her private parts throbbed so much at the vision in her head she pressed her legs together. She would have to seek out a quiet place and relieve her longing with her own clever fingers, if she were unable to find herself a willing young buck to ease her discomfort. She hid a sly smile. There was soft hay in the barn and she often liaised there with one of the fine lads in the burh. There was a time she had two take a turn on her. It was heavenly. Rowena would not understand; she was like her pure Irish mother. Neither of them knew how to have fun.

Rowena coloured, her heart palpitating at the picture Gilda had placed in her brain. Would Sigurd's tool be too large for her? She glanced at him from beneath her lashes. He was the largest man she had ever seen, so it was possible. A mixture of terror and anticipation burned within her, one warring against the other. Whatever happened she would have to submit to him eventually, but first of all she would put up a good fight.

She longed to wipe Gilda's stupid grin from her face. The girl knew nothing. She had no more sense than the geese that honked outside in the yard. 'So you would wish to change places with me, cousin?' she whispered in her ear, lest her husband hear her and think her fearful. 'And would it not bother you to be taken from your family and friends? Would it not bother you to sail to a foreign land where you would be stranger to all and sundry except the man who has sworn to beat you into submission?'

Gilda smoothed her kirtle with an unsteady hand. 'I must admit I had not thought of it.' She patted Rowena's arm. 'I'm sorry, cousin, I have been foolish. I was carried away with your husband's strength and good looks. And now that I dwell on it, it's true; I don't envy you your lot.'

Rowena gave her a watery smile. 'Nor I, but I have little choice in the matter.'

While her silly cousin continued to dream about Sigurd, she gazed around the great hall. Soon she would be taken far away from all she knew and loved. She had helped her mother embroider the tapestries that adorned the walls, frolicked with her brothers in the sunshine. Her whole life had revolved around the burh. She could not bring herself to think of those she would be leaving behind, for the tears would fall and she had promised herself that Sigurd would not see her cry.

Sigurd laughed at something her father whispered in his ear, and Rowena glared at him with hate in her heart. He was a great warrior, tall and far too strong for her to resist for long. But she would make him sorry he had ever taken her in marriage. Her eyes misted and to hide her feelings she left her seat and went to feed Ede some titbits.

Ede was lying contentedly enough, her pup's nibbling greedily on her teats. It was such a beautiful scene she became even more emotional.

'Wife.'

He was towering over her, looking every bit the bird of prey he was named after. 'Sigurd,' she said, a sour taste in her mouth, quite unable to call him husband.

'I feel like some air and would like my wife to accompany me.'

Although the words were simple enough, the threat with which he spoke them made her tremble. 'I slept little last night,' she replied, 'and wish to stay in the comfort of the hall.'

'It's an order, wife,' he said, loud enough for some guests to hear and turn their heads in surprise.

One woman giggled, wishing it was her being ordered around by the imposing warrior, for her mate was stick thin, and his tool small and ineffectual. Judging by the gleam in the Norse chieftain's eyes it was obvious he was unable to resist their thane's daughter any longer. Her cunny heated and she found her skinny husband's hand and thrust it beneath her kirtle, knowing the trestle would hide them.

Rowena doubled her fists at her sides, smiling sweetly at their guests; she did not relish her mother being aware of her misery. 'Wife I might be, but I will never take orders from you,' she hissed. 'I hate you with all my being.'

'Then ours will indeed be a tempestuous mating.' He curled his top lip to reveal his white teeth. 'I find that appealing. There is nothing more tiresome than a weak and willing maid. A warrior becomes used to battle and I like my women feisty.'

Rowena's shoulders drooped. She was inflaming him all the more. But she was unable to go to him with a song in her heart and a smile on her lips. She wished she were taller and stronger, able to face him eye to eye on the battlefield, wipe the smile from his arrogant face. 'Would that I was a warrior,' she snarled. 'I would grind you and your ilk to a pulp.'

'Your fine Saxon warriors were unable to get close enough to tickle my beard, wife,' he smirked. 'Had there been one brave enough to do so we wouldn't be having this conversation.'

'How dare you even speak of the militia so? They are the finest in the country.' He hooted loudly and Rowena snapped. Her fists whipped out and beat at his chest. 'I despise you... you cur! Would that you had died at the hand of a brave Saxon!'

A dull roar rumbled from his throat and he lunged for her. Rowena tried to back away but she lost her footing and landed on her rump on the floor. She sprawled before him, her dignity in ashes. Ede whimpered and Rowena fought back her tears. She would never best him, but she would never stop trying.

His face was thunderous, his mouth a thin line. Reaching forward from his great height he swooped and, grabbing her bright curls, began to drag her from the hall, caring nothing for her feelings or her delicate flesh. While her husband sought his revenge the noisy revellers in the hall ate and drank their fill, completely unaware of her plight.

The filth outside stuck to her clothing, scratched her tender skin, and slipped into her mouth when she tried to protest at his treatment. Her hair, she was certain, was being pulled out from the roots.

'You... you heathen, unhand me!' she shrieked.

Sigurd took no notice of her distress. When he had dragged her halfway across the yard he swooped again and bundled her under one stout arm, carrying her as though she weighed no more than a feather. While she kicked and spluttered, spitting out bits of straw and mud, he threw her to the ground in the mire near the pigsty. He laughed down at the sorry plight she made, lying in animal excrement, her wedding finery ruined. 'You will learn to respect your husband, bitch. Now get to your feet.'

The sound of merriment rose from the great hall. Her friends and family were celebrating her wedding, while her new husband strove to demean her. She struggled to her feet, slipping and sliding before she was able to gain purchase. Sigurd's enjoyment at her plight only served to harden her heart even more.

'Come, wife,' he commanded, ''tis time I claimed my dues.'

Rowena lifted her muddied kirtle and made to run. 'I would rather die.'

His answer was to catch her by her red-gold curls. 'Do not tempt me,' he spat.

To her chagrin he lifted her from her feet and deposited her once more beneath a muscular arm. With the other he lifted her kirtle, bearing her creamy cheeks to the elements. Rowena's tears flowed down her face, wet his mantle, but Sigurd's ire was up. Holding her firmly he brought a huge hand down on her buttocks, the first slap soon followed by many more.

A white-hot fire surged through her bottom, and each time he slapped her it got worse as the delicate flesh became more tender. She screamed with pain. 'Unhand me! Unhand me, I beg of you!'

Another slap, even harder this time, made her gasp, but her husband neither noticed, or if he did, cared less. His laugh was a deep rumble in his throat. ''Tis too late for begging, wife. I've reached the pinnacle of my patience and will stand no more.'

'You are nothing more than a beast!' she railed; her bottom stained with red from his slaps, her misery complete.

As before his reply was to slap her naked cheeks. 'Then it is well past time you tasted my animal passions.'

She was carried screaming to the nearest barn and thrown carelessly onto the hay. Her body was racked with pitiful sobs, her bottom raw from his beating. The smell of excrement smote her clothes and she wanted to die. 'Take me if you must,' she told the enormous Norse, 'but I will never submit my heart.'

Her girdle had been lost in the midden and Sigurd ripped the muddied kirtle from around her legs, exposing the red-gold hair that hid her sex. 'I have not asked for it,' he spat back, pausing only to rip the rest of her kirtle and her smock away from her trembling form. She was left with no covering, save for the caress of his eyes as they drank in the twin beauty of her breasts.

'Although your tongue spits poison you are pleasing on the eye. My luck is not all bad. Your face could have been covered in warts, your body twisted and repulsive.'

Despite her pain Rowena wondered at his words. If she had been such a sight he would have refused to marry her, wouldn't he? Instead he would insist on all his payment being in silver and her father would have had no option but to pay him. 'I am glad one of us has a bargain,' she whispered, defiance still burning brightly in her breast. 'For I find nothing attractive to delight me in your features or physique.'

He eyed her with evil intent. 'Your opinion is of no interest to me. Now, silence your mouth and open your legs, bitch. I will take my pleasure of you.'

She was completely at his mercy. Her heart pounding like a drum, she opened her thighs and Sigurd flung off his mantle. She watched fearfully as he stepped out of his breeches. Even in the gloom of the barn she was able to see his strong thighs, his huge member. Letting out a terrified wail she tried to dig herself into the hay, ignoring the pain in her buttocks, wanting nothing more than to run from this place, from the heathen who sought to enter her. There was no way his enormous tool would fit inside her body.

'Does the sight of a man's cock frighten you, virgin bitch?' he asked, obviously delighting in her fear. 'Or is your cunny throbbing with excitement?'

She was hard pressed to form words through her parched lips. Cowering away from him, her courage momentarily deserting her, she choked back her sobs. 'I find you as exciting as a duck's behind!'

'We will see.' He bore down on her, his teeth gleaming in the shadowy barn, the length of his tool forcing itself between her slim thighs.

There was no thought for her or her virgin state as he roughly found her entrance and ploughed his way inside. Rowena thought she would be torn in two and her screams were muffled in the shoulder of her husband. But as is the way of nature, her vagina stretched, though be it agonising, to accommodate the man. When she was filled with hard, throbbing flesh, her insides were raw with pain, her sobs pitiful.

'Be still,' he grumbled as she wriggled beneath him, and without any preamble began to drive into her.

Her cries became louder as fresh torment racked her frail body. He ground deeper and deeper, faster and faster and as her virgin blood soaked the hay, Rowena was certain she would die. But to her disgust her traitorous body began to react strangely to his onslaught. Her sex vibrated with pleasure, sent out such wonderful signals of delight she wanted to scream with exultation. The pain in her bottom seemed to add strangely to the enjoyment of her flesh and, though she hated herself, she was incapable of doing anything but following the dictates of her libido.

He rode her hard and fast and she matched his every stroke, crying out loudly. When he squeezed her breasts she tingled and her nipples peaked shamefully to meet his questing fingers. But she cared not, for she was in a fever of desire, such a burning desire that had not been on her before. She strove with him to reach the pinnacle, to reach the very peak of human enjoyment. And when he shot his load into her she shuddered with passion. She lay in the barn a willing victim to whatever he would do to her.

Sigurd got to his feet and adjusted his attire. ''Tis a shame you hate me so much, wife,' he said sarcastically.

Still exposed to his gaze, her shapely form bruised from his ministrations, her red-gold curls tangled and damp from her exertions, she blushed deeply. Shamefully she tried to pull the remnants of her clothing over her nakedness, her head down, tears of fury sliding down her cheeks. How was she to know the pain he wrought would release another woman inside her, a woman who was so in tune to Sigurd's body even now she longed for him to take her again.

'Lost your tongue, wife?' His derogatory tone did nothing to ease her shame. 'For a genteel lady you have the appetite of a whore.'

'And you are too good to be dragged through the midden,' she spat, her desire turning quickly to disgust, to hate. 'Animals do not treat one another with the disrespect you show me.'

He cocked his head to one side. 'You have to earn respect, little witch.'

With those words he strode out of the barn, leaving her bleeding and broken.

Rowena, praying she would not be seen, made her way to her bower. Mildred, who was busy sorting her clean linen, stared with disbelief. 'Mistress, what has happened to you?' The servant's fingers lifted to her face in distress upon sight of the fair Rowena, tattered and muddied as she was. 'Lord in heaven, you are such a mess.'

Rowena was still trembling. 'My husband, the devil,' she whispered, and falling into Mildred's arms was received with tender care.

'If your poor mother could see you now,' she said, clicking her tongue in disgust, easing the filthy tattered clothes from her lady, weeping herself when she saw the cruel bruises on Rowena's bottom. 'Someone should whip the heathen; give him a dose of his own medicine!'

When she was bathed and clothed, the handmaiden held some mead to her lips. 'Drink, lady,' she urged. 'Purge your mind of your distress. Your mother has been looking for you and will be worried if I cannot pinch some roses back into your cheeks.'

Rowena clutched at Mildred. 'Fetch Cwendritha, for I shall not be able to sit in the hall lest she can heal the pain in my buttocks. And she will know how to disguise my swollen eyes.'

When Mildred hurried the old woman into the bower she took one look at the wan face and muttered a spell. 'Death to the Norseman!' she railed. 'Were my predictions not correct?' she demanded. 'Had I been left in peace in the forest mayhap you would not be in such a muddle now.'

Rowena moved uneasily on the bed. Her buttocks were still stinging from her beating, and she had a dreadful headache. 'Do not preach, Cwendritha. I need your help.'

'I am not here to congratulate you on your good fortune. Mildred has informed me of your malaise. Turn over and I shall rub in some potion.' When Rowena wearily lay on her front Mildred gently raised her kirtle, and Cwendritha swore roundly when she saw the cruel marks from Sigurd's hands.

'Handsome is as handsome does,' she sniffed. 'And this man who does the devil's work must taste a little of Cwendritha's power before night falls.'

The old hag grinned, and Rowena turned her head away from the putrefaction of her breath. 'Would that you were able to equal such a power as he has over me.'

Cwendritha's grin widened. 'The old ways are often the best and so sorely misunderstood by the young. But I am here to help you through the rest of your ordeal. I have something for you to drink.'

Rowena rubbed her swollen eyes. 'You have? What is it?'

Cwendritha held out a goblet. 'An infusion of balm, lavender and lime blossom. It will calm you and make the spasms in your insides go away. It will elevate your mood and ease the dread in your heart.'

Rowena smiled gratefully. Cwendritha was a great favourite with her mother. 'Then it will be very welcome, dear friend.'

The old woman was eyeing her covertly, and Rowena arched a brow. 'You have something more?'

Cwendritha nodded, and reaching into a large bag tied around her waist, she brought out a small linen bag, which she quickly pressed into her hand. 'Slip this into your lord's ale and I can guarantee he will give up all thoughts of being a lusty buck this night.'

Rowena clenched her present tightly. One night's respite would be better than nothing. 'Would that it would last forever,' she sighed, easing herself from bed and smoothing out her kirtle.

Cwendritha cackled. 'Just make sure and add it to the chieftain's ale when he is not looking. But first of all let me bathe your swollen eyes.'

Rowena was shaking when she took her seat at the board beside Sigurd. She could barely face him after what had gone on in the barn. He was busy sharing a joke with her father and she knew she had to do the deed now or lose her nerve completely. Secreting the linen bag in her palm, she pulled down the full sleeve of her tunic and, giving a small yawn, stretched her arms over the board. When her one hand rested over Sigurd's leather tankard she quickly tipped the contents of the package into his drink.

Sigurd was swift to acknowledge her presence and she blanched when his keen eyes assessed her. 'The excitement of the day has exhausted you, wife,' he averred, a sarcastic smile lighting the saturnine face.

A guilty flush rose in Rowena's cheeks and she let the empty package slip from her hand to the dirt floor at her feet. How dare he refer to the act he forced on her that day! 'Very amusing,' she remarked with as much derision as her spouse, and kicked the object from her to lie undetected beneath the table.

'You will seek your bed eagerly this night, if your earlier performance is anything to go by.'

His eyes twinkled and her colour deepened. 'You are insufferable!'

'And you have not yet learned your lesson. Happen I will need to paddle your backside until you are more dutiful.'

His words sent a chill right through her. Thank the Lord for Cwendritha and her potions!

No one seemed to notice that she wore a different tunic and kirtle, they were obviously too merry to notice anything much. Her mother had laid on a feast fit for a king, indeed the last time she had seen such a sight was when the king paid them a visit. The trestles groaned with venison, wood pigeon, larks in a delicious sauce, eels, salmon, apple and blackberry tartlets, nettle soup and succulent roast pig. But none of it held any appeal for her.

It sickened her to see her father cosying up to the cur he had forced her to marry, to see him stuff his belly, his face glowing ruddier with every sip of mead. It had been within his power to pay the heathen off, but he would sooner keep his riches than lose a daughter he had never loved. She sat stony-faced as the two men cracked jokes and drank their fill, caring not that her life had been turned upside down.

Apart from a little mead, nothing had passed her lips all day. She was too full of misery to eat. The hall was stuffy and she slipped outside to breathe some air. The low rectangular buildings of the bowers, guesthouses and food-stores clustered around the hall and she wrung her hands soulfully. In outward appearance nothing had changed.

'Rowena.'

'Mother.'

She looked up into the anxious face of the woman who had borne her, and for the first time noticed the fine lines that etched her skin. Her beautiful mother appeared suddenly old and vulnerable.

'Your husband told me you had a headache and had gone to your bower. Are you feeling better?'

Rowena nodded, forcing a smile to her lips. 'It was just the excitement of the day and the stuffy hall, that's all.'

Grainne missed nothing and, although she did not remark on it, her Irish eyes noted immediately that her daughter had changed clothing. 'Are you happy, child? Your father tells me you are taken with Sigurd.' A worried sigh escaped her lips. 'I would like to hear it with my own ears.'

Rowena was dumbstruck. Why had her father lied? But when she saw Grainne's tortured expression she knew the answer. She also knew she must lie too. Her mother did not need to suffer any more.

''Tis the truth,' she replied. 'Sigurd is everything I could ever want in a husband.'

Grainne expelled her breath gratefully, and immediately looked younger as her features relaxed. 'It does my heart good to hear it, my daughter. Sometimes people are thrown together in strange ways, under awkward circumstances, just like your father and I. It was fated that we should meet just as you and Sigurd are fated to be together.'

Rowena shuddered inwardly. 'Yes, mother.'

'His customs are strange to us, it is true, but he is a good man for all that. Your brother, Athelstan, tells me he was at Sigurd's mercy during the battle, but he pushed him aside, declaring he did not kill children. It has shown me that not all his race is bad.'

She frowned in puzzlement. So her husband did have some good qualities. She squeezed Grainne's fingers reassuringly. 'You have seen how strong and handsome my husband is,' she said, recalling Gilda's words. 'How could I not help but love him? I am the envy of every maiden in the hall.'

There were tears of joy on Grainne's cheeks. She recalled how strong her own feelings had been for the red-bearded Norse chieftain who had taken her from her land. His gentleness and tender loving quickly won her heart. The thought made her blush but she soon came back to the matter at hand. God willing her own daughter had found such a man. A man who would refrain from going a-Viking and settle down now that he had a beautiful wife to build a home with. She smiled. 'Then mayhap you should join him in your wedding celebrations.'

'I will follow in a moment.' Rowena struggled with her conscience, but not for long. It was bad enough that one of them suffered. Grainne must be protected at all costs. Her mother left her, and she jumped just moments later as Sigurd's voice broke into her thoughts.

'I was not aware you thought so well of me, wife.'

She gasped in dismay, he stood grinning down at her, his blue eyes challenging. 'Do not believe everything you hear, husband,' she spat, hating every self-assured inch of him. 'I love my mother and wanted to put her mind at rest, nothing more.'

'Don't be coy,' he urged. 'You may admit your passion for your new mate.' He seemed amused while she spluttered and fought for composure. 'Mayhap the beating did you good after all. That and the time you spent beneath me in the hay.'

'I would as soon sleep in a hornet's nest as with you, Norse dog.'

His face darkened and she thought he would beat her again. But in the space of a heartbeat he changed his mind and took her arm. 'I can see you will keep me amused, Rowena. Come, our guests are waiting.'

He guided her back to the table and his laughter boomed across the hall. Many turned to see the chieftain's pleasure in his new bride. Rowena held her tongue as her goblet was refilled. She wanted to run from the burh, run from the tall man at her side and seek her freedom. But she dare not. Instead she smiled a smile that hid a deep well of resentment and frustration. All around her people were making merry; they had been saved from the dogs of war and she was the sacrifice.

Athelstan, her youngest brother, who was fourteen summers, seemed to be the only one to read her. She could see the sympathy in his eyes and her own signalled their gratitude.

Sigurd was talking again, acting as though nothing bad had happened between them, as though they were truly happy newly-weds He spoke of his morning ride with Athelwine, of the fine hawk he'd been given. She could only nod and feign interest until he changed the subject, capturing her full attention.

'Let us drink to a fruitful union, Rowena.'

His large hand covered hers and it was as though she had been struck by lightning. She turned from him in anger, but he caught her wrist, forcing her to face him. Her hatred overflowed. 'I will do no such thing,' she snapped, her eyes flashing green fire. 'For I will never go to you willingly.'

His grip became firmer, a fierce scowl marring the handsome face. 'And who can say what a man will do when he is driven beyond his patience?'

Her wrist throbbed and she trembled at the threat in his tone. What else could he do to her? What was worse than being beaten and taken with force by a man you hated? When he freed her, to help himself to more pigeon pie, she rubbed the fresh marks on her skin, annoyed that his appetite had not been affected.

When would Cwendritha's potion work? The thought of what was before her that night ran round her mind in vivid circles until her stomach was so cramped she wanted to scream. A minstrel played a romantic tune on his harp, singing of their wondrous match. It did nothing to relieve her tension and she was pleased when she spotted Cwendritha in a knot of people further down the hall.

Gilda chose that moment to attempt to flirt with Sigurd, but Rowena had the satisfaction to see that she approached him with much caution. She hid a bitter smile; her cousin was a man-eater. Apart from seeing her with Eadred, she had heard tales about her lying with the lads from the village, and wondered what Gilda would do if Sigurd decided to bed her too. It would suit her purpose if they did spend the night together; she would cross her fingers and wish her cousin good luck in seducing her new husband.

Gilda had drunk too much spiced ale and was rubbing her hand up and down Sigurd's leg, her fingers pausing over the muscled thighs, wondering what he would do if she should dare to reach higher. She longed to feel the strength of his tool, to test him out before her cousin had the chance. After all, men liked her; she was not as stuck up and untouchable as Rowena.

'What are you about, lady?' Sigurd asked quietly. Unlike most of his guests, his speech was not slurred, his movements not slow and awkward.

Gilda hiccupped and giggled. 'I think you know, my lord,' she whispered in his ear, brushing the flaxen hair from his forehead. 'Would that I was able to open my thighs for you this night I would make you a happy man.'

Sigurd smiled at her and her heart fluttered. 'But I have a new bride, lady.'

'Fie!' she exclaimed, extending her tongue and playfully sticking it in his ear. 'You will have a cold night with that one. Her cunny is so tight she walks cross-legged. As for me,' she purred, caressing the soft lobe with her lips, 'I am well schooled in the art of pleasing a man.'

Sigurd enjoyed the attention. Most of the assembled company was far from sober; a few were still upright, while others slept where they sat or had slid beneath the board, curled up on the hard-packed dirt floor.

'So, tell me how you intend pleasing me, Gilda.'

Gilda rested her head on his broad shoulder. 'Why, my lord, I would take your cock and lick its glands until it was sopping wet. I would place kisses on the tip and suck and massage it until your seed shot into my mouth. Then I would swallow it, enjoying every last drop.'

Sigurd was impressed. He glanced at his wife, who was conversing with one of the guests further down the board. 'And what would you like me to do with you, fair lady?'

Gilda was in her element now. Let her stuffy cousin go hang, she would take her place in Sigurd's bed this night. She slipped her shoe from her foot and, with her head on one side, in what she thought to be a coquettish pose, slid her bare foot up and down Sigurd's thigh. 'Why, lord, I would like you to eat my cunny, then to run your tongue over my nubbin until I came. After that I would like you to enter me and ride me until we both came again. Does that sound good?'

'It sounds very tempting,' he admitted. 'Your words have me hard, lady.' He took her hand and led it to the stiff tool in his breeches.

Gilda gave a sly grin and slid to the floor. Opening his breeches she almost swooned at the length and width of his cock. It pressed into her face impatiently and she licked the glans with her eager tongue, swirling and tonguing him until he was wet. Then she wrapped her fist around the fine male tool, not in the least surprised that she was unable to fit her fingers together. Her cousin spoke rubbish. Why, any woman would follow a man like this anywhere. Each night spent with him would be the biggest thrill she could imagine.

Her fist worked up and down the slippery shaft, massaging the wonderful length of him, and then she took him into her mouth and sucked until his seed flowed onto her tongue. She swallowed it with as much satisfaction as she'd promised.

'Oh, lord,' she sighed, resuming her seat beside him, creamy spunk running down her chin. 'Did you enjoy that as much as I did?'

Sigurd viewed the woman with distaste. 'You disgust me. But there is a place for you in my camp. You would be useful servicing my men, for you are nothing but a whore.'

Gilda was stunned. With her chin still coated by his emissions, she got to her feet and stumbled away from the great northern warrior she now hated with all her being.

Rowena was busy remonstrating with Cwendritha. 'Nothing has happened. He is as strong as a bull. You promised me he would be rendered useless and you have failed. What shall I do?'

Cwendritha soothed her. 'Do not panic, lady. I have read the runes well and they are on my side. Everyone in the village and burh come to me when they want something to ease their aches and pains, or when they require a love potion, or something to rid them of bad luck. They all go to church to pray for their souls, but no one thinks it amiss to ask for extra help in times of stress.' She winked conspiratorially. 'Have you ever known me let anyone down? Your own dear mother has great faith in me. When she has the megrims my door is the first place she comes, and she is never disappointed.'

Rowena sighed. 'This is true. I do have faith in you, of course I do. But I also have fear in my heart that this man is mayhap too strong for your potions.'

Cwendritha mulled this over. ''Tis true a lesser mortal would have already succumbed. But your lord is stronger than most and you must have patience, lady.'

Just then Rowena noticed Gilda making for the door, her face a strange shade of puce. She clicked her tongue, she had obviously failed to seduce Sigurd, and judging by her awkward gait had indulged in too much ale.

Athelwine, who had just picked his head up from the board, held his leather tankard up high and began to make a speech, completely oblivious to the fact that no one was listening. His voice rose higher and higher as it gained momentum, loudly proclaiming the excellence of their match, boasting about his part in bringing the couple together. Rowena felt nauseous, he had bartered her to a complete stranger to save his fortune and he was acting like a benevolent sire. What a hypocrite the thane was.

She pressed her fingers to her temples, as the headache that had started earlier threatened to overtake her. The noise of snoring and drunken laughter only accelerated the throbbing, and the smoke from the fire seemed to have wended its way down her throat. But most of all she feared the man favouring her with the look of possession.

When she joined him he took her hand. 'Come, wife,' he said with a covert smile, ''tis time we left our wedding feast and made merry on our own.'

Her hand went to her sore buttocks and she almost disgraced herself by fainting clean away. Instead she gazed on him nervously. Cwendritha had failed; she was his to beat and abuse at will. Her mouth as dry as dust she nodded. 'As you wish.'

His eyebrows rose in surprise. 'So, you are to be an obedient wife after all.'

She held her tongue with great difficulty. Her fate was sealed.

Sigurd turned to take his leave of Athelwine, but before he could utter a sound his face paled and he sank back onto the bench, one hand grasping his middle. Rig was at his side immediately, calling his men to attention. The Norse, who she had thought to be drunk and incapable of anything but sleep, rallied swiftly and surrounded their chieftain, weapons appearing as if by magic.

The hall was filled with tension and Sigurd was helped out, his brow perspiring freely, his powerful body doubled with pain. Six strong Norse were left to guard the door, their demeanour threatening. One after the other guests were roused, for great danger had beset them. It was whispered that the great warrior chieftain had been poisoned, and if that were the case they would all perish before morning.

Chapter Three

Athelwine staggered to his feet, sorely shaken by events. His mind was still foggy from drink and he fought for composure.

There was much muttering and shaking of heads in the great hall, much fear to see the northmen carrying weapons and barring the door. Athelwine tried to appear in charge of the situation. Holding up his hands for quiet he spoke a few soothing words to the assembled company, ending with what Rowena thought to be a tasteless pun about some men being unable to take their ale. His statement only served to anger Sigurd's men, who moved forward, their hands on the hilts of their swords. Too late Athelwine saw the error of his words, and as angry foreign voices rose, tried to make amends.

When he finally managed to appease the northmen he turned an anxious face to Rowena. 'What ails him, wench?'

So filled with remorse was she, she could only shake her head. Athelwine sighed impatiently and with ashen features tried to march after his sick son-in-law. He was forcibly restrained, his chest puffing with anger and frustration. How was it this could happen in his own hall?

In the furore that followed Rowena was motivated to seek Cwendritha, who she'd seen sidle out through the side door. She caught up with her and demanded she accompany her to her bower. Once inside Rowena wrung her hands in agitation. 'What was in the package, Cwendritha? What did I give Sigurd?'

Cwendritha shrugged her shoulders noncommittally. ''Twas just a little something to help you out.'

'But Sigurd is very ill,' she averred angrily. The old woman tried to avoid her gaze, which immediately made Rowena suspicious. 'You must tell me.'

A gleam of triumph lit Cwendritha's eyes. ''Tis of no

consequence because it has served its purpose and you are free of him now.'

Fear gripped Rowena. She shook the woman. 'What do you mean?'

She blinked her disapproval of Rowena's tone. 'I'm old and sometimes lose track of my ingredients. This happened not long since, so I despaired of what I was doing and fell asleep. When I awoke there was a dead rat on my hearth.' She cackled. 'It had eaten some of my mixture and soon learned to rue the day it stole from me. I kept the rest thinking I might find a use for it. I was right, was I not?'

Rowena cried out in horror. 'Are you telling me we gave Sigurd some sort of poison?'

Cwendritha's mouth turned down in discontent. 'I thought only to please you.'

'I've been such a fool! Oh, Cwendritha, what have we done?' She dropped her head in her hands. 'What if Sigurd dies? It will be all my fault.'

Cwendritha viewed her in confusion. 'You do not want him to die?'

Rowena shook her head violently. 'Of course not! If he dies we will all suffer. You have heard tell of the wrath of the northmen?'

The old woman nodded, suddenly understanding the problem. 'Aye. I suppose I wasn't thinking straight. Seeing what that cur did to you, revenge was my only concern.'

'Is there something you can do for him, Cwendritha?' she asked hopefully.

'We can try.'

With a sinking heart Rowena followed her to her hut, grateful there was a bright moon to show their way. The campfires of Sigurd's army glowed eerily against the night sky and she shuddered, knowing the earth would run with blood if she were unable to undo the wrong she had wrought.

When they reached Cwendritha's hut the old woman lit

a tallow, before taking some of the herbs that hung from the rafters and setting to work. First she put them into a pot of water, which she placed over the fire. When the water boiled she simmered it for a few minutes before removing it from the heat. 'It must be left to infuse for a while,' she explained.

After the fiasco in the hall Rowena was suspicious. 'What is it?'

'Rest easy, 'tis just blood root and a few other harmless herbs.'

'Are you sure it will work?' she asked anxiously.

Cwendritha shrugged helplessly. 'Nothing is certain. And there is a long way to go yet.' She paused uncertainly. 'There is a sacred place in the forest which I visit in order to cast spells. It leads to the centre of the earth and has much power. You must go there this night to align yourself to the Spirit of the Earth from whence you are come.'

'Rowena gave a hysterical laugh. 'You want me to go to the forest in the dark?'

'Aye, there is no other way. It is your husband who is stricken, so it must be you who begs for his life.' Her small eyes were grave. 'Listen carefully, lady. There is a clearing with a mud pool, near the giant oak where we met just a day ago. 'Tis this you must seek. Once there you must be brave, and take off all your garments. You must give yourself to the Spirit of the Earth. As you go to meet the great one you must say these words.' She whispered them to Rowena. 'If you please him he will grant your wish.'

An icy tingle shot down her spine. It was a dream. Or mayhap nightmare would explain it better. 'How shall I find my way?' she asked shakily.

'The moon is high; it will guide you. Take care, lady, for it is a dangerous place you seek and I know not how the spirit will react.'

Trembling with fear and apprehension Rowena went to fetch her cloak, for the night was cold. She crept quietly from the burh and made her way to the forest, the fires of her husband's army seeming more welcoming than her destination.

The forest path was stony and uneven. Tree roots made humps to trip her and bracken tore at her clothes and tender skin. Rotting vegetation warred with the scent of pine needles. Wild animals made strange noises in the undergrowth and the canopy of trees hid most of the moonlight. She was almost convinced to go back to the burh, but thought of the responsibility she carried forced her to do otherwise.

An owl hooted and her heart flipped in her breast. She was so small and insignificant in this mystic, leafy land, where Cwendritha seemed to be at her best. And although she had always been fascinated by the place, she also had a healthy fear and respect for the dangers that lay there.

When she came to a part of the forest that was even darker than the rest she lost her footing. She fell headlong to the mossy ground, wrenching her ankle and bruising an elbow. Tears were very near but she refused to cry. Her own stupidity had been the author of her fate, and when she was rested she must continue her journey.

There were dark, irregular shapes all around her, and she listened wide-eyed, lest something less than human was lying in wait. She had foolishly thought this woodland a silent area, but there were far too many alien sounds for her liking.

A loud snuffling at her back brought motivation to her limbs, and forgetting her injuries she limped onward. After a little while, and to her great relief, the trees thinned out and a silvery path stretched ahead of her. She smiled up at the moon and speeded her gait. It wasn't long before she reached the old oak, hugging its girth with thanks.

Casting her eyes nervously around for the pool she saw a low mist and threaded her way towards it. Thin, wispy fingers seemed to beckon her, and she found herself beside a muddy bog. Bracken and small plants grew around its edges. The mist was suspended a few feet above and she shivered violently, knowing what she must do.

Casting her clothes aside she stood shivering, naked and vulnerable beside the filthy mire, realising that if she paused in her task she would be undone. Carefully stepping over the vegetation she dipped a toe into the murky depths and felt a tugging sensation. It was so strong; it sucked her foot right into the bog. This unbalanced her and she was soon completely immersed in the slime, her breath coming in short sharp gasps.

Convinced that she would be swallowed whole she began to struggle and thrash around, but then Cwendritha's husky voice penetrated the fog of her mind and she became calmer, recalling what was expected of her. Slowly and succinctly she repeated the words the old woman had taught her. 'Flame and flood, fire and ice, spirit of darkness, spirit of light, receive your lowly maid, relieve my sin that Sigurd may rise whole again.'

The mud began to quiver and Rowena struggled to extricate herself, but each time she tried it sucked her further in, surrounding her until her limbs were completely immobile. She tried to breathe slowly, to stay calm, but it was difficult with the mire sucking at her. She had heard of people being lost forever in these bogs and she prayed she would not meet the same fate.

The mud began to revolve, slowly at first, then faster, picking up speed until it was whirling, nudging her with a violence that was vastly disturbing. It surged and rotated and Rowena was caught in a downward spiral, quite unable to extricate herself from her predicament. Bright colours played on her eyelids as her body swirled and spun. The thick gunge sucked at her, its slimy fingers ensnaring her, surging into her most private places, and Rowena's terror was indescribable.

She was helpless, incapacitated. The bog was violating her, sapping her strength as it took complete control. Her vulva was forced open and the gunge rushed into her vagina, stretching it to capacity. Before she had time to come to terms with this it slid back out, only to repeat the assault time and time again. It was as though a huge staff was thrust deep inside her and it hurt even more than the first time with Sigurd.

Her breasts were being pummelled to distraction. Even her bottom hole was not sacred, and if she were able to scream she would, as the mud surged into that most private and sacred of places only to retreat and return again and again, just as it did in her vagina. Her whole body was under attack, her head the only part of her visible. Tears rolled silently down her face, for she was unable to open her mouth for fear the filth would enter and choke her.

She began to despair, there was no way out of her predicament, and she was stuck fast. But despair gave way to pleasure as her perverse nature took over and her body began to enjoy what was being inflicted upon it. The pain was a potent aphrodisiac, its dynamic aggression a tempest that brought strange satisfaction.

She wasn't allowed her smugness for long. The pummelling grew worse, the mud became more demanding and she cried out, 'Release me! Please take pity on me and let me loose!'

Just as she thought herself incapable of withstanding any more pain, the mud changed its motion. It spun faster still, but the touch was much lighter, much softer. It caressed that which it had tortured and she let out a sigh of relief.

It was as though she had a thousand lovers. A thousand tongues licked her skin; a thousand lips kissed and sucked her flesh that had never been so sensitive as it was now. She was flung into a thousand pieces and made one again all in the blink of an eye. And yet it was an eternity.

The mud spun even faster and Rowena was caught in its momentum, caught in its soft yet powerful embrace. As it swirled it seeped into all her delicate folds, caressing her vulva, stimulating her clitoris as it had never been stimulated before. Her breasts peaked with pleasure as they were caressed and massaged, tweaked and explored.

The mud was in her, around her. It was taking her body for its own, mastering her as forcefully as any man ever could. She cried out as it made her come over and over again, her love juices mixing with the mire. Her body and mind in a frenzy of desire, of fulfilment – and agony! It was too much to bear. She sobbed, asking to be spared, begging and pleading, but the Spirit of the Earth was her master and it didn't choose to deliver her from its strong arms.

Somewhere in the depths of the forest a bird sang. Rowena awoke and stretched out her arms with a loud yawn. Dawn was breaking above the leafy boughs, pink and orange splashed colour across the sky. She was stiff and cold, muddy and – naked! She looked down at her filthy, mud-caked skin in confusion and horror. What was she doing sleeping in the forest without any clothes?

Hugging herself for warmth she looked around and found her garments. They were on the banks of the mud pool. Memories rushed back to haunt her and her body tingled and burned. Shivering, she picked up her clothes and nervously skirted the mud. She had to find somewhere to wash some of the filth away. It would not be prudent to return to the burh in such a state.

She had not walked far when there was the sound of running water, and over the next rise she found a brook. Her heart lightened and she immediately rinsed her hands and, cupping them, slaked her thirst. The water was icy as it danced over its stony bed, but she had little choice but to step in and try to scrub the mud from her skin and matted hair.

When she was done she dried herself in her mantle and quickly shrugged into her clothes. The brook had brought her fully awake and her body pulsed and burned as memories of the previous night assuaged her. Her nipples began to bloom and became like small nuts beneath her bodice. She covered them with her hands, flicking gently at the little points with her thumbs.

Her belly was on fire and one hand sneaked down to feel the fever that was on her. It stole lower to where her clitoris burned and throbbed with desire. She sank to the ground, and opening her thighs rubbed the nub, stimulating her love juices. As she got wetter and wetter she remembered her spirit lover of the bog, who had taken her over and over again, plunging into her vagina like a mighty staff until she begged for mercy. At her memory her fingers moved faster until she lay spent and exhausted beneath the mighty oak.

It was easier to find her way through the forest in daylight, fingers of brightness darted through the branches, leading her away from her adventure. It was all so clear, frighteningly so, from her first tentative steps to her complete possession. If she closed her eyes she was still able to feel the mortifying yet intoxicating vibrations.

Cwendritha had known what was ahead of her, had warned her in her own way. It shocked her that the old hag had been right all along. The old ways were still pertinent. They were all beings of the earth that would eventually reclaim them. Their souls, with the help of Father Edwin, would travel elsewhere.

Her thoughts turned to Sigurd. Would Cwendritha's potion work? She must hurry back to the burh and find out. She ran through the forest, wondering if her husband would recognise her now with her tangled hair and creased clothes. No doubt even her mother would disown her in her present state.

Cwendritha was waiting for her when she arrived back. 'I've been worried,' she admitted, scanning the young woman's face anxiously. 'Thankfully it appears my concern was wasted. You must have pleased the spirit to be here now.'

Her words were sobering, but Rowena refused to dwell on what might have happened. 'Have you heard how

Sigurd is?'

'The news is not good. He is still very sick. You must take the potion and persuade him to drink it or he will not last the day.'

She took the remedy from the old woman. 'Pray to whatever gods you worship, Cwendritha, or we are all doomed. A cold hand of fear clutched at her heart and, without pausing to groom herself, she made her way to the guest hut.

Sigurd was well guarded, but she made herself known and after a few moments a grave Rig came to the door. She gave him a brief nod, ignoring his surprise at her dishevelled state. 'Rig, I have something to cure your chieftain,' she said, holding up the jug that held the potion.'

Rig shook his head firmly, his demeanour telling of his resentment, his distrust for his lord's new bride. 'Take it away,' he said gruffly.

She begged but he remained stubbornly barring the door to her. 'You cannot forbid me from visiting my husband on his sickbed. It is my right,' she averred hotly.

Sigurd's general gave a sardonic laugh. 'You have no rights. Now go.'

Upset and weary she went in search of her father. Surely he would help; it was not in his interest to see Sigurd die. She found him in the great hall with her eldest brother, Ethelwulf, and explained her abortive errand. 'The potion is our last hope, father.'

'The northmen believe him to be poisoned.' He banged his fist down on the board. 'If he dies we will all perish!'

Rowena's hand went involuntarily to her mouth. 'I did not realise the consequences when I mixed herbs with Sigurd's ale.' Her green eyes darkened with guilt and Athelwine's mouth slackened with shock.

'You mean to tell me he was poisoned? And by your hand?'

Both Ethelwulf and her father glared at her, and Rowena haltingly retold what had happened and why. 'I did not mean to harm him,' she added wretchedly. 'I merely needed time to get used to being his wife, before... before...' She could not bring herself to say the words.

Athelwine struck her viciously; the force of the blow knocking her to the floor, where she lay stunned. Ethelwulf took a step forward but Athelwine's withering glance forestalled him.

'You have been a burden to me since the day of your birth,' he spat angrily. 'But even you have excelled yourself this time.' He slammed his fist down once more and Rowena trembled.

She held her hand up to her throbbing cheek. 'I am sorry, father,' she said miserably.

'Sorry?' he thundered. 'Sorry? You are an imbecile if you think your contrition will relieve us of this tribulation.'

As Rowena struggled, head bowed, to contain her shame and tears, Grainne arrived on the scene. She pushed her way through the spectators to Rowena's misery and demanded an explanation for her daughter's upset.

Athelwine lost no time in expounding Rowena's crime. 'So, wife, you now see the bitch you gave me to rear in her true colours,' he finished bitterly.

Grainne tenderly helped her daughter to her feet. 'She has done wrong, husband, but she realises the folly of her ways and only wishes to make amends.'

Rowena closed her eyes dazedly, she had lost count of the times her softly spoken mother had tried to protect her from her father's rages. She was usually innocent of the crimes he attributed to her, but this time she was wholly guilty and her entire being longed to undo the deed.

'Please, father,' she interrupted, when he began another tirade at her expense. 'I am guilty as charged. But time is of the essence. Sigurd desperately needs the potion if he is to live.'

She glanced meaningfully at the jug she'd thankfully

placed on the board before being punished. 'Can you not try to see him and administer it?'

Athelwine did his best, but all his pleadings went the same way Rowena's had, so she had no recourse but to try once again. As before Rig refused, so she took a deep breath. 'Rig, if you bar my way you and I both know he will die.'

'He should have never come to this place, never made you his bride,' Rig snarled venomously.

Rowena sighed, and lifting the jug to her lips, swallowed some of the contents. 'You see it is quite safe. Let me in to see Sigurd,' she asked once more.

'If anything happens to him it will be on your head.' With a snort he grabbed the jug and went to his lord.

Rowena chewed her lip. There was nothing else she could do. With dragging steps she made her way to her bower, where nausea overtook her and she lost the contents of her stomach. As she wiped her face her handmaiden was surprised at Rowena's smile.

'Mistress?'

'It does work, Mildred. The remedy does work, there is hope.'

The air was charged with fear when Rowena set forth to the church the following morning. She found no peace in her prayers as she usually did, even though she confessed all to Father Edwin and received absolution. Outside again the sun was strong and its rays smote her, as though it too was out to punish her for her misdeed.

She had visited the guest hut earlier, and to her utter dismay Rig's news was not encouraging. Shading her eyes from the fierce sun she decided to search out her mother; her soft voice would be a panacea for her troubles.

As she approached Grainne's bower her Aunt Elfrida's voice carried clearly to her through the unshuttered window. 'You must tell her, sister. Rowena will better understand Athelwine's attitude if you do.'

Grainne's tone was tortured. 'I cannot, Elfrida. Rowena must never know about Godmund the Red. I have kept the secret this long, do not ask me to tell her now, it would destroy her.'

The pain in her mother's voice disturbed Rowena. What did she mean? But she had little time to concentrate on anything else when all their lives rested on Sigurd's fate.

'Rowena.' She turned to see her brother Athelstan coming towards her. 'Father wants to see you,' he announced gravely.

Fear clutched at her heart. 'Has Sigurd's condition worsened?'

Athelstan shrugged his shoulders. 'I only know father is in a fine temper.'

'What's new?'

She hurried to the hall, a great foreboding riding over her like a dark cloud. 'You wanted to see me, father.'

Athelwine was striding up and down before the hearth, his expression grim. As soon as he saw Rowena he let out an enormous roar. 'You have brought destruction on us all!'

She was too stunned to reply. So the worst had happened; Sigurd had succumbed to the poison she had unwittingly administered. Her shoulders drooped. Her father continued to rant, but she was oblivious to anything but the thought of the danger she had brought to them all.

'Dimwit! Are you deaf?' The veins stood out in Athelwine's neck.

Rowena looked at him with confusion. 'Sorry, father.'

'I was telling you what happened when I tried to go hunting this morning. Your husband's men had the audacity to turn me back.' He glared at her. 'A prisoner in my own home!'

She bit back a smile. Athelwine did not relish being thwarted. 'I am sure it will end soon. Sigurd has

Cwendritha's potion and with the Lord's help all will be well.' She tried to inject a lightness she did not feel into her words.

Athelwine grunted. 'Pah! That is how this ungodly business began. I swear to you, girl, if the Norse do not punish you for your part in this I shall.'

As he pounded his fist into his palm Rowena recoiled. If he had his way each blow would be rained on her; and who could blame him? The Norse were ready to revolt at any moment. 'A little patience is all that is needed in order for the herb to work,' she insisted.

'Patience!' Athelwine laughed sarcastically. 'Would you care to be the one to tell the fine warriors of the north that they must have patience?'

Rowena hung her head. She knew what he was implying; it would be like putting your hand in the fire and hoping the flesh would not be singed. 'No, father.'

Her quiet words served to aggravate him all the more, and picking up a switch he raised it over his head. 'Mayhap I have been far too lenient with you. Justice should be seen to be done.'

Rowena closed her eyes and waited for the switch to bite into her back, but a familiar voice she had thought not to hear again caused her to snap them open. Sigurd was coolly snatching the switch from her father's hands, his blue eyes impaling her.

'I do not think that will be necessary,' he grated. 'If anyone chastises my wife it shall be me.'

Chapter Four

The whole hall was hushed into silence upon sight of the chieftain. Rowena fought to keep her composure. 'You are well?' she asked shakily.

'Aye. No thanks to you, wife.' His tone told of his anger and she cowered before him.

Athelwine pumped him on the back. ''Tis wonderful to see you back on your feet. We were worried.'

'With good cause,' Sigurd grunted. 'Your daughter is a witch who tried to take my life.'

Athelwine poured him some mead from a jug on the board. 'Be seated, my friend. Help yourself to bread and cheese,' he gushed, pushing the platter towards him.

'How do I know I'll not be poisoned again?'

Rowena swallowed and Athelwine fidgeted awkwardly, worried by the fierce demeanour of Sigurd's general, who hovered nearby. He sliced some bread and cheese and chewed on it. 'See, it is good. I would do you no harm.' Sigurd remained standing and Athelwine said nervously, 'My daughter is a worthless chit and I will punish her in any way you see fit, my lord.'

Sigurd viewed Rowena through narrowed eyes. 'What say you, wench? Shall I leave your discipline to your father? Or will I use the switch on you myself?'

Rowena faced him fearfully; she had forgotten just how large her husband was. 'I am glad to see you recovered,' she replied meekly. 'I had not meant to do you harm. The herbs were stronger than I bargained for.'

'So I heard tell.'

There was much muttering from the benches. The reeve who had come to speak to her father, and had always made her uncomfortable with his lingering looks, seemed overly excited. Athelwine put up a hand for silence. 'You have not answered your husband, wretch. Do so, or I shall whip you till your flesh parts company with your bones.'

'Aye, and take much pleasure in doing so,' she retorted, knowing her mistake as soon as the words were uttered.

Athelwine's face went red with rage and he barely held himself back from striking her. 'You are a feckless bitch and I would not blame your husband if he flayed you to death.'

Rowena blinked back her tears.

Sigurd watched grimly. 'Get to your feet, wife. I would speak with you in private.'

Without a word to anyone he marched out, the switch still clutched in his hand. Rowena was left to lever herself from the floor, disgraced and demeaned in the eyes of everyone, and tread after him with great reluctance. Although she was glad to see him recover it was not from love. If the safety of her people were not at stake she would gladly poison him again.

Breathless from trying to keep up with his long strides, she followed him to the forest, wondering why he would pick such a place in which to chastise her. Her clothes and hair were snagged on bushes and low branches and the putrid smell of leaf mould made her nostrils twitch with distaste. Her temper was rising by the minute.

When he finally came to rest in a dark and densely populated part she sighed with relief. 'If you wish to punish me, lord, let it be soon. I can't walk much further.'

Sigurd's lips rose in a delighted smirk. 'You are much bedraggled, wife. Though still as beautiful as ever.'

A squirrel, disturbed by their arrival, scampered across the leafy ground, and digging its claws into a nearby tree, made its escape. Even in the dim light she was able to see the lust in the man's eyes. Part of her wanted to run from him, but her belly burned with the same desire as before. 'What ails you, Sigurd?' she asked boldly. 'You're not in the habit of praising me.' She brushed twigs from her mantle, leaves from her hair.

'You do not deserve praise,' he shot back just as swiftly. 'I am merely making an observation.' He caressed the switch with wilful intent and Rowena shrank back against a tree. 'You are fortunate, wife. Had I died from your hand my men would have used you well before putting you to death.' He took a step forward and she lent against the firm oak lest her legs refuse to support her.

His mantle was thrown back from his shoulders and she had to admit he was a fine looking man. His huge erection made an impression in his breeches, making her wonder if he was always so well primed. The sight of this, and the image he had implanted in her head of many muscled warriors ripping her clothes away, and taking her roughly, increased the burning. Her vulva throbbed and leaked profusely and she silently castigated her rogue body. What was it about this ruffian that inflamed her so? But she didn't have to question it for long; deep down she already knew the answer.

'Your cheeks are burning, wife. Are you so eager to impale yourself on my cock you have taken a fever?'

Rowena's back stiffened. 'How dare you? I would rather be beaten senseless than have your vile body near me.'

Sigurd regarded her grimly. 'Your crimes are on the increase and I thank the gods I have the strength to tame you.'

Despite the fact that her fear was mounting fast, Rowena faced him regally. 'I will never be tamed by you or anyone else.'

Sigurd laughed so loudly crows took flight from their nests. 'I could snap your pretty neck with the crook of a finger. But you fascinate me. Come, let your husband begin your education.'

He picked her up from his great height as though she were no more than a babe and, sitting down on a fallen tree trunk, deposited her over his lap. Before she had time to protest his meaty hands had lifted her kirtle, leaving her bottom, still rosy from his previous beating, naked. And although it was a small consolation, she was extremely glad that he hadn't destroyed another kirtle.

His palms ran over her blushing cheeks with great possession, causing her so much pleasure she had to fight back her sighs of delight. Then, ignoring the switch he'd let drop to the forest floor, he grabbed at a nearby fallen branch and holding her firmly snapped off a sturdy length.

Rowena squealed when she realised what he was about to do. 'You cannot think to whip me with such a thing!'

'Wild women are best dealt with in a wild manner,' he rejoined, bringing the stick down with great gusto on her naked buttocks.

Rowena's screams matched the squawking of the crows and tears spilled from her eyes. The skin on her bottom cheeks, already sore, stung worse than any bee sting she'd ever had. She did not expect to survive the assault, for though her spirit was strong her body was fast weakening. It was as though a thousand devils spat their fury on her tender buttocks with red-hot tongues, and her screams became even louder.

'You must have some pity inside you,' she cried weakly. 'How can you use me so?' But she might as well have saved her voice, for Sigurd ignored her pleadings and carried on wielding the stick until she thought her skin would soon be stripped from her cheeks.

Then as before the pain did something strange to her insides and they buzzed with even more desire, so that each stroke of the stout stick brought more emissions from her vulva, and she cursed her traitorous flesh.

Sigurd gave a lusty laugh that shook her even more, especially when she realised he was laughing at her. 'You can't resist the feel of something hard, can you, slut?' he remarked triumphantly. 'Be it on your arse or up your cute cunny that even now spurts like a waterfall.'

Rowena's face flamed with shame and she tried to twist from his grasp. But he was far too strong and she gained nothing but his wrath, so that he beat her even harder. 'Stop,' she cried. 'Have mercy.'

A few slaps later he gave up beating her and inserted a

finger in the sticky dew that coated her nether lips. 'Such a noise for one so small. And such a slippery pathway for your husband to follow.'

She kicked her legs furiously. 'Unhand me, you wretch. I am the daughter of a princess and unused to such violence.'

Unimpressed, Sigurd clicked his tongue. 'So 'tis time you lived a little.'

Rowena's reply was smothered in a gasp as he slid one finger into her vagina, then two. He began to slide them in and out, and at the same time he reached for her breasts and began pinching her nipples, one first then the other. Her cries of agony soon turned to ones of passion and Sigurd grunted his satisfaction.

'Shall we try a little variety,' he suggested, and to her horror reached for the switch and stuck it into her juices. Before she had time to demure he began to slide it into her vaginal passage, tentatively at first, but when it was in a good few inches he eased it back out. The action was repeated time and time again until Rowena realised he was actually ravishing her with the stick.

At first she was appalled by what was happening to her. What more degradation would he heap on her? But Sigurd wielded the stick as cleverly as he wielded his own tool and she began to rock to his rhythm, pushing down onto the switch so it would gain more purchase in her vagina. She sobbed as her wanton body welcomed the intrusion, as her clitoris strove to feel the cloth of his breeches.

Realising her intent, Sigurd slid a finger beneath her and found the nub of her arousal. He began to rub the slippery flesh, still keeping up the momentum with the switch. Her predicament began to appeal to her; it was so rude, so utterly disgusting. What, she wondered, would they think back at the burh if they could see her now with her body draped inelegantly over Sigurd's lap, while he diddled her boldly with a switch and tickled her clitoris with his finger?

The thought merely increased her excitement and she clung onto him for all she was worth, concentrating on that finger as it rubbed her pleasure zone, enjoying the switch as her muscles sucked it further and further in her vagina.

When the spasms of her climax began to radiate around her clitoris he dumped her unceremoniously on the forest floor. She gaped up at him in surprise. 'Sigurd, what are you doing?' she asked, disappointed that her pleasure had been taken from her.

Although she was sprawled on the damp ground she was able to think of nothing but the heat that surged through her private place. She opened her thighs to him, welcoming him like a siren, and she suddenly knew what made Gilda like she was; she had obviously discovered the diversities of the flesh and refused to deny herself such pleasures. It had taken her a long time to work her cousin out, but now she had she gave a secret smile of understanding.

Sigurd was grinning down at her, releasing his huge tool from his breeches. 'You are nothing more than a whore, wife. And one of my missions in life will be to punish you for being such a slut.' Approaching her with his enormous erection he knelt between her thighs, nudging them even further apart.

Rowena was appalled at his tone and whimpered at the size of his member. The memory of it ripping into her most tender part brought mixed feelings. But she knew that to fight him inflamed him even more and lay back passively, knowing it would be over much sooner this way.

Sigurd raised an eyebrow. 'The blushing maiden has gone from me,' he taunted. 'In her place I have a bitch on heat. Open your portal, wife,' he groaned, bearing down on her, 'for I have needs of my own.'

Sigurd pushed into her eagerly. Rowena grimaced against the great pain that was to come, her muscles clenched against him with apprehension. But because it was not the first time he had stretched her and because she was wetter this time, the pain was not as bad as before.

He was tireless, and continued to lunge into her long after most men would have collapsed. Despite her dire hatred of the man and all he stood for, Rowena's insides began to thrill to his ministrations and she matched him stroke for stroke, her inner muscles sucking him in, her young body riding with him to fruition.

He came with a loud shout, pumping his seed into her. Without a word he rolled away and she lay exhausted at his side. How she hated herself for her animal desires, hated him for using her so. As a new bride she should be able to expect tenderness and concern. Instead she was treated no better than the beasts in the fields.

Sated, Sigurd appeared relaxed, his head resting on his arms. She clicked her tongue with annoyance and without pausing to think how dangerous it would be, sat up and pummelled his chest with her fists. 'You are impossible,' she intoned miserably. 'How can you ever expect me to settle into wedlock when you treat me so?'

'I think you have forgotten the reason for your being here,' he remarked coldly. ''Tis not a lover's tryst. If my memory serves me right I was laid low by your own fair hand.'

The dark cloud of his face issued a stark warning. Rowena scrabbled to her feet but was brought down by his hand grasping her ankle. She tried to stand with little success. Each time she gained a little ground Sigurd's hand toppled her.

'You are a no account lowlife,' she railed, out of breath after being pushed over for the umpteenth time, her eyes brimming with tears from the pain inflicted by her father's switch. How apt, she thought ruefully, even though Athelwine was absent he was still able to have a hand in her misery!

Sigurd's eyes narrowed to slits. 'Be silent, wife,' he said nastily. 'You will learn to be obedient. It is clear that you have not been chastised enough. Mayhap I will give you over to my men, after all. Olaf, Magnus,' he called, 'show yourselves.'

Rowena's heart sank and her face flamed when two lusty Norse came from behind some trees. Both wore swords that hung from their baldrics and one carried an axe. They were dressed similarly to Sigurd, in smocks and tight breeches. The one carrying the axe also wore a sheep's fleece.

Rowena tried to cover herself with her clothes, but Sigurd lifted her kirtle and she was left lying on the forest floor, her sex covered only by a triangle of red-gold hair. 'How... how long have they been out there?' she stammered, embarrassment flushing her skin.

'Long enough.' He grinned at his men. 'I am a chieftain; my warriors are trained to watch my back.'

'What we did should have been private.' She covered herself with her hands. The thought of the two men witnessing her most intimate moments with her husband sickened her. They had seen him beat her naked bottom. They had watched while he used a switch like a cock to abuse her with. They had seen her sprawling before their chieftain, begging with her wanton body for more. Her tears flowed freely; she would never live down so much shame. Not long since she had been a chaste virgin, she knew nothing of men. Now, thanks to the Norse who had taken her to wife, her body was sport for all.

Sigurd viewed her silently, his head on one side. Magnus and Olaf looked as if they were getting ready for a feast, their eyes glowing with expectation.

'What if we make this more interesting?' Sigurd declared with a roguish wink, inclining his head towards the trees.

To Rowena's surprise another man approached, dragging a dark-haired girl.

'Has your whole army been watching us?' she asked, as disgust and despair washed over her.

'I suggest you rest your tongue and take note of what

will happen to you should you continue your disobedience.'

Knowing she was not strong enough to put up with any more violence, Rowena said no more. Instead she directed her attention at the dark-haired girl being held by the bulky Norwegian. She was very beautiful, with skin like milk, but her eyes were the strangest shape she had ever seen. They were like almonds and instead of reducing her attraction they merely emphasised it.

'Who is she?' she asked quietly, lest she anger him some more.

'Just another slave I captured and decided to keep to pleasure my men.'

'What do you intend doing to her now.'

'I'll use her to show you what will happen should you not behave.'

The girl's eyes were glazed and Rowena wondered what they had given her. She had seen people with that same look when Cwendritha used her skills to ease pain. Rowena kept her own council and Sigurd looked satisfied.

'That's better,' he chuckled. 'Now then, wife, which one shall I order to punish her first?'

She was aghast. 'You cannot be serious! Even you would not be churlish enough to force your own wife to witness the poor girl being beaten.'

Sigurd grinned. 'Would you rather I had Eiric punish you instead?'

Rowena got to her feet shakily. 'I would see no one hurt.'

Her eyes were brimming with tears but Sigurd was unmoved. 'It is for your own good. A wife should be demure and mindful of her husband at all times. I think Olaf should take a turn first,' he said, beckoning the tallest man of the three to come closer and addressing him in his own language. 'My men are always eager to have a hand in the disciplining of a woman, so be warned,' he said, turning back to Rowena.

Rowena paled. Ignoring her Sigurd slapped him heartily on the back. 'Show her how we deal with females who do not please us, Olaf.'

He spoke in the two languages once again so she'd know what was going on. The girl was handed over to Olaf and forced to lie over the fallen tree. Her clothing was ripped from her, leaving her perfect flesh on display to all. She said nothing when the hefty blond Norwegian took the switch from Sigurd, and using it like a sword, swung it in an arc over her body.

Rowena saw it cut through the air, heard the snap it made, saw it connect with the lovely bottom and choked on her tears. The Norwegian's mouth was turned up in a sly smile and she shrank away from her husband in terror. She knew that no matter how much she remonstrated with him nothing would save the girl. But she also knew she had to try.

Running towards the brute she tried to put herself between him and the girl. But Sigurd was faster than she was. With a loud snort he caught and dragged her back to her original position, holding her in a cruel arm lock.

'That little performance will earn her a more severe beating,' he promised, curling his lips in satisfaction.

He nodded at Olaf, who was thrilled at having an audience. He swung the switch, this time catching the girl right across her secret entrance. Her cries only made his smile wider, and Magnus and Eiric looked on approvingly. More so when he decided to tease her, swinging the switch one way without striking, then swinging it again, catching her when she was not expecting the blow. He would snap it down either on her thighs or on the darkly fringed sex, and take great delight in her distress.

Sigurd put up a restraining hand and Rowena thought the girl's ordeal was over, but he merely ordered Olaf to hand the switch over to Magnus. 'Pay close attention, wife,' he commanded.

Rowena's entire body seemed to throb with pain. She

did not want anyone else suffering as she did. 'No, do not do this,' she begged. 'I will be obedient.'

Sigurd snorted disdainfully. ''Tis too late for that,' he said sternly. 'Now watch.'

Wearily she did as she was told, wondering just how much pain the lovely dark-haired girl would be able to stand. Magnus, who was slightly shorter than Olaf but every bit as strong, lifted what was left of her kirtle with the switch until her red-striped bottom was on show to all. With an excited breath he swung the switch and brought it down again and again, torturing the skin that was already sore.

Rowena imagined the agony and bit into her hand to stop from crying out. The girl screamed, but the more she cried the more excited they became and the more she was hurt. Rowena watched in pity, knowing she had probably taken far more punishment than she could stand, and that she would probably faint. The prospect filled her with relief; there would be no pleasure in abusing an unconscious girl.

Sigurd released Rowena, and approaching his slave gave her sex one hard slap with his hand. Sweet dew leaked from her vulva. He slipped a finger into her juices and offered it up to Magnus. 'Taste the honey of her sweet nether lips, my friend. Then you can stick your cock right up her. Let my wife see what she is missing.'

Rowena couldn't believe what her husband was saying; it was bad enough making her endure what she had, but urging them to have sex with the girl in front of her was demeaning. She swung away from the scene, but Sigurd pulled her back and forced her to face Magnus and his poor victim.

Magnus did not need telling twice; tossing the switch aside he released his stiff member and fed it home. Still draped over the fallen tree the girl whimpered. But in spite of her tears he rode her long and hard, while Sigurd watched with a broad grin on his face. Finally, Magnus shot his seed into her and rolled off.

Sigurd chuckled. 'See, wife, how the minx wiggles her rear, how her cunny floods with lust. At this very minute she is hoping Eiric will give her a good ride too.'

Rowena had to admit that the lovely girl did seem to have a smile on her lips and her bottom did seem to wiggle quite a bit. Sigurd gave Eiric a signal and he took Magnus's place. But the last Viking, excited by the display of his friend pumping in and out of the bruised bottom of the slave, did not last as long. He quickly reached his climax with a long, loud cry of triumph that Rowena imagined echoed through the entire forest.

She hung her head in misery. Her life was in the hands of barbarians and there was nothing anyone could do.

Chapter Five

Rowena opened her eyes and stretched wearily. She had been asleep for hours but she did not feel refreshed. Everything had happened so swiftly since Sigurd's unexpected arrival in the great hall. After just one day's grace he declared himself well enough to travel, and Rowena found herself and her belongs being transported in a sleek sailing craft with bright striped sails and a fierce dragon carved on the prow.

It had been like a dream as she watched its sister ships driven along by oar and wind like multi-coloured butterflies. She gave a wry smile; Sigurd's dragon fleet was certainly not as innocuous as those iridescent creatures. And it was not a dream; the strange land she'd been brought to after six long days of travelling had proved that. Iceland – it was a place she had never heard of.

When they landed the men escorted Rowena and their chieftain into the hills. 'Iceland,' she said aloud. It sounded as forbidding as the man himself.

She turned restlessly and sat up in bed; a bed like nothing she had ever known. It was huge and hewn of wood with four posts at either corner. The posts at her head were carved in the likeness of an eagle. Down-filled pillows cushioned her back, fine linen and wool covered her. Furs lay at the foot of the bed to warm her feet if the nights grew cold.

Sigurd had not joined her in that bed, she was thankful to say. Upon their arrival she was given a meal in the place they called the fire-hall, and shown to the bedchamber that was partitioned off the entrance hall, where exhausted she had quickly fallen asleep.

But it had not been a peaceful sleep; a cold-eyed eagle that reminded her of Sigurd haunted her dreams. It roamed a land surrounded by ice floes where fire-breathing dragons lived.

Sigurd had certainly resembled the creature when he emerged from his sickroom. His eyes were threatening, his nostrils flaring with suppressed anger.

The door to the chamber opened and Rowena cowered in the bed, afraid of seeing her husband and being punished again, but a flaxen-haired woman entered. She looked up cautiously, wondering what tongue she would be greeted in, and the woman surprised her by speaking perfect English.

'I bring you food, mistress,' she said shyly.

Rowena thanked her and took the soapstone bowl from her, which contained a thick broth. 'Sigurd...' she said awkwardly. The woman gave her a blank look and Rowena blushed. She did not want her to think she was missing the caresses of her new husband, not when her rear was still so sore. 'I was just wondering where he was,' she explained.

'You slept late. It's almost noon. The chieftain's been up for hours. He is out in the pastures. The men go a-viking for adventure and gain, but when they return they are farmers again.'

Rowena combed her fingers through her tangled hair. She had never slept so late in her entire life. Feeling hungry she tasted the food. 'Mmm,' she said appreciatively, and received a pleased grin in return. 'What's your name?'

'I am called Algitha, mistress.'

'And you are Saxon too, are you not?'

Algitha smiled. 'Yes. I was taken from my village a long time ago.'

Rowena wondered at her composure, she certainly didn't sound like a slave. She almost choked on the broth, for what else was she, Rowena, if not Sigurd's slave. 'We are a long way from home,' she said soberly.

'Yes, mistress.'

'How do you stand it?'

'I am happy here.'

'How is that possible?' Rowena absently chewed her food.

'I often went hungry before,' Algitha explained patiently. 'Here I eat well and am treated kindly.'

'I'm glad to hear it.' Rowena strove to hide her surprise.

When the meal was finished the woman brought her some water for washing, in a bronze bowl. Still feeling tired and ill used she gave a little cry when she tried to move from the bed.

Algitha was immediately concerned. 'What ails you, lady?'

Rowena missed Mildred. Sigurd had forbidden her to bring her handmaiden to Iceland. She knew it was another form of punishment, and deep down hoped she would bond with Algitha much as she had with Mildred. 'I had an accident,' she replied nervously, thinking that Algitha might be able to relieve some of her pain.

Turning over on her front she lifted her shift to reveal her curvy but striped bottom. Algitha's hands went to her mouth in shock. 'Mercy me, what has happened to you?' Though she had a good idea that Sigurd had beaten the poor lady badly. 'I've just the thing,' she said. 'I'll be back in no time.'

True to her word, she was soon smoothing a cooling salve on Rowena's buttocks. Her hands were so soft and gentle Rowena sighed her pleasure. 'Oh, Algitha, how well you do your job.'

'Thank you, my lady, I know what pain feels like and can sympathise with you.'

Rowena turned slightly to see the woman better. 'You have been beaten?'

Algitha flushed. 'Yes.'

'I don't understand,' Rowena declared in confusion. 'You said you have been well treated.'

The young woman's colour deepened. 'I... I am usually,' she stammered. 'The last few months have been good.'

Rowena picked up on the woman's distress. 'You mean things were easier for you with the army away?' Algitha dropped her head and Rowena immediately knew who the culprit was. 'Sigurd beats you, doesn't he?' The woman was obviously reluctant to implicate her husband, so she tried to allay her fears. 'Don't forget, I know from experience just how much Sigurd enjoys humiliating women. I did not marry my husband willingly, Algitha. I was forced into it; so don't be afraid of offending me. The man is a beast.'

Algitha's nose flared in anger. 'He *is* a beast! He has rigged restraining chains in one of the store cupboards to hang his victims from.'

Rowena trembled; it was worse than she expected.

Algitha patted her shoulder. 'Now is not the time to talk of these things. You need to rest. Let me help you.'

As the woman began to cream her again, Rowena relaxed. Her eyes closed and though she winced occasionally, the pain soon eased. 'That's wonderful,' she said gratefully, a smile lifting her lips.

Algitha stroked the delightful cheeks, tutting at the bruises that stained the perfect skin. Rowena was beginning to fall asleep when she felt the woman's fingers slip into her private channel.

'You are in need of some tender care,' Algitha clucked over her. 'A massage will send your megrims away, relax you.'

Rowena was about to protest when Algitha's probing fingers found the centre of her desire and began to stroke it gently. Rowena gasped and, despite her reservations, her thighs opened wider so she was able to attend to her more easily. As the fingers stroked her vulva she cooed over her like a dove. 'Lady, you deserve to be loved not beaten. Let Algitha show you what joys await you at my hands.'

Rowena knew her channel was beginning to fill with her secretions; as for the first time in her life she was being shown what it was like to be touched there by another female. She sensed it was wrong, but after her punishment and the cruel lovemaking of her husband, she was enjoying the gentle caress.

She felt Algitha's breath on her thighs, as the handmaiden knelt on the bed and put her head between her legs. Her tongue flicked to her nectar and she felt her lick, smacking her lips in enjoyment.

'Oh, lady, your honey is delightful, so sweet and warm, it fair turns me to mush. But I wonder if you would mind getting to your knees so I may reach you better.'

Rowena was bewitched, and without demure she changed her position on the bed.

'And if you can elevate your bottom I'll put a pillow under you for your further comfort,' the handmaiden urged.

A pillow was wedged beneath Rowena and her bottom was raised. She found she liked the position and wiggled a little. Algitha gave a cry of delight, and Rowena became speechless as the woman's head ducked between her thighs and she licked to find her throbbing nub. Her clever fingers began to caress her breasts with such tenderness Rowena was completely under her spell. Algitha stroked her nipples with her thumbs and Rowena sighed, then gave a little cry when the soft wet tongue circled the nub between her thighs. Her bottom rose even higher and, with her two hands grasping the other pillows, she concentrated on the wonderful feelings that spread right through her.

Algitha lapped her like a cat laps milk, and Rowena's stomach tightened as she gave in completely to the sensual pleasure. The clever tongue teased and tantalised with great expertise. Algitha had learned well how to please her mistresses and if she were lucky, as she often was, they would return the favour.

This lady was new to Sapphic pleasure but she could tell by her abandonment she was one of her successes. Men were far too keen to obtain their own release to bother with the feelings of their ladies. It was little wonder many turned to their own sex for gratification.

One of her hands left Rowena's breast and slid into her wet furrow. She coated a finger with juice, and then finding the opening to her vagina began to probe inside. Her finger went deeper and deeper before sliding quickly in and out. Another finger slid into that warm place and she smiled again as Rowena began to pant. Algitha was pleased; after all, she was only there to serve her mistress.

Rowena had never known such ecstasy, and as wild spasms ran through her muscles her legs began to shake with the power of her climax. Afterwards she lay in her bed in utter bliss. It was true she was a little embarrassed and shy, but Algitha soon cured that by taking her into her arms and kissing her soft lips.

'Girly love is the best, don't you agree, mistress?'

Rowena was able to taste her own juices on the sweet mouth. She had never been kissed so passionately and she clung to Algitha gratefully. ''Tis a wonderful experience,' she agreed quickly. 'But is it quite, um, well you know... is it normal?'

Algitha gave a little giggle. 'Much more common than you would think. Many of my ladies were glad to spend time with me in private so I could ease the longing between their thighs. 'Tis the most natural thing in the world.'

Rowena was still a little uneasy about her new experience, so Algitha gave her a little shake. 'Do you not touch yourself, my dear?'

Rowena blushed. 'I have done.'

'There now, what is the difference? We know what we enjoy, don't we? So what can be better than two women sharing their pleasure?'

It sounded sensible, and Rowena lay in her handmaiden's arms feeling more happy and relaxed than she had in a long time.

Before she left, Algitha gave her a bright smile. 'We must do this again soon. It's good to see the roses blooming in your wan cheeks.'

Rowena nodded. 'Yes, and it will be our secret.'

Algitha kissed her cheek. 'Our most sacred secret, my lady.'

Rowena liked the idea. She had a secret. No matter what Sigurd did to her she would find succour and pleasure in Algitha's arms. She hoped he wouldn't notice her sudden glow, for she could hardly tell him her maidservant had been in her bed – though it would be great fun to see his face. She dissolved into giggles.

Feeling much better she decided it was time she explored her new home, for she had to grudgingly admit it was just that now.

She walked into the fire-hall with burgeoning curiosity. Dour faces met her shy smile. Several ladies were sat or stood around a hearth, spinning. In the burh they'd had a weaving shed, where thralls spun the wool and wove it into cloth. She looked around in interest, only slightly dispirited by her lack of welcome.

The walls of the hall were panelled with wood and intricately carved, as were the roof posts and doorposts. The longer walls curved inwards towards the gable ends. The ladies were sat on silk cushions that adorned the benches around the walls. Beautiful wall hangings added warmth, and weaponry was hung at intervals.

No one made a move to speak or make themselves known to her, until an older lady, who had been deeply absorbed in her spinning, seemed to notice her for the first time. She gave Rowena a warm smile and Rowena walked over to her.

'You seem very busy,' she said pleasantly.

The woman shook her head and shrugged her shoulders, and Rowena realised she was trying to explain that she was unable to understand what she was saying.

The women soon resumed a noisy chatter, and from their pointed glances Rowena was certain most of the conversation was cantered upon her. She knew they would soon tire of the subject however, and kept herself occupied by studying her surroundings.

Although she had the grace not to stare at the Norse, she did notice that like her they wore more than one layer of clothing. All wore beads, some coloured glass, some gold or silver. They were adorned with many rings, bracelets and armbands. And whereas she wore but one brooch, the Norse wore one on either side of their chest and a different shaped one between. From the right hand brooch there hung an unwieldy assortment of objects: keys, knives, combs, scissors and needles.

She wondered if any of the beautiful younger ones had slept with her husband. She doubted that the chieftain would be refused anything. She began to study the women more closely, and decided there were one or two he wouldn't be able to resist. She was curious as to whether he'd beaten any of them; he liked having a woman at his mercy.

She also wondered how many of them had been satisfied by Algitha's clever fingers. There was an extremely curvaceous young woman in the group with a very pretty face, who it seemed to her had the look of sensuality about her. She watched her walking up and down with her spinning, as she noticed many of them did, by holding the distaff in the crook of the left arm, while the spindle, weighted at one end by a disk of stone, was set spinning in the right hand and sank slowly to the floor, drawing the wool out to a thread.

Yes, she thought, of all the ladies she would pick this one out as having a strong libido. Her hips swayed sexily and her breasts jiggled fetchingly. The picture of her with her ample bottom perched over Sigurd's lap, while he delivered one stinging slap after another, came into her mind. She guessed by the colour of her hair that a fair thatch would hide her sex and that in her cleft her clitoris would be pouting with desire.

She would shed a few fie tears when he slapped her, smiling secretly between each slap as the pain turned to stunning pleasure. Her sex would be weeping for his thick member to burrow inside, and when it did she would scream and cling to him as though her life depended upon it.

The girl gave Rowena a knowing smile, and she blushed; it was almost as if she were able to read her mind. Or was Algitha pleasuring her too? If so, mayhap it was a smile of complicity.

Rowena was quite able to imagine the lovely girl spread wide on her bed, while Algitha stuck her experienced tongue into her channel, and played with her nipples. She wondered what colour her nipples were, and whether she liked them flicked or sucked, or maybe both in quick succession.

Rowena began to fan herself; her sensual musings were beginning to make her quite hot. She knew if she didn't stop her train of thought directly she would be driven to look for Algitha and indulge in some more girly fun.

She was on the verge of doing just that when she wisely vetoed her decision. Everyone would find it peculiar if she retired to her bedchamber at this time of the day.

She was feeling quite sorry for herself when another lady entered the fire-hall. Her friends met her with enthusiasm. Rowena expected her to sit with them, but she moved towards her instead. She was dignified and very attractive, in a long linen kirtle topped by a fine shawl. Like her sisters she wore lots of jewellery, though hers, Rowena noticed, was all made of gold and precious stones.

She sat beside her. 'I expect you are finding your first day very strange,' she remarked kindly.

Rowena sighed with relief. 'You speak English.'

'My husband taught me,' she said graciously. 'And I often converse with the thralls who are of your land. I find it relatively easy. Our languages are quite similar, you know.'

'I am glad you're here,' Rowena admitted. 'I was beginning to feel a little lonely.'

The woman pushed a strand of fair hair behind her ears,

where it was gathered into a knot at the nape of her neck before flowing down her back. 'It is naughty of Sigurd to leave you like this. But I'm afraid men think of the land first.'

Rowena shrugged. 'I know little about Sigurd,' she said quickly. 'As you can imagine, we have not been married long.'

The woman started. 'Forgive me, I have omitted to introduce myself.' She smiled. 'I am Gunnhild. And of course you are Rowena. Rig has told me all about you.'

Rowena paled. 'Rig is your husband?' Gunnhild affirmed that he was and Rowena wondered if he had told her about Cwendritha's poison. She would not want to lose her only friend because of such a thing. Gunnhild continued to chatter on quite happily, so she thankfully decided he had kept that titbit to himself.

'I expect everything is alien to you,' Gunnhild remarked sympathetically.

Rowena agreed with her and glanced despondently at the other women still deeply immersed in their gossip. 'It would help if I were able to converse with everyone.'

'That's no problem.' Gunnhild's eyes lit up. 'I could teach you our tongue.'

Rowena brightened. 'That would be wonderful!' At least she would not feel so cut off if she were able to understand what was going on around her.

'I suppose Sigurd's told you we stay here in the shieling for the best months of the year.'

'Sigurd has been a laggard and failed to enlighten me about his home,' Rowena replied quietly, knowing better than to complain that her husband preferred to beat her instead. 'Shieling, is that what this place is called?'

'Aye, it's the largest in Iceland. The home farm is much bigger of course. But then it has to be. He has his own army, as you know.'

Rowena nodded. 'My father is a thane and our warriors farm the land too. They take it in turns to go out on campaign, all except for my father's personal bodyguards.'

As Gunnhild talked some more about Sigurd's army and the farm, Rowena's attention unwillingly strayed to the other girl in the fire-hall again. Her eyes followed the spindle whorls as they rose and sank to the floor. It was such a homely scene she felt more homesick than ever.

'Would you like me to find you some needlework?' Gunnhild offered, noting her distress. 'Then mayhap we could go for a walk.'

Rowena smiled her gratitude. 'Thank you, I'd like that.'

The light in the hall came from the fire and several torches. There was also an opening near the gable end that was covered in calf membrane, so there was sufficient brightness for her to do her stitching by. Thus occupied, they sat contentedly side by side until Gunnhild was called away, so bored by her embroidery by now, Rowena decided to go and explore her husband's domain on her own.

She found that part of the hall was partitioned off into sleeping areas. But she was certain there weren't enough for everyone, and assumed they were kept for those with the greatest authority.

Leaving the fire-hall she saw that two small storerooms and a kitchen opened off the back. She peaked inside the first storeroom and found that it held three large vats for dairy produce. The interior of the second room was quite chilly, and was crisscrossed with two deep stone gullies. They were packed with ice and she surmised it was where they stored the meat.

Rowena noted the chains that dangled from the walls, and shivered. This must be the place Algitha told her about, and she resolved to keep away from it at all costs. Her husband was a fiend and she would not wish to be caught up in any more of his sport.

Walking outside in the fresh air she tried to shut her mind off from what she'd seen by studying her surroundings. Outside the shieling were two old women, busily making lace with their bone needles. They smiled at her and said something in Norse, which she was unable to understand, so she returned their smiles and gave a polite nod.

Behind the shieling and some outbuildings was a wood that burgeoned with tall birches, rowans and willows. As she watched an intricately carved wagon trundled over the hillside, drawn by a cute brown pony, the man who drove the wagon waved at her and she waved back. Sigurd's people appeared to be very friendly and industrious. She breathed in deeply, the air was good in the hills, but nothing could blow away the scene of the wicked chains she had seen in the storeroom.

No matter how hard she tried she could not come to terms with what she'd seen, but it wormed through her every thought and she was laid low with a bad head, forced to seek out her bedchamber. Algitha ministered to her, but nothing would help. Sigurd did not come to her that night and she thanked the Lord he did not. She cared little for his whereabouts as long as she was left in peace.

It was the early hours when she awoke from a restless sleep, her mouth dry. Her tongue rasped over parched lips, and by the light of the candle that still burned, she foraged for something to ease her thirst. The water jug was empty. She clucked her dismay, and wrapping a mantle around her shift, ventured out into the fire-hall.

The fire still burned brightly in the centre of it, and around this were many straw-filled mattresses upon which some of the Norse reposed. The rest were obviously in the partitioned-off bedchambers. She glanced at the sleeping men and women and wished she were able to sleep so peacefully.

A loud sneeze made her jump, and then giggle, for the woman who'd sneezed was twitching her nose and rubbing it violently in her sleep. Even in the dull light Rowena could see that her quilt had received a tear and some feathers were poking through, tormenting her.

A movement on the other side of the fire pit attracted her attention, and she moved back into the shadows fearful of the animalistic grunts that came from there. When her eyes focused better she realised it was a man and a woman having sex.

At first she was overcome with embarrassment and wished herself anywhere but there. Then she realised the couple was either so overcome by passion that it made them oblivious to anyone else, or they cared little for modesty.

Rowena's curiosity got the better of her and she tiptoed nearer. Thinking of the way Algitha had made love to her, and of her tenderness, set her to wondering about this couple. Were they gentle lovers, or did all Norse take their woman as roughly as Sigurd did?

She felt odd witnessing that which should be done in private, but instead of filling her with shame she was beginning to feel a burgeoning excitement.

Having worked her way quietly around the hall she was able to see the lovers more closely. The man she recognised as Olaf, and he was balancing on his knees, his penis moving in and out of the woman's mouth as she sucked with relish. He grunted something in Norse and she released his shaft reluctantly.

The woman's breasts were huge, her teats erect and rosy-red. The man, who was as muscled as the rest of his ilk, grabbed them roughly and she groaned with delight as he suckled on them, his head bobbing from one to the other. The woman sighed loudly and Rowena was able to see that the man's legs were furred with thick hairs, and his cock stuck out from a wheat-coloured thatch. It was long and thick, the bulbous tip purple-hued. Rowena bit her lip; he was a fine specimen and she felt a pang of envy, wishing it were her breasts being sucked by him, her cunny that throbbed with expectancy.

As Rowena watched he grabbed his lover's breasts and pressed them inwards, making a channel into which he stuffed his member. As she gave a small scream of excitement he began to pump into that fleshy pink tunnel. 'Brynhild,' he groaned. 'Brynhild,' his hairy bottom rocking back and forth.

Rowena licked her lips wantonly. She was able to see his balls as they jiggled between his thighs. Fanning herself, and quite unable to stand any more frustration, Rowena slid her own fingers beneath her shift and into the wetness of her womanhood. Finding her pulsing nub she began to stroke it just as Algitha had, taking care not to cry out lest the lovers become aware that they were being watched.

Olaf came with a loud snort of pleasure, shooting his seed over his lover's throat and breasts. She smiled wickedly and began to massage the creamy fluid into the fleshy mounds that had been well fucked by her warrior.

Gilda had once told Rowena that a man's spunk was good for the skin, and that she always saved what she could to keep her body wrinkle free. Rowena had sent her off with a flea in her ear, Gilda's sexual boasting disgusting her. She gave a wry smile; marriage to Sigurd had certainly changed her.

Olaf snuggled down into his bed and began to snore and, to her astonishment, someone else began to sweet talk Brynhild. Soon his hand began to sneak between her thighs, to slide into her damp core. Brynhild wrapped her arms around the new male, opening her thighs wider for his ease.

While Brynhild abandoned herself to her new lover, Rowena was surprised to see another man and woman coupling, swiftly followed by another and another. Olaf and Brynhild's loud lovemaking had obviously awakened them. Rowena wondered if they had silently observed them as she had, then having seen their fill and been sexually aroused, decided to seek their own fulfilment.

Rowena retreated further into the shadows, her heart beating like a drum, her libido in overdrive. When she'd set out to quench her thirst she had not expected to see such carryings-on in her husband's fire-hall.

What happened next caused her to give a little cry of surprise, and to clamp her hand to her mouth lest she be heard. For even more couples were waking and beginning to make love. Then some began to exchange partners, rolling off one body and onto another. But it did not stop there, for as more couples awoke so they became lustier.

Hands began to wander from one pair of breasts to another, from one hard member to another. Rowena saw one woman take a man into her cunny and welcome another into her mouth. Another voluptuous female lay back on her straw bed, her legs wide apart, while one man after another fucked her, the smile on her lips as wide as her thighs.

Rowena thought she had seen enough when two women, far too close to her for comfort, fell on each other and began to kiss passionately. Then their hands and tongues began to frantically explore each other's curves and valleys.

One of the women reached beneath her mattress and brought forth a piece of wood shaped like a man's penis, and Rowena fought back gasps of shock. Slipping the object into her mouth the woman wet it well, then held it up in the firelight, talking softly to her partner – no doubt bragging at what she was about to do to her.

She gently slid the fake penis into her partner's vagina and Rowena could see the woman was already wet with desire. Her dark pink vulva was glistening in the firelight. The observation made her feel even sexier, so that her own love juices began to seep. How she longed to join in, to be cast into that sea of writhing bodies and feel strangers' hands caress her, strangers' mouths suck her nipples and her clitoris. She imagined what it would be like to open her legs and sit on one of the many cocks that were rampantly primed and ready for use.

She sighed; it would have to remain a fantasy. Deep down she would never willingly subject herself to such depravity. She decided that retreat was her best action under the circumstances; it would not do to be discovered spying on the Norse at play.

She turned quietly and, keeping to the shadows, began to make her way back to her bedchamber, her breath coming in shallow gasps. There had never been a sight so welcome as that of Sigurd's huge bed when she reached it, and shrugging out of her mantle she dived beneath the covers.

Too late she realised that she was still thirsty, and silently castigated herself for having stayed to watch the orgy in the fire-hall, instead of going in search of something to quench that thirst. But her first day in the strange land had exhausted her, and she soon succumbed to sleep's welcome arms. However, the thick quilt and the added layer of furs made her far too hot, and she tossed and turned restlessly. Her dreams were filled with visions of naked men and woman frolicking in a large pool. They were beckoning to her, teasing her by pointing to the teats of the women and the cocks of the men.

Rowena shook her head. She was well brought up and would not be tempted into joining them. But her clitoris begged attention and her breasts swelled with need. A man, bolder than the rest, walked up to her and inserted a finger into her sex. Rowena threw her head back in abandonment, thinking that perhaps she would give in to temptation, when someone began to shake her shoulder.

Simply furious for being interrupted she slapped at them irritably, but she was shaken more insistently. 'Wake up, Rowena, wake up.'

Her eyes flickered open and for a few moments she felt completely disorientated, but she soon came rudely awake when dragged roughly from the bed, and the shadows in the bedchamber turned into human form, lifting her, tipping her over a shoulder like a sack of rubbish.

'Put me down!' she cried. 'Put me down at once!'

She kicked and screamed and was slapped on the rump. At the same time someone covered her head with some sort of hood that frightened her all the more. What was happening to her?

'Be still, or you will suffer far worse.'

The gruff male voice silenced her. He did not sound the type to make empty threats. Who was he? Where was he taking her? But with the suffocating hood shutting out the night she could only hope and pray she'd be spared from too much harm.

Chapter Six

He carried her a good few paces and she soon felt the night air on her body. She longed to tear off the suffocating hood, be free of any constraints.

'Where are you taking me?' she demanded, her teeth chattering despite the balmy weather.

There was no reply, and she was carried a goodly way before she was dumped on the ground. She lay there trembling, the cold surface penetrating her thin shift. The hood was loose around her neck and the odour of blood and incense wafted up her nose. She felt about tentatively, but found no clues as to her whereabouts. Then, in the distance, she heard rustling noises.

Her captor was very close, she could hear him breathing. She began to wonder what his next move would be when she heard crunching and snapping noises, and the sound of footsteps and voices coming closer. She was certain there were at least ten to twelve people, maybe more, about to join them.

Rowena tried to reason with her captor again. 'Who are you? What are you going to do with me?'

No one answered, and the sounds came nearer. Suddenly she was dragged to her feet and her hands untied. She gave a sigh of relief that didn't last. She was made to lean against what felt like a thick pole, her hands embracing it behind her, before being tied again. This time the rope was wound around her waist and the pole, making sure she was unable to escape whatever fate they had planned for her.

The rope was rough, it rubbed her through the thin material of her shift, chaffed her delicate skin. There were noises all around her now, people's voices, and the glimmer of light seeping through the garment over her head. The voices were indistinct, sinister sounds that made her spine crawl. Then silence, except for the sound of breathing quite close.

What was happening? Were they watching her as she stood helpless and blindfolded, enjoying her weakness and their control?

Suddenly the hood was torn off and she blinked rapidly. It took a few seconds for her eyes to become acclimatised to the light. When they did she froze, for there was a circle of people around her carrying flaming torches of fire. They were clad in loose black garments, with hoods from which eyeholes were cut, and slits for their mouths. She seemed to be in some sort of a temple, a large building, every bit as large as the fire-hall. In the middle of the floor was an altar bearing fragrant candles and a gold arm ring. Around the altar stood carved figures of all the gods they worshipped, the largest of all being Thor. He was resplendent in a gold and silver chariot drawn by two goats. Odin stood at one side of him and at the other was the naked squatting figure of Frey, the god of peace and sensual pleasure, sporting a huge erect phallus.

They had tied her to a post in front of the gods and she trembled, realising this was the sacred temple of the Norse. It was surreal.

'Wh-who are you?' she asked shakily, her throat dry with fear. 'What do you want?'

'You've been a bad girl, Rowena,' came the reply, the voice a sibilant whisper that chilled. 'A very bad girl. And you have dared flout the rules of Sigurd's household.'

'What are you talking about?' She swallowed hard, aware of the thud of her heartbeat.

As if she hadn't spoken he went on sombrely. 'You have flouted the most important rule.'

'You're mad, I've not been here long enough to do anything wrong,' she spat angrily.

'You go against the laws and still proclaim innocence! Think hard before you reply again.'

The voice was heavily accented and she was unable to

make out who it was. She shook her head, the overpowering fragrance of the candles making her nauseas. 'Leave me alone. Untie me; I just want to go back to bed.'

The group mumbled disapprovingly and he spoke again: 'A good wife is respectful of her husband. A chieftain's wife more so.'

Things became clearer. She bit her lip anxiously; she was to be punished again for accidentally poisoning Sigurd! 'Have I not suffered enough? Will my discipline go on forever? I did not mean to harm my husband, it was a mistake.'

'You have been brought to the council for ignoring the privacy of Sigurd's people.'

Rowena reddened. 'I... I'm sorry. I woke up thirsty and went to the fire-hall in search of a drink.'

'And when you realised that people were indulging in lovemaking you chose to stand and watch.'

A shaking began in her limbs. She had crossed the wrong people. 'I was too embarrassed to move straightaway,' she lied. How could she explain that she was so turned on she was unable to do anything but watch?

The light from the torches flickered unerringly against the darkness. Rowena was sure she would be sick as her stomach lurched in fear. No one spoke. She dropped her head, realising for the first time that her shift was wet with perspiration and clinging revealingly to her body, so that to all intent and purpose she was virtually naked and open to the perusal of the assembled company.

Thinking she glimpsed the glint of eyes in the slits in the hoods, eyes that were zoned in on her nearly naked curves, she stared back. To her utter shame her breasts tingled and her nipples ripened like spring fruit.

The leader stepped forward, just in front of her. 'Perhaps the truth of the matter is that you are immoral, Rowena. That you enjoy watching.'

Rowena's temper flared. 'You dare to accuse me, when

you all knew I was there and enjoyed performing your lewd acts in front of me?'

'Quiet!' the voice ordered angrily. 'You have not been given permission to speak. And it is not your place to question our motives.' There was a pregnant pause before he said, 'Did it not occur to you that you were being tested?'

She flexed her arms, but she was held fast. 'I request permission to speak,' she said miserably, and the man nodded. Rowena adopted a more subservient tone, knowing she was only incurring their wrath by fighting back. 'I am sorry if I upset Sigurd's people and beg forgiveness.'

'Does the group accept the apology?' he asked, turning to the circle. They nodded one after another. 'We are in agreement. But you must perform a penance to erase your sins.'

She was so tired she would willingly agree to anything. 'Of course,' she sighed, thinking she'd be given demeaning cleaning tasks to perform, things beneath the station of a chieftain's wife.

'So, you agree to your punishment?' She nodded. 'Good. So be it.'

He made no move to untie her and she pointedly glanced at her arms. 'Release me, please, so I may have my sleep and awake refreshed and more able to be disciplined.'

'You may not be released. 'Tis far too soon.' The other figures nodded and mumbled their agreement.

'Then I refuse to stand for any of it,' she said, utterly fed up of the whole business.

He took a deep breath, and sounding almost regretful said, 'Then your husband will be informed of your immoral behaviour.'

'No!' That was the last thing she wanted. If Sigurd were made aware of her actions he would flay her within an inch of her life. She stared at the black figures, at the burning torches. Why hadn't she run from the fire-hall when she had the chance? Why hadn't she left them to their heady pleasure instead of watching them?

He laughed mirthlessly. 'You thought you could satisfy your more basic instincts without paying a price. That is not possible. Come, Rowena, you must make a choice.'

'Choice?' she asked caustically. 'I have none. You all know what would happen if Sigurd were to find out. No, I elect to be punished by the group.'

The spokesman nodded his acceptance and she wondered again who he was. She could feel his eyes roving over her helpless form. Was he imagining himself on top of her, rolling on the temple floor, his robes picking up pieces of straw and dirt while he fumbled beneath his robes for his male member?

The itch began between her legs, that wretched itch that made her out of control as she searched for ways to appease it. But it did her little good, those dark eyes still raking her and she was able to do nothing.

But her weakness didn't last. Stiffening her back she glared at him. She would face up to her punishment. Do what they wanted. He stared back and she was frustrated by not knowing who he was. She had seen no one in Sigurd's hall anywhere near his size. He was far taller than any of the others, his voice and manner full of authority. Being tied up and so helpless while he stood towering over her made her so hot for him, it was impossible to ignore.

'When is my punishment to begin?' she demanded.

'I can see that your body is excited by the prospect,' he drawled. 'See how your breasts peak, how your belly rises and falls as your vulva contracts.' She blushed. How dare he?

The group began to whisper, but the man put up a hand and they were instantly silenced. 'You will have your first taste of discipline this night.'

Rowena started. 'First?'

'Of course. Your sin was a major one. Your discipline must be harsh.'

She closed her eyes; she was so weary. Mayhap it was a nightmare she was unable to awake from, but the flaming torches proved it was all too real. She just had to face facts and hope she was up to whatever it was they intended for her.

'Open your eyes, Rowena,' he instructed. 'We want you fully aware of what is happening to you.'

'I do realise that,' she snapped irritably, and his answer was to bring the torch so close she thought her shift would catch alight.

'You are completely at our mercy,' he warned. 'To compound your errors would be extremely foolish.'

How could she feel so sexy at a time like this? But she knew why; he had such an air or superiority, such strength about him he was irresistible.

The figures resumed their whispering, eerie, sibilant whispers that resounded around the temple. Then they began to chant. A clap of thunder roared in the heavens, followed by a jagged fork of lightning that did nothing to sway the group from their plan, even though it left Rowena feeling even more shaken than before.

The chanting ceased as suddenly as it had begun, and the circle parted. Out of the darkness came another robed figure, carrying some sort of container. As it came closer she realised it was a wooden bucket. Without any preamble the contents were thrown over her, and her breath was taken away as icy water soaked her. She was left shivering, her shift clinging even more obscenely than before.

The circle began to move, and she tried to contain her fear as they formed a line that silently approached like a huge snake. Was each one going to take her right there in the temple? The thought terrified her, her trembling intensified.

The first figure stopped, holding a torch so that she was completely visible, her shift hugging each curve, each valley, making her look far more vulnerable than if she'd been completely naked. The eyes moved over her in fascination, following every form-fitting path of the material. The figure didn't touch her. It didn't have to; the eyes mauled her as thoroughly as any touch.

Rowena's trembling body heated, but not with shame. She was reacting to the people just as disgracefully as she had earlier when she watched them fornicate in the firehall.

The leader was watching her too, watching her closely, taking in every traitorous nuance of her flesh, just as the figure in front of her seemed eager to commit every last detail of her form to memory.

The first of the group stood aside, the movement obviously a silent command for the line to move forward. The next hooded figure did more than look; it touched her hair, smoothing the silky strands as if in wonder. The fingers began to massage her scalp, and from the faceless hood came a lilting sound, almost like a lullaby.

Rowena whimpered as she was completely captivated by the weird but enjoyable actions. And she was mistaken about the strange song sounding like a lullaby; it was far too sensual for that. The hands moved from her scalp and began outlining her lips, forcing fingers into her mouth, gliding over her teeth and gums, her palate, making her mouth tingle with the same need as her sex.

The line moved on again. The next person reached out and pressed her stomach, kneaded until her thighs parted hopefully and her clitoris swelled insistently. Her breasts and nipples were prodded and pinched so hard she cried out, but the pleasurable pain flooded her wet furrow. A hand dug into the shadow between her thighs and knuckles rubbed her sex.

She cried out with pleasure, her musky waters flowing onto the Norwegian's skin. Then to Rowena's misery the delightful stimulation ceased, and knuckles were thrust inside her mouth so she could taste her own salty dew. She was on fire, burning and shaking with need. She struggled to break free of her bonds, longing to stick her own fingers in her aching sex, bring herself to orgasm.

But the rope bound her too firmly to the post.

And still they came; fingers and mouths pinching and licking, sucking and biting, tempting and testing her to distraction, so she was a mass of unfulfilled flesh.

The last and final member of the group, the leader, stepped forward and, although the enveloping robes were sexless, there was no mistaking his maleness. The powerful shoulders belonged to no female.

He stood there for a few moments, his eyes glinting, and she felt as though the little will she had left was being drawn from her and into those hypnotic orbs. His face moved closer still and she was able to smell his clean male scent, that set up a primeval urge so strong it seemed to drum right through her. Before he so much as touched her it was as though his fist was deep inside her, wrenching her insides out, dissolving her bones.

When his hands slid teasingly over her curves he pushed his body against her, grinding back and forth until she thought she would die if he didn't remove his robe and possess her.

Inflamed to breaking point she tried to block her feelings; think of the things Gunnhild told her about life in the shieling. But it was so difficult when he was doing everything he could to excite her. 'Stop it, you fiend, leave me alone,' she begged.

The deep voice was like honey when he whispered, 'What is it you really want, Rowena?'

'You know exactly what I want.'

'Tell me, Rowena. Spell it out for me.'

He wanted her to beg, to forget her dignity and plead with him to make love to her. But there was no way she would. 'Go to hell!' she spat.

'Why are you so afraid of admitting your desires?' he goaded.

There it was again, that teasing tone. He was still expecting her to give in. She had been weak in the shieling when unable to turn away from the orgy, she would not let herself down again.

Seconds passed. The pain of her bonds was nothing to the agony of wanting him. When he bent forward and skimmed her lips with his own it was like the touch of a butterfly's wing, but nonetheless, so intoxicating her legs seemed to turn to water.

He took a step back in order to study her. Seeing her eyes glaze over he repeated his action. But this time it started slowly, softly and more firmly, the pressure building until the kiss took her over. She had only ever dreamed of being kissed like that, had never experienced it until now. It left her totally disorientated, hanging from her bonds like a bundle of rags.

The possibility of him untying her and laying her on the temple floor, so he could assuage the agonising hunger in her, was foremost in her mind. And it was the most thrilling scenario she had ever imagined. Her heart began to palpitate, her pulses to race. Every part of her was ready to dissolve into him, to become one with the masterful, hooded figure.

She closed her eyes during the kiss, and when he removed his lips her lashes slowly fluttered open to find he was no longer there. She felt drugged and totally surprised to see no one left in the temple. During the kiss they had all filed off leaving her with the leader, and now even he was gone.

Rowena waited, her breath catching in her throat when she realised this was her punishment. He had taken her to the edge of paradise and, just when she had sight of the portal opening to welcome her inside, it was slammed shut in her face.

Her head dropped and tears rolled down her cheeks, her flesh in a delirium of need. She had never felt like this before, could never feel worse. Wouldn't someone take pity and release her from her torment?

As though hearing her inner voice, two figures moved into the circle of light radiated from the candles on the altar, and she sighed with relief. He had come back for her. But she soon saw by the slightness of their build she was to be disappointed. Even so, if they released her she would search Algitha out and let her comfort her.

'Thank goodness,' she sighed when they came nearer. 'I knew you wouldn't leave me here too long.'

She wasn't sure they understood her language until one said gruffly, 'You accepted your punishment and there can be no going back.'

'Yes, but I didn't expect to be left here,' she sobbed. 'Do anything you like, but for pity sake don't leave me here.'

They ignored her, but the one who seemed to understand English held his torch over her. The other one, the silent one, reached deep into a linen bag and brought out what looked like a piece of jewellery that glinted in the dull light. Then, taking the material of her shift, he ripped it from neck to hem and cradled one of her breasts in his palm. She inhaled swiftly at the glorious contact.

She wondered if they were going to tease her some more, or if the sight of her near-naked body had brought them slinking back to take their pleasure of her, despite the brave words. Shame and anger warred with her body's desperate needs.

Her breast bloomed in his hand and she tried to brace herself against her natural sensuality. But her mouth slackened and her breath quickened. When he clipped the piece of jewellery to her nipple she gasped, the pain making her eyes water. She glanced down at the cruel metal as it dug into her delicate flesh. So they hadn't finished with her after all. They had come back to torture her some more with their fiendish tricks.

Tears ran down her cheeks, they were so hateful. She wouldn't be surprised if Sigurd had arranged all this. The leader told her she was being tested in the fire-hall, and it would be just the kind of prank he would pull, leaving her naked and helpless in front of his people. She gasped and her self-pity dissolved, for the strangest thing happened, a divine signal was darted to her pleasure centre.

'That is good, yes?' the one who spoke English asked,

and she imagined him smiling beneath his hood, watching her nipples bud and blush as the strange object held her in its embrace.

Rowena closed her eyes against the flickering torch, against their smug eyes. But she was unable to shut out the pain as he clamped some more gold to her other nipple. It was so uncomfortable she gritted her teeth to stop herself from crying out in agony. Then to her dismay the same thing happened, the gold bit into the roseate tip, bringing her other breast alive to its clawing, hedonistic effect.

The one holding the torch gave it over to his partner, and taking the bag also reached inside and brought out more sparkling metal.

'What are you going to do?' she asked nervously.

'Give you more stimulation until your beautiful body is begging to be relieved.'

Rowena almost laughed, her vagina wet from the pressure of the strange jewellery and the men's eager eyes. 'You're wasting your time,' she lied, her denial useless.

They smiled, their breathing uneven at the sight of her naked beauty. One parted her legs and insinuating fingers into her furrow.

'All right, you've proved your point,' she said raggedly. 'Now let me go.'

The one who spoke her tongue shook his head and slid his fingers into her wetness again, more firmly this time, and tears of delight filmed her eyes. 'You are wet,' he observed smugly, speaking in Norse to his partner, who made an excited hoot and laughed.

The front of their robes tented and she rolled her head back against the post. When would it end? 'Does my husband know of the liberties you take with his wife?' she demanded.

'I am sure he'd be more interested in what we had to say,' he reminded her nastily.

She was about to reply when the quiet man caught his

friend's elbow and said something urgently, nodding to the shadows. His partner hurriedly knelt at her feet, then to her consternation he took one of her vaginal lips and attached a piece of jewellery to it. She gave a cry as even more pain surged through her body. How much degradation was she supposed to suffer?

'Don't,' she begged. 'No more, I can't...' She paused; as with the nipple jewellery the pain became secondary and she was becoming completely in tune with the new sensations. Nevertheless, she was unprepared when he attached yet another, leaving both lips of her vagina clenched tightly in gold teeth. She writhed against the pole as the pressure did its work.

'Is the task completed?'

The husky voice came from the edge of the light, and the men immediately nodded and said something in Norwegian. Rowena thought they sounded rather guilty.

They were dismissed, and she was just able to make out the tall figure of the leader as he emerged from the shadows. She wondered if he'd been there all along, watching her. 'And you call me a voyeur,' she said derisively.

Keeping his distance he asked, 'Do you want something?'

Rowena laughed mirthlessly. 'What could I possibly want trussed up like an animal?' He stayed where he was and she laughed again. 'Are you afraid of getting too close in case you're tempted to finish what you started earlier?'

'You are even more beautiful in anger, Rowena. And yes, I'm very tempted. I don't think there is a man alive who wouldn't be. I'm only human, after all. But we must abide by the rules and tonight is not the time for you and I.'

The pleasurable pains of her restraints were driving her to despair. She gave a deep sigh of frustration. 'So, you admit your weakness for me.'

'I do.'

'Then prove it.' She hoped that if he got closer the sparks she knew flew both ways when they kissed would rekindle and burst into flame.

'You are the wife of the chieftain,' he reminded her solemnly.

'We both know Sigurd has little regard for me. He even sleeps elsewhere.'

'I know.'

She gave a mirthless laugh. 'He's probably with other women as we speak. No doubt my husband has many mistresses.'

'Does it worry you, Rowena?'

His question was unexpected, but she was honest with him. 'I care nothing for Sigurd. He has treated me with disrespect since the hour of our marriage.'

He moved to her, and lifting his robe to his waist she saw he was completely naked beneath and his stiff member was superb. She began to tremble; the overwhelming maleness of him drowning her saturated senses. They were skin to skin, his magnificent arousal pressing against her stomach. She imagined it nestling inside her, imagined him moving until it slid easily in and out, setting up a rhythm that was satisfactory to them both.

'Is this proof enough?' he asked as pre-come started to weep from the eye of his penis.

Rowena sighed. 'It would feel so much better inside me.' She spoke her thoughts aloud, determined to capture the enigma of a man, make him hers.

'All in good time.'

The dark hairs of his chest tickled her breasts, rubbed against her nipple jewellery, causing it to hurt and make her tingle with lust. His thick weapon stood proudly and she almost screamed her frustration. 'How can you stand so calmly with your cock straining when we both know you want me? It would be so easy to slip between my legs. I could wrap them around your waist and we could make wonderful love.'

'That is not about to happen.'

'Then untie me,' she snapped. 'This rope is chaffing my skin.'

'Pain is good discipline,' he retorted. 'And I don't need to bury myself inside you when I can obtain relief like this…'

He rubbed his cock up and down her stomach and she thought she would go insane with desire. It felt so good as it glided against her. He was taunting her and she was completely at his mercy.

'You're not really enjoying yourself, are you?' she challenged, her head resting wearily against the wooden pole, her hips moving with him, trying to bring her sex closer to his erection.

He chuckled. 'Oh, but I am. The thought of seeding all over you is a great turn on.'

'I hate you.'

He laughed louder and she longed to lash out at him. But instead all thought of dignity deserted her, and her will fast draining she writhed against his erection. 'Such a waste,' she sighed. 'While the chieftain sleeps elsewhere there is nothing stopping you taking his wife.'

'Ah, but there is. You're being disciplined. None of this is for your pleasure.'

'You're nothing but an oversized oaf,' she railed, his reply to breathe quicker as his orgasm began.

She tried to shrink away from that slippery shaft, to deny him what he denied her, but the post and the rope held her firm. One last rub produced the desired effect and his sperm spurted up her belly and over her breasts. He lent against her for a few moments resting from his exertions, and the warmth of him, the wonderful feeling of skin on skin delighted her.

He began massaging the creamy discharge into her stomach and breasts. 'Is this what you want?' he asked thickly. 'Does it help ease your longing?'

'Bastard,' she hissed. 'You know exactly what you're doing to me.'

'Of course.'

His reply was calmly cool and she forced back a cry of anguish. 'You will regret this.'

'I think not.' His fingers ceased to work their magic and lay idly at her waist. 'It's my job to see that you suffer for your misbehaviour.'

'Why?' she asked miserably.

'Because I choose to,' he said simply. 'Because taming you is fascinating, watching you suffer a great aphrodisiac.'

His lips captured hers roughly, but even so she gravitated to him body and soul. There was no way she was able to resist him.

He pulled away. He surveyed her steadily while she tried to compose herself. 'Until the next time, Rowena,' he intoned softly.

Just as dawn came with a rosy glow, so two robed and hooded figures released her from her bonds. She was so stiff they helped her back to the shieling. Once more in her own bed she tried to ease her aching body, stop from crying out at the excruciating pain in her limbs as her circulation began to return.

She had taken her first bout of punishment, but she would live from day to day in fear of those hooded figures until they came for her again.

Chapter Seven

Sigurd breathed in the air of the land he had decided to settle, and feasted his eyes on the rolling hills that hugged the sky to their breasts. From his position he was able to see the turf-topped shieling and the other buildings clustered around it. He was pleased with the unobtrusive way they blended in with the countryside. Children played on the grassy mounds, their dogs slumbering in the sunshine.

He was delighted to be back. The pirate in him had been satisfied by his last trip; besides bringing back a good haul in coins and jewels, he had brought the greatest prize ever, the seed of the Serpent.

'Sigurd, you have paid me little attention since your return. Mayhap your new bride has tired you out.'

Sigurd looked down at the feisty woman at his side, and grinned. 'Who's a jealous little puss? I have to see to the land first, you know that.'

Maeve shook her long black hair and scowled. 'I recall other times you have returned impatient to fuck me.'

Sigurd eyed the doe-eyed Irish beauty who was his mistress with amusement. 'Has your cunny been aching for me, sweetheart?'

Maeve took his hand and, lifting her kirtle, thrust it between her thighs. 'Feel how wet I am, love. I've been dying with longing for you.'

'Enough to have been waving your arse at every cock in the district, I'll be bound,' he growled, his flaxen hair turned to gold in the sunshine.

Angered at his suggestion, Maeve dropped her kirtle and swung away from him. 'What difference would it make, when you've been raping every Saxon wench you've laid your hands on?'

'Temper, temper,' Sigurd warned. 'I don't recall your Irish lips complaining when I took you.'

Maeve swirled her skirts coquettishly. It was true; when Sigurd's army had invaded her land she was terrified of the huge Norwegians. But when the fair giant rode up on his horse her heart beat so fast she thought it would burst out of her breast.

She watched his men raping the village women and found it exciting. She abhorred their screams, and far from pitying them, wondered why they had not relaxed and enjoyed the rigid pricks jammed between their thighs.

He had taken her right there in the middle of her village, and she was more than willing, her vulva slick and welcoming for the handsome lord. Back then she was sick and tired of pretending to be a blushing virgin, when she had enjoyed many a secret tryst. She usually chose married men whose wives were far too prim and tight-arsed to make them happy. They weren't disposed to having their sins aired in public any more than she was. When Sigurd stole her away from her land she was a willing victim. She went as a slave and fast became his mistress.

She had been happy in Sigurd's land of fire and ice until now. All that changed when he brought back a bride. Although she knew he could not marry a lowborn slave, she had stupidly put any thoughts of his matrimony from her. She had woven daydreams about him when he was away, and none of those contained a Saxon bitch with red-gold curls and a face that sent men mad with longing.

Bringing her back from her reverie, Sigurd grabbed her and swung her off her feet. She giggled and beat at his chest. 'Let me down, you great lump.'

'And have you complain of being neglected? I think not.'

His lips bore down on hers and she clung to him, savouring the taste of him, the feel of his mouth as it devoured hers. There was not another man in the land, or any other, who made her body sing like Sigurd did. He lowered her gently to the grass and lay alongside her, throwing a thigh on top of her.

Maeve thrilled to the intensity of her feelings; she was ready to explode with love for him. The others, the ones before him, had been nothing in comparison. She was an extremely sensuous person and had needed those diversions, but since falling in love with the great chieftain there had been no one else. He had spoilt her for any other man. In her heart it was and always would be Sigurd, whether he was married or not.

When his hand began to wander up her thigh beneath her kirtle she stopped him. It was important to her that she pleasured him first.

She pressed the firmness of his erection through his breeches, satisfied by his sharp intake of breath. She had yearned for this moment for a long time. Releasing him from his clothes, laying the cloth he sometimes wore in his breeches aside, she took his shaft and licked along the silken skin, at the same time cupping his hairy balls in her hand. He tasted of sweat and man and her thighs trembled with her emotions.

Taking him in her mouth she worked on the bulbous tip, teasing and tantalising him with her tongue and lips. He grew even larger and Maeve surrounded his hardness, her skin glowing as her tongue danced firmly around his heated manhood. She sucked and sucked at his engorged flesh, welcoming him even deeper until the length of him was in her throat. Soon he was convulsing with his come and almost choking her with his seed, which she swallowed as though it was her life's blood.

Her reward was to have his tongue inside her, heating her feminine core, thrilling her with each pull of its silken strength. When he lapped her womanhood she whimpered and held the flaxen head, urging him on. Her clitoris surged into his mouth; her love dew was his mead. His ministrations soon brought the desired effect and the most wonderful sensations built within her. Her climax came like a shooting star, for it was far too wonderful to be of this earth.

Afterwards she lay in his arms, knowing that whatever mood he was in, whether he chose to make love to her or punish her, she was his to command. And she was always open to a little discipline. Her bottom had often warmed to the feel of his switch or his calloused hands, for with each stroke came an intense longing to be possessed by him.

Sigurd parted her thighs; he never needed to rest for long, and inserted her favourite weapon between her nether lips. Soon he was riding her to distraction, the most wonderful stallion she had found.

Afterwards their game began again, the game he always needed to play when he came back from his travels, the game that was their deepest and darkest secret.

Maeve helped him dress, making sure to slip the soft cloth back in his breeches. Sigurd snuggled his head in her lap, sucking on her nipples like a newborn babe, and as always she was sad she could not supply him with mother's milk. She crooned a soft song and he seemed to rest easier. When he emptied his bowels she attended to him as tenderly as she would any babe, washing his skin until he was clean once more. For when the game was over he repaid her by making love to her again and it was more than she could ever ask for.

It was a long time before they parted, and although her lover had taken her to the heights, satisfaction would not truly be hers until she obtained her revenge on the redheaded Saxon bitch!

Algitha was mortified to see her lady so ill-treated, and rubbed her with her special oils to help relieve her painful joints. She could not understand why Rowena was so stiff and tired, and it irked her that she kept her own council. ''Tis wicked to see you so. What ails you?'

'I can only think my body is in shock from Sigurd's ill use,' Rowena replied weakly, having the need to keep her secret for the present. She was far too tired to battle with questions, and her limbs ached so badly she was utterly miserable. Even so, her mind dwelt on thoughts of the leader, of his voice, his manly stance, the feeling of his hands and manhood on her skin.

Algitha went around with drooping shoulders and a hard done by look on her face that drove Rowena to distraction. It was obvious that her handmaiden thought she was keeping something from her, so fed up with her manner Rowena bade her sit down.

'I can't bear to see your miserable face any longer,' she complained, 'so you might as well know that something did happen last night.'

Algitha clapped her hands. 'Oh, mistress, I knew it had. Do tell.'

Rowena took a deep breath. 'It started quite innocently. I needed a drink and was on the way to the kitchen when I heard a sound in the fire-hall. When I went to explore I found a couple making love.'

Algitha giggled. 'Ooh, were they naked?'

'As naked as the day they were born. But the strange thing was that they knew I was there and one couple after another followed suit and began fucking as though there was no tomorrow.'

'And you stayed and watched it all?'

Algitha's mouth gaped and it was Rowena's turn to giggle. 'If the wind changes you'll stay like that, you know.'

The handmaiden closed her mouth, and asked, 'Was it good?'

'It was very interesting. And judging by the reactions of the women the Norse must have the biggest cocks anywhere.'

'Oh, I think they have.'

Algitha blushed and Rowena nudged her elbow. 'What's all this then?'

'I slept in the kitchen last night with one of the warriors and he stretched my cunny like it's never been stretched before.'

Rowena rolled her eyes. 'It seems the shieling is a hotbed of lust.'

'They're always at it in that hall,' Algitha agreed. 'And the way they creep from one bed to another I'm sure no one knows who's sired what child half the time.'

'I forgot to mention,' Rowena remarked in a whisper, lest anyone was passing and she was overheard, 'there were two women making love with a wooden penis.'

Algitha smiled knowingly. 'A dildo. I will use one on you when you're feeling better. Then you can tell me who has the biggest cock of all.'

The women tittered, and although Rowena felt slightly guilty for not mentioning the charismatic leader or what had taken place after the orgy, she was determined to keep it her secret.

Algitha gave her a soothing potion and she fell asleep and her dreams were full of him. She was on a verdant hillside where goats and sheep nibbled the grass. He wore a long flowing cloak, but although he was minus the concealing hood, there was a mist where his face should have been. Her arms reached out for him, and in the surreal world he came to her, his erection as large as she remembered.

She knew she had to have him and that this time she would take the prize. As he was a few inches from her the mist began to dissipate and she caught sight of dark-blue eyes and mocking lips. His arms went round her and she inhaled his skin, the scent of his tumescent prick. She was about to sink to the ground with him when she was taken from behind and tied to a pole.

'You have sinned in Sigurd's hall.'

The voices were heavily accented as the dark cloaked figures circled around her, their torches lighting hollow-eyed faces. Their cloaks opened to a breeze that whipped around the green hillside, revealing that beneath their dark covering they were completely naked. The women had long legs and trim waists, their breasts beautiful globes. The pelts that hid their feminine secrets were wheat-coloured, all except for one, whose mound was completely free of hair.

Rowena struggled to free herself, but as before the ropes that held her were too strong to break. She looked to the leader to help her, but he smiled slyly through the mist that hid most of his features. 'You are here to be punished. The time is not right for you and I. But it will come.'

She stubbornly battled against her restraints. 'I want you now,' she retorted, wondering why he was unable to see that.

'We will have you.'

The cloaked figures circled her with intent, before marching towards her. In their hands they carried sticks. Rowena cried out in fear. 'Go away. I don't want you near me.'

'You have sinned and must be punished.'

The chant went on and on until she wanted to cover her ears. The leader untied her and she rubbed her sore wrists, glad she was free. But the feeling of euphoria wasn't to last, for she was pushed to the ground on her face and her clothes were torn away. One of the women lay over her, stroking her with her large breasts. A man lay beside her and kissed her roughly. Someone wormed his way beneath her and bit and caressed her nipples. Another sucked her clitoris.

The leader watched, his dark eyes sparkling with lust. 'Look at her,' he urged. 'Have you ever seen such a perfect bottom? It is the way with redheads; they have lovely skin. And look at her dainty waist, my hands could quite easily span it.'

Rowena bathed in his praise, in the ministrations of the group, as her body was driven to insensibility by the stroking and caressing. 'Don't stop,' she begged, afraid they would leave her with her desires unsatisfied like the last time.

The leader bent over her, his robes tickling her back. Rowena sighed happily as he began to dabble his fingers

She sighed her relief, and aiming to keep him sweet said, 'She is an elegant and lovely person.'

'So you do not hate all the Norse?'

He indolently reached for his breeches and stepped into them. Rowena was surprised by his easy manner. 'I am merely wary of anyone who comes to my land to plunder.'

His head snapped round. 'This is your land now.'

His jaw squared stubbornly and the part of his scar that was not hidden by his beard looked white and angry against the rest of his skin. She sat up, and covering her breasts with the quilt asked impulsively, 'Your face, was it done in battle?'

'Yes, when I was not yet a man. The cur that did it took advantage of that. But I've not forgotten the debt I owe him.' He smiled a cruel smile. 'One day, my Saxon wife, I will tell you the story that surrounds this scar.' He fingered it thoughtfully. 'Do you find it disagreeable?'

'No, why should I?' If anything it enhanced the roguish looks, but she was not about to tell him that, any more than she would give him the satisfaction of asking whose bed he'd been in when hers was empty.

He seemed pleased by her answer. 'I'm glad to hear it. I will not get an heir with someone who finds me distasteful.'

Rowena quailed. 'An heir?'

'Of course. You're not barren, are you?'

He appeared anxious and she struggled to reply. 'I... I have not had the opportunity to find out.'

'That is something we must remedy.'

His voice was threatening and Rowena held her hot cheeks. She had been far too absorbed in her misery to so much as think of having a family with him. The thought appalled her. 'I would not wish my child to be brought up a heathen.'

His eyes narrowed. 'Be careful, wife, I still have the paddle at hand and will not hesitate to use it should you need discipline.'

Rowena lowered her gaze. She wanted to tell him just what she thought of him and his paddle, but the memory of her beating was still too fresh in her mind.

'By the way,' he said, his eyes slanted curiously. 'What are you doing lazing in bed at this time of day? Everyone in the shieling and farm share the work, even though we have thralls aplenty. As the chieftain's wife you will be expected to supervise.'

She sought her mind for an excuse. She could not tell him she'd been up half the night eagerly watching an orgy in his fire-hall. Or that she'd spent the rest of the night tied to a pole as punishment, a burning longing plaguing her loins.

'I am not used to sailing the seas,' she said quickly. 'I think the journey exhausted me more than I realised.'

'Then let us see if your rest has given you an appetite. Come, 'tis time to eat.'

Sigurd's fire-hall had been set with trestles and benches and delicious smells were coming from the kitchen. They were given water and towels in order to wash, then Sigurd led her to an intricately carved settle near the hearth and the largest roof pillars. When seated Rig and Gunnhild sat on a similar settle opposite them, with the hearth between.

Rowena turned to Sigurd enquiringly. 'The seating plan is interesting.'

'The settles we use are called high seats and only for the use of the master and mistress and honoured guests.' He pointed to the rest of the household, who resided at trestles arranged in two rows along each side of the fire-hall. 'The places near the centre are considered more honourable than those far out.'

'I see.' Rowena studied her fellow diners carefully, and was just as thoroughly inspected in her turn. She wondered who, among these people, had been in the hall during the orgy, and more importantly, who had been part of the group who tied her to the post, and messed with her mind and body until she begged the leader for sex.

She spoke a few friendly words with Rig and Gunnhild while the servants were serving the food. Sigurd peered suspiciously into his drinking horn, and Gunnhild asked innocently, 'What ails you, Sigurd? Is something amiss with your drink?'

He swirled the contents of the horn and crooked an eyebrow at Rowena. 'What say you, wife? Is there anything amiss with my ale?'

She hated him for the joke, which was in poor taste. 'Nay, husband, I'm sure it's fine.'

Gunnhild was about to question their strange conversation, but was silenced by a dig in the ribs from Rig.

A latecomer joined them, a man with attractive dark-blue eyes who was every bit as tall and broad as Sigurd, though leaner in the hip. Rowena trembled when he sat opposite her, a mocking smile on his handsome face. It was he, she was sure of it. Yes, he was definitely the 'leader'. She had never seen eyes quite like his before. They were the colour of sapphires and they glinted as magnificently as any jewel.

'Forgive me for my tardy behaviour,' he excused. 'I lost track of time.'

Sigurd grinned. 'I wager a beautiful wench kept you, Leif. 'Tis the only reason that would keep you away from your food.'

Leif smiled and Rowena's heart seemed to miss a beat. 'You do me a disservice, Sigurd. The ladies will think me a wastrel.'

He slapped the bottom of the pretty young Irish girl who served him and she blushed. Sigurd picked up his ale. 'Rowena, allow me to introduce you to my cousin, Leif. Cousin, meet my new wife, Rowena.'

Rowena prayed her cheeks would not give her away but she felt them burning.

Leif raised his horn. 'A toast to the newly married couple.'

His eyes were guileless and Rowena wished she were

as clever at hiding her feelings. She lost her appetite after that, but managed to taste a little of most things put in front of her, hoping to allay Sigurd's suspicion. And she couldn't fault the food, for there was meat aplenty, all well cooked and tender, and the buttermilk was the best she had ever tasted.

'Try some of this,' Leif said, pointing to some cheesy curds in front of her. 'It's called skyr.'

Amusement played at the sides of his mouth, and Rowena could not help but blush when she recalled how close they were the previous night. How he had her stripped naked and brought himself to climax by rubbing his proud manhood on her stomach.

Sigurd was watching her carefully, almost as though he suspected something, so she smiled and tried the curd. 'Extremely palatable,' she said graciously.

'I'm relieved it meets your approval,' Sigurd remarked, an eyebrow raised slightly.

Rowena knew it was a warning sign. He was beginning to wonder why the innocent remarks flowing back and forth seemed charged with tension. She tried to lighten the atmosphere by telling a joke one of her brother's had told her, and for once she told it skilfully and Sigurd laughed heartily and seemed more relaxed.

Then people took it in turns to tell stories. Sigurd told her that they were known as sagas. Rowena kept a smile on her lips, though extremely bored after the third saga, for they were all related in Norwegian and she was unable to understand any of them.

The gathering grew noisy but nothing could distract her from the handsome man who was her husband's cousin, the man who could manipulate her with just the blink of his blue eyes.

Then someone began to play a harp, and a lovely dark-haired woman halfway down the hall got to her feet and began to sing in a voice so sweet Rowena thought she sounded like an angel. With a start she realised she was singing to Sigurd, and that she was able to understand every word, for the woman was singing in Irish.

From a small child she had been told that she was half Irish, and Grainne had tried to explain to her about the beauty of the country she came from. She taught her the Irish tongue, and up until the day she left Wessex they had conversed in that language when alone.

The woman was looking at Sigurd with passion in her eyes, and the words she sang were words of love, of lovers' trysts and joys shared. It was obvious to Rowena that Sigurd understood every word, for his mouth had softened and his eyes held a glazed look.

Rowena was surprised to see that her husband had a heart after all. It was obvious that the lovely Irish girl was his mistress, and Rowena admired her, for anyone who was able to find a soft spot in that granite body deserved her prize.

All eyes were turned on her for her reaction. She smiled sweetly; why would she care who Sigurd slept with when she only had eyes for his enigmatic cousin? Leif was watching her closely too, his handsome face grim and his knife digging absently into his trencher.

She wondered what had displeased him; surely Sigurd's mistress and her love ballad had not disturbed him. The hall was stuffy and Rowena excused herself; she needed fresh air.

Sigurd didn't seem to have any objections, so she made her way to the stables. The horses whinnied and she patted their velvet noses. 'You're so beautiful,' she said, feeding one a honeyed cake from the table.

'She is called Syn, for one of the goddesses.'

She turned, her spine thrilling to his voice, his body so near she was able to feel his breath on her neck. 'She's quite lovely.'

Leif fondled his own mount. 'And this is Alsvid, who is named for one of the sun's horses because he is immensely strong.'

Rowena lifted a dainty eyebrow. 'The sun has horses?'

He laughed. 'Oh yes, and she's always in a great hurry

because she is chased by Skoll, the wolf who is always snapping at her heels.'

Rowena shook her head in bewilderment. 'The sun is chased by a wolf?'

'Aye. One day soon I will tell you about our gods and how it all began.' He smiled at her and her stomach seemed to somersault. 'Do you ride?'

'I like to ride,' she replied lightly.

'Would you come riding with me?'

She blushed. 'What will Sigurd think?'

'That I'm sniffing after you like a dog on heat. But he will feel safe in the knowledge that I'll do no more than flirt and enjoy your company, because I am family.'

She gave a whimsical smile. 'And what is the truth?'

'The truth is I want to feel your naked skin close to mine again. And I will spend every waking minute trying to persuade you to sleep with me.'

He caressed her neck and she trembled. 'I thought punishment was your only aim.'

He shook his head. 'Had I not led the group in the shieling you would have suffered far worse than you did. I don't usually get involved in their games, but when I saw the vision that was my cousin's bride, I wanted to protect you from them. The only way to be sure of that was to take the lead.'

'If you wanted me so much, why did you not take me when you had the chance?'

'Don't you think I would have laid you on your back and stretched your lovely cunny if it was at all possible? But every move I made was being monitored, so I had to play out the game in order to please them and, by so doing, save you from their true wrath.'

'I didn't think the Norse feared anything,' she said flirtatiously.

'You're right,' he agreed. 'But had I fought every one, Sigurd would have found out and the reason would have soon come to the fore.'

Rowena sighed and leaned into his kiss. 'So that's what

you meant when you said the time wasn't right for us.'

'That was exactly what I meant.' His hands caressed her breasts and she clung to him, welcoming his knee as it nudged her legs apart and insinuated itself just at the apex of her thighs. It slid back and forth over her sex and she was wet in no time.

'I want you, Rowena,' he breathed. 'I want you more than any other woman I've ever met. And I think you want me too.'

'I do want you, Leif. I felt something between us from the beginning. It was as though we were in a magic place where only you and I existed.'

She was moving with him, and as his knee slid against her wet furrow, so she pressed down on him. His hands grabbed her bottom cheeks and pulled her closer, squeezing them, his knee moving faster. Rowena's breathing became ragged and he muffled her screams of passion with his mouth as she came, her thighs shaking.

He lifted her in his arms and took her then, up against the wall of the stable, his hot meat ploughing into her warm wet centre. It was how she expected it to be with her husband; exciting, scintillating, gentleness mixed with passion.

Her hands were on his muscled back and she thrilled at the strength of him. 'Why couldn't it have been you who came to my land instead of Sigurd?' she wondered aloud.

'If only,' he groaned, and shot his seed inside her.

Afterwards, knowing she must look bedraggled from her loving, she tidied herself. 'What if Sigurd comes looking for me and finds us together?'

'I don't think you need worry about my cousin,' he said, with the same grim smile she'd seen earlier, 'for as you know, he's not a faithful husband. Maeve has his attention this night, so don't be surprised if he warms her bed and not yours.'

'You don't approve, do you?' she asked in surprise.

'I only know that if I had you for my own I would never look elsewhere.'

'Is that why you flirted with all the pretty girls in the hall?' she asked teasingly.

He kissed the top of her head. 'It was a ruse. If Sigurd noticed I only had eyes for you he'd flay me alive.' He winked wickedly. 'Or should I say he would have died trying.' He studied her carefully for a few moments.

'What is it, Leif?' she asked, sensing he wanted to tell her something.

'I just wanted you to know that Sigurd has changed. As a boy he was kind and gentle, but something bad happened to him and he hasn't been the same since.'

Rowena tried to imagine Sigurd as a kind, gentle person, and failed abysmally. 'What was it?'

'Come, 'tis a nice evening, we shall walk by the river.' He saw the flicker of alarm in her eyes. 'Don't be afraid, Sigurd will be occupied elsewhere. Besides, what can be wrong with becoming acquainted with your husband's cousin?'

It all sounded innocent enough, so she acquiesced and they took the path that ran alongside the river. Leif picked up some flat stones and skimmed them along the water, and she clapped her hands at his expertise. Then they sat on a rock overlooking the fast moving current.

'I hope you don't regret this,' he sighed deeply.

'Please,' she urged, 'I might feel better if I understand some of his past.'

He capitulated. 'Very well. A long time ago, when we were both children, Sigurd's mother, Helgi, fell in love with someone else. His father, Thorkel, found out and as you can imagine was very angry. After a while Helgi could no longer live with that anger, so she took Sigurd and fled with her lover.'

Rowena's eyes were wide. 'What happened then?'

'They took a ship, planning to go to Russia, where her lover's brother was jarl of Kiev.' His expression sobered. 'But the ship was attacked by Estonian pirates who enslaved them all.'

She gasped in dismay, surprised to find herself still

beside the river; Leif had almost made the past come alive for her. 'How did they survive?'

He shook his head sadly. 'Helgi was not strong and died soon after her capture. My uncle searched ceaselessly for his son and eventually found him six years later, and was able to buy him out of captivity.'

Rowena blinked away her tears. 'Thorkel must have been overjoyed to be reunited with Sigurd after so long.'

'Aye, but Thorkel was full of bitterness. He never took another wife, and I fear he passed some of that animosity on to Sigurd. For although he had his fill of women like any other healthy male, his emotions have always remained separate.'

Rowena folded her hands in her lap, feeling something sap out of her. 'That accounts for a lot.'

Leif nodded. 'And there are his years of captivity to take into consideration. He never talks of them, but from what my father said he was treated like an animal. When they found him he was nothing but skin and bone.'

Leif noted her tears and hugged her to him. 'Poor Sigurd.' She tried to visualise the young child after having spent his formative years enslaved, back with his father, a man changed, twisted by bitterness and hate. How Thorkel must have hated his wife for her infidelity, for running away with her lover, taking his son, a son he was made to search six long harrowing years for. It was little wonder he had become embittered.

And Sigurd was the logical one for him to confide in, the one to be indoctrinated with Thorkel's own feelings on womankind. He had grown up with it day and night until it was a canker in his insides eating away at him like a disease.

'Mayhap I will be able to help him a little now,' she said hopefully. 'Sometimes he makes it so hard I cannot bear to even look at him.'

'Does he beat you?' Leif asked in concern.

'Sometimes.' There was no way she was able to tell him how badly.

He slammed a fist into the palm of his hand. 'Then I will speak to him. I will not have you hurt.'

'No!' she wailed. 'You will make things worse for me. If Sigurd finds out I have spoken about it he will be very angry.' He looked doubtful but she tugged his sleeve fearfully. 'You must promise me, Leif.'

'All right, but this must be addressed soon.'

Rowena looked nervously over her shoulder. 'I had better return to the hall, just in case he has not sought Maeve's bed and is waiting for me.'

'Come riding with me tomorrow,' he pleaded.

'I'll try,' she promised, and they parted on a kiss.

Sigurd was no longer in the hall, but she found Algitha in her bedchamber, lighting candles and turning down the bed. She looked embarrassed, but Rowena smiled. 'Don't fret on my account. If Sigurd's gone to his mistress this night I am pleased.'

'Then I am pleased you feel so, for he is the sort to break a kind and loving heart.'

Rowena wasn't quite sure how to broach the subject, but it had to be done. 'Sigurd wants a child,' she said, quailing at the thought of bearing his infant.

Algitha smiled knowingly. 'And you don't want to fall pregnant by your husband. Of course it would be different if it were to be a handsome fellow who has just come to the fire-hall.'

Rowena stiffened. 'What are you talking about?'

'I know you well enough to recognise the signs.'

She wrung her hands. 'I cannot risk getting pregnant by either one. What shall I do, Algitha?'

'I can mix a douche for you to use whenever you make love. But don't let your husband know or his wrath will be felt all over Iceland.'

Algitha massaged her shoulders, allowing her fingers to graze her nipples. 'Of course, I can love you,' she said, finding the hot furrow between her legs that Leif had enjoyed earlier, 'and you will have no worries.' She felt some of the seed that seeped back out of Rowena's vagina, and sighed. 'But first it would be wise to give you a douche to use now. You have obviously been a naughty girl this evening.' She chuckled. 'I envy you.'

Rowena sighed. 'Tomorrow we go riding.'

Algitha giggled. 'And who knows what you might get up to on a horse with that one beside you?'

The thought made Rowena cross her legs and smile. 'What indeed.'

Chapter Eight

The following morning Rowena was aglow with the expectation of riding with Leif. But there was no sign of either him or Sigurd in the fire-hall. Algitha presented her with an assortment of keys. 'What are these?'

'Sigurd bade me give you the keys of the household, mistress.'

Rowena attached them to her belt, muttering angrily beneath her breath; no doubt he thought them a fair exchange for her beatings. 'Where are Sigurd and Rig?' she asked Gunnhild when she appeared. 'Are they out in the pastures?'

Gunnhild raised her eyebrows in surprise. 'Sigurd has taken some of the men and journeyed to the coast to trade with the merchant ships. He will also be bartering dairy products with the seaside farmers for dried fish for the winter. The packhorses were fair straining under the weight of their packs.' Her eyebrows rose. 'Didn't he tell you? They left very early.'

Rowena sighed heavily. 'He didn't think fit to inform me.' Her heart sank. 'And what of his cousin, Leif?'

'Sigurd invited him and he was obliged to accept. Though I must admit he didn't appear overly keen.'

Rowena wanted to throw something – Sigurd always ruined everything! She cast her eyes around the hall. Had her husband taken Maeve with him? She was annoyed to see the woman was nowhere in sight.

'Of course, Sigurd will be entertained in a nearby farm.'

'Of course,' Rowena replied dryly. And his mistress will be made most welcome, she thought miserably. It was one thing to flout their affair in the hall, but to actually go away with the woman was, in Rowena's eyes, completely disrespectful to her.

A passing Norsewoman caught Gunnhild's attention,

and when she turned back to her she gave Rowena an encouraging smile. 'I can see Sigurd's leave-taking has upset you. We must remedy that. What do you say to beginning our lessons today?' Rowena stared at her blankly. 'You wanted to learn our tongue,' Gunnhild reminded her. 'Just think how pleased your husband will be when he returns to find you've taken the trouble to learn some Norse.'

She nodded half-heartedly, wanting nothing more than to hear the sound of Leif's voice, the feel of his strong body lying next to hers. 'How long will they be gone?'

'A few days.'

Rowena wanted to scream; she would die with waiting for her new love. But then it occurred to her that while Sigurd was away she would be free of his cruel beatings, so it wasn't all bad.

After the meal Rowena was taken on a tour of the shieling and its outbuildings, so she could correspond the keys in her possession with the locks they turned. She was fascinated by the bathhouse and promised herself a visit as soon as was possible.

Gunnhild was as good as her word, and part of the day she instructed Rowena in Norse. She was pleased to find it much easier than she imagined, and she began to envisage her husband's expression when he returned and realised she was able to understand a few words of his tongue.

When they tired of this Gunnhild showed her how to spin wool. She taught her how to hold the distaff in the crook of the left arm while the spindle whorl was set spinning by the right hand and sank slowly to the floor, drawing the wool out to a thread. This thread would be wound up and the process repeated until a large ball of yarn had been produced.

Rowena was awkward at first, but soon a rhythm developed and she let out an excited squeal. The Norse ladies, whom she had already learned to say good day to, smiled warmly at her efforts.

'What are they saying?' she wanted to know, when they bombarded her with a string of Norse.

'The ladies are pleased that their chieftain's Saxon wife should take such an interest in their simple spinning,' Gunnhild informed her happily. 'They say you have accomplished much in one day.'

Rowena smiled. 'Tell them they are very kind to say so.'

While Gunnhild was thus employed, Rowena noticed that not all the women were eager to be friendly. A few of the younger ones regarded her slyly, and she was convinced they were the women who had taken part in the orgy in the fire-hall.

Having thrown off her disappointment she was eager to learn all she could in her new home. 'I wish to know more,' she averred animatedly. 'I have noticed that although you have many thralls everyone does their share.'

'In the old country we would have left all manual labour to the thralls,' Gunnhild replied. 'But this is a new land and we have much pleasure in it, so we all do our bit. But you are Sigurd's wife; I'm not sure, Rowena.'

But Rowena was hard to refuse when she had her heart set on something and Gunnhild gave in graciously. 'The weaving and the dairy can wait until tomorrow,' she said, laughing at the younger woman's energy. 'The evening meal will be ready soon, and Sigurd will not thank me to find his wife has overtaxed her strength in his absence.'

While Rowena learned the workings of his shieling Sigurd was being wined and dined by Gunnar Egilsson and his sister, Freyjr. The voluptuous, yellow-haired beauty stood beside him at the shore watching the boats unload their cargo. She was at her most desirable with jewelled combs in her flaxen hair, and a red kirtle that billowed out behind her in the sea breeze, showing her breasts off to perfection.

'You don't visit us often enough, Sigurd,' she complained, tugging at the sleeve of his tunic.'

'It sounds as though you miss me, Freyjr,' he replied with a winning smile.

Freyjr grazed her fingers along his bearded jaw. 'If only you knew how much,' she purred, pressing her breasts into his chest. 'The farm is so boring sometimes I could scream.'

'It sounds as though you need to find yourself a husband. He will keep you occupied.'

She cast her eyes around the shore at the men who busied themselves at their task. 'Not one of these compares with the great Sigurd Thorkelsson. How is a poor body to manage when the handsomest and bravest man of all lives elsewhere?'

Sigurd grinned down at her; she was a fine wench, well padded in all the places that mattered. It looked like his luck was in. 'Your flattery will give me a big head.'

She plucked excitedly at his chest and giggled girlishly. 'Oh, I do hope so.'

Sigurd's eyebrows rose. 'I had thought you an innocent, Freyjr.'

'What man longs for an innocent in his bed?' She gave him a smouldering look. 'I am all woman, Sigurd, and anxious to prove it to you.'

Sigurd's cock surged. 'Then who am I to stop you?' he growled, pressing her buttocks to bring her closer, so she was able to feel his stiff shaft dig into her stomach.

'Ooooh,' she cried, 'you are hard!'

'I am always ready to oblige a lady,' he boasted, grabbing a handful of breast, much to the amusement of some nearby sailors.

Freyjr was completely unfazed by them – if anything it made her more excited. 'Come with me behind the rocks, Sigurd,' she suggested, nibbling his earlobe. 'For I'm bursting with need.'

'Whatever you say,' he replied, giving the seamen a sly wink.

Freyjr giggled as waves lapped at her feet. She danced away from them, dragging Sigurd with her. It began to drizzle, but she was aware of nothing but the longing she felt for the famed warrior and the ache between her legs that she wanted him to ease.

When they were hidden from sight she began to undress. 'Hurry, Sigurd,' she urged, slipping her kirtle and smock from her shoulders, licking her sensuous lips. She knelt on the wet sand in front of him, her body white and wanton against the lapping tide.

He couldn't believe the force of her desires; it was a distinct turn on to have a woman with such a healthy sexual appetite. Not that Maeve wasn't keen, but sometimes her devotion bored him. Sigurd gazed on her dark-tipped breasts and shapely hips with pleasure, but the fair hair at the apex of her legs was his target, and he knelt in front of her, taking the nipple of one breast in his mouth and the other in his hand, foraging with eager fingers between the lips of her pleasure zone.

She was as wet as the thundering ocean, and his fingers soon dripped with the salty tang of her. While he frigged her nubbin so she took his huge staff, a gasp on her lips at his size. They masturbated each other and she came with a loud scream that drowned out the sounds of the gulls.

'Lay back, my love,' she sighed. 'Let me ride you.'

'Whatever you say,' Sigurd said, surprised; he was always the one in charge and this forward bitch was a revelation to him – though not an unpleasant one, as she sat on his cock and rode them both to satisfaction.

Rowena's fingers felt clumsy as she practiced weaving on an upright loom propped against the wall in the fire-hall. Sigurd and Leif had been gone for many days and she was trying to keep herself occupied to stop herself pining for her new love.

'Very good.' Gunnhild applauded her fervently. 'Now let me just show you once more.' Rowena moved over and Rig's wife repeated the steps of weaving 'See there are two sets of warp threads,' she said patiently, pointing to the threads held taut by stones that hung off the ends.

Rowena nodded her understanding; she picked things up quickly and it would be good to show off to Sigurd when he returned.

'Horizontal rods control their positions as the woof is slipped through and beaten upwards with the wooden sword.'

'I like the cloth best when it's dyed,' Rowena said, feeling the more valuable material that was tossed over a nearby trestle.

Gunnhild's forehead furrowed. 'That reminds me; we need to dye up some more later. 'I hope we've enough madder to make up the red dye. Violet's my favourite,' she said with a sly smile. 'It was the colour I was wearing when Rig proposed. Violet and reddish-brown dyes come from certain lichens. I'll show you when we have the time.'

Gunnhild continued her instruction on the use of the loom, but a stocky man who had just walked in carrying a carved chest interrupted her in full flow. He laid it at Gunnhild's feet, wheezing loudly at the effort. 'I was contracted to make this chest by the chieftain,' he managed, wiping sweat from his brow with the sleeve of his tunic.

Although Rowena could not quite understand him, Gunnhild translated for her. She felt the patina of the wood excitedly. 'How wonderful. The one in our bedchamber is rather shabby, but Sigurd never mentioned anything about a new one.'

Gunnhild laughed. 'Trust me, just be grateful. Men are so forgetful.'

Rowena smiled at the carpenter. 'Tell him it's lovely.'

He puffed out his chest with pride when Gunnhild told him what the pretty young woman had said, and happily followed her to the bedchamber where he installed the new chest. She paid him with some un-dyed twill that was often used as an alternative to silver, and he went away whistling a merry tune.

True to her word, Gunnhild took her out onto the hillside later and showed her the lichens they used for dying the twill. 'We get the black dye from bog-mud impregnated with iron.'

Rowena was taken to see the smithy, who was a grumpy old man with a greying beard and a gouty leg. He showed them how he ground red and green tufa-stone to powder to make mineral dyes. 'Anything else you want to know you come and see me,' he told Rowena, showing his stumpy black teeth.

Gunnhild giggled and led her outside. 'He's taken a shine to you.' She scolded some rowdy children and chased some cattle and goats from the turf roof.

Rowena hurried on before her. 'I'd better see how Gerd is getting on with the meat.'

They went indoors and Rowena walked over to the hearth. 'Take a rest, Gerd,' she told the cook, in the Norse Gunnhild had taught her. Gerd smiled and nodded her thanks.

'Sigurd will be delighted to see his shieling so well run,' Gunnhild remarked, watching Rowena turn the spit over the fire upon which roasted a succulent sheep.

Rowena was unable to tell her friend that she couldn't care less what Sigurd thought, though she supposed it would be nice to show her proficiency to the man of the house when he decided to return. By the end of the week her hands were as calloused as that of the thralls, who were looking at her with a new respect.

The following morning she watched some of Sigurd's men wrestling outside the shieling, testing their feats of strength. They all looked harmless enough, even the berserks. It was hard to imagine these seemingly even-tempered men acting like frenzied wolves in battle. Gunnhild had told her that they were devotees of the god Odin, from whom they derived their power.

Her happiness was spoilt when one of the men blocked her path, his meaty fist holding a flashing spear he'd been using for target practice. 'Need any help?' he asked slyly. 'I'm good with my hands and my cock. Take your pick.'

Another man joined him, flexing his stout arms. 'Take a look at my muscles, girly. But I've got a better muscle in my breeches. Do you want to feel it?'

'Go away, you're detestable,' she grated, pushing past the two men, hiding her blushes as best she could.

She made her way to the stables; she wouldn't let those two morons upset her. And although she missed Leif, it was nice not to have anyone to answer to while Sigurd was away. Leif had reminded her how fond she was of riding. And as she hadn't been out on a horse since her husband brought her to his land, she had the stable lad saddle up Syn for her. She took the bridle path through the wood, delighting in the freedom and beauty all around. Great oaks towered over her as she coaxed the gentle mare into a trot. She hadn't felt so good since being taken from her homeland and she relaxed in the familiarity of a good leather saddle beneath her. She didn't ride far, though, for she hadn't told Gunnhild of her plans and she would be sure to worry that she was out riding alone.

She spent the rest of the day in earnest labour, and after the evening meal she decided to take advantage of the bathhouse. It was set a little way away from the shieling with a stone flagged floor and a drain to carry away the water. In the centre was an open hearth over which a pile of stones was heated in a peat fire.

Rowena removed her clothes and threw water over the hot stones, as Gunnhild had shown her to do in order to fill the room with steam. Afterward she lay on a platform that was built around the wall as the steam swirled over her, and she thought it the most heavenly feeling in the world. If it wasn't for her cruel husband she realised she could be quite happy in this place. The older ones in the shieling were beginning to show her more kindness; but she still had trouble with the younger ones who appeared indifferent to her overtures of friendship.

'You seem very relaxed.'

Rowena started in alarm at the strange voice that spoke her language in a heavy accent. The woman was dressed in a blue strapped cloak set with a myriad stones. On her head was a black lambskin hood, her face old and much wrinkled.

'Rowena trembled and her hands moved to cover her nakedness. 'What... what do you want?' she asked fearfully.

'You, Rowena, we want you,' said the woman, her voice strong and deep despite her age.

More people joined her, and from outside came the sound of chanting. The Norse were all gowned in black, with black hoods from which holes were cut for eyes and nose. They were as intimidating as before, and this time she did not have Leif to protect her. 'I have done my penance,' she replied shakily.

'You have only received a small amount of punishment,' the woman said gravely. 'It is not considered sufficient.'

Rowena refused to bow down before them. 'Nonsense. Leave me now. I am the chieftain's wife and command you to do so.'

Her brave speech was ignored and one blue-sleeved arm caught her, holding her firmly. 'Do not try and hide from us, Rowena. It will only make things harder for you. We are inclined to see every part of you. To use every part of you as we wish.' A goblet was held to her lips and she was forced to drink from it. It tasted a little like mead, but there was a bitter aftertaste.

A broader figure stepped forward and she was sure it was a man. 'You must listen to the volva, for she is wise,' he ordered, and Rowena cowered when she saw the bunch of twigs he was holding menacingly. 'You are right to look afraid,' he averred snidely. 'You have been a bad girl. Bad girls are always disciplined.'

His arm rose and the twigs were brought down hard on her bare legs. She cried out as her skin smarted and stung.

'I am sorry for offending you! Please, no more.'

'How can anyone resist a body like yours?' he asked, caressing her ankle. His hand wandered insolently up to her knee, where he caressed the tender underside. 'Is that good, Rowena? Do you like to be touched like this? As I recall, your body is that of a goddess but you have the morals of a whore.'

Rowena strove to block out the feel of the fingers that touched her with such sensual knowledge. She set her mouth determinedly and struggled against the woman who restrained her. 'You're wrong, for only a whore would accept such a loathsome touch,' she snapped. 'I'd rather be fed to the fish that swim around your shores than be mauled by such scum as you.'

The fingers that had been warming her skin were snatched away, and she whimpered as the bunch of twigs was once more poised threateningly over her head. 'Do your worst,' she challenged, her cringing body belying her feisty words. 'I am much stronger than I look.'

The old woman forced her onto her back, and with a loud snort of anger the man brought the twigs down on her legs, arms and breasts. Gunnhild had informed her earlier that all the Norse used the twigs after luxuriating in the bathhouse because they were invigorating, but Rowena's skin burned with pain. He beat her with enthusiasm and tears coursed down her face at the indignity and cruelty of the act.

'Poor Rowena,' wailed a darkly gowned and hooded woman from the group, who came nearer and began to dab her sore skin with a soothing solution the old woman gave her. 'You must find pleasure in our bathhouse. Your beautiful body deserves to be pleasured as well as tortured. It's good for your soul.'

While everyone watched the woman continued to apply the solution to the inflamed skin, cooing and fussing over her like a mother hen. Rowena's nerve ends began to sing with desire and the woman massaged her with more vigour, paying special attention to her breasts, dipping into her furrow with persistent fingers that set every part of her buzzing.

'Sweet, pretty, Rowena,' she purred. 'Let me heal you. Let me love you.'

Rowena was enjoying her ministrations, but all too soon the tender touch ceased and the woman stood aside allowing the man access. He forced her to lie on her front and began slapping her bottom with the twigs. He started with one rosy cheek, that bounced and glowed deep pink from the marks of the scourging. Then he slapped the other one, his eyes sparking with lust as he watched the plump globes jumping and staining with colour.

Rowena took a deep breath, trying not to cry out, unwilling for them to think she was unable to stand a little discipline. If she were able to sustain pain from the great Norse Chieftain, Sigurd Thorkelsson, they would not bring her down.

The man changed his tactics and the bundle of twigs was brought lower so that each time he wielded them they caught her sex lips. Pain sliced through her and tears slid silently down her cheeks.

But then she felt light-headed, suddenly tired and dizzy. The man stopped his assault and she let out a sigh of relief. She glanced up at him, and as before the eyes that stared out of the slits in the hood sent darts of fear through her. The man was studying her in return, and took his time, peering down at her insolently, dipping his bundle of cruelty into her wetness.

'Rowena is ready for fucking,' he said. 'How does this feel, Rowena?' he asked, slapping the twigs against her secret place with great aplomb.

Rowena blinked rapidly, her eyes blurred and she seemed to swim through the pain to the other side, where there was a pleasure that coursed through her veins. 'Oh yes,' she moaned. 'Oh yes, that's good.'

He nodded his satisfaction and cast the twigs aside. 'She is almost ready for my purpose,' he announced. 'But first of all, she must be cleansed.'

A strange powder was thrown over the peat fire and a potent odour was expelled. Rowena's head swam, but her dreamy state soon dissolved when she was lifted and hung over the fire. Her feet and arms were splayed wide and her skin felt the heat rising from the stones. 'W-what are you doing?'

'You must be bathed and purified.' The group spoke as if with one voice, that seemed to echo around her like an evil spell.

Water was poured over the stones and steam billowed from them in a frightening whoosh of sound. She screamed and the old woman cackled. They held her high and the steam enveloped her, just as the swamp had in the forest in Wessex. It moved around her eerily, its damp tendrils creating beads of water and sweat on her pearly flesh.

'Even through the steam your hair gleams and your skin dazzles,' the man remarked, running his fingers through the long, damp, red-gold strands. ''Tis a pity the beauty is so badly tarnished by the wickedness inside.'

'Aye, 'tis a great shame.'

The response was echoed all around her and she tried to tell them it was not so, but her body seemed to move slowly and her brain soon forgot what it wanted to remember.

'We will strive to cleanse you, Rowena.'

'We will strive to rid you of your evil.'

The voices came through the steam that veiled her eyes, that reached out its damp fingers to the cloaked and hooded figures, as if in supplication.

'Aye, it is agreed by us all,' they said in unison.

Her breasts were pinched, her clitoris was sucked and she felt a finger being inserted into her anus. Someone began to suck her toes as though they were the juiciest fruits, licking between each one with great relish. Someone else licked her legs right up to her sex. Her skin was feverish. She tossed her head, silently begging release, for she could stand no more.

She was turned over and the twigs tapped lightly over her body. It was a good feeling, and she was beginning to relax when the twigs were brought down harder and faster, lashing her. At the same time she was being fingered and stroked until she was on fire with longing.

Just then the old woman clapped her hands. ''Tis time to give thanks.'

The group suddenly stopped their work and Rowena was bereft. There were strange mutterings around her and she realised they were praying to their gods. Thor was mentioned often and she was turned like a piece of meat on a spit, and then Odin was called upon. Their chanting rose and Rowena's limbs felt as though they were being pulled from her body, and her head ached.

When she thought she could stand no more they began to call upon Frey, and Rowena quaked in fear, for Frey was the god of fertility and the last thing she wanted was to be impregnated. She longed to castigate them, tell them that these gods were not hers, but the pungent scent from the fire made her head swim and her mouth would not form the words.

Suddenly all was quiet and she was carried outside where the rest of the group waited. They placed her on a mound of the greenest grass she had ever seen. She wished her head would clear, but she was forced to drink more mead, which the volva doctored with some powder from the skin pouch at her waist.

'Drink deeply, Rowena,' she urged. 'Drink deeply, let the volva's magic sustain you throughout your ordeal.'

Rowena swallowed, pulling a face at the bitter taste of the potion. But the hallucinatory effect was far more potent this time. Everyone around her, except for the volva, removed their gowns and hoods and their skin seemed to glow with bright colours. She knew that if she could focus her eyes properly she would be able to see the identity of them, but everything wavered and danced in front of her vision, rendering it impossible.

Her legs were forced apart and a thousand butterflies

seemed to be dancing on her body, their luminescent colours rendering her breathless, their touch seeming to reach every fibre, every nerve-ending. They settled on her nipples, sucking her, and the lips of her sex were lightly bitten, tantalising her until she cried out with pleasure.

Then the butterflies turned into human shapes again that seemed to swirl around her, dazzling in their brightness. The dreamlike quality of her position intensified, and although she still felt the pain of her beating, it was through a pleasured haze that eased it.

'Cease!'

The order was stern enough to calm them. The volva held a staff with a knob on the top that sparkled with stones. On her feet she wore calfskin shoes, her cloak belled out around her, the myriad gems gleaming magnificently. Moments passed when nothing was heard but the soughing of the breeze through the trees nearby. Then the volva struck the ground with her staff and began to chant.

A large hammer was held over Rowena, the symbol of the god Thor. The naked figures, still bright waves of colour, joined in the chanting, dancing around her. Then he was on her, his weight a surprise as a knee parted her thighs, his large member pushing its way inside her vaginal lips. Rowena gave an involuntary gasp as he filled her, grasping her shoulders firmly.

Prayers were uttered as he rode her hard and fast, pushing into her as though it was to be his last mating. Incense was waved over them, adding a mystical quality to the proceedings, and Rowena panted and gyrated beneath him as her body came to life in his arms. He tasted of ale and spices and, though he had disciplined her with severity, he took her now with much fervour.

It was another kind of discipline, one she was not averse to. Mayhap Sigurd was right when he said she was only happy when there was something hard between her thighs. It was as though something in her psyche longed for that creamy male seed to make her whole.

When he reached his climax and climbed off her she watched dazedly as the group dressed, their images still blurred. The volva held her staff over her, circling her head twice. 'You have weathered your ordeal well. And you're much respected for your hard work around the shieling. Your sins are forgiven. Go in peace.'

Rowena waited until her head cleared before she was able to dress and make her way back to the shieling, grateful that she would suffer no more at their hands.

Algitha awaited her anxiously in her bedchamber. 'Where have you been, mistress? I looked everywhere for you. Since you told me what happened in the fire-hall I've been worried about you.'

'With good cause,' Rowena replied weakly, and wearily related her tale.

Algitha rushed to fetch the douche. 'Do not delay, for this is another night's work that would have been best avoided!'

A few days later Rowena, with reservations, was persuaded by Gunnhild to accompany her to the bathhouse, where they lay on the platform built around the wall.

Gunnhild appraised her warmly. 'Before you came the heart was draining out of Sigurd's halls, Rowena. As you know Maeve was Sigurd's mistress, and when their relationship began she made sure everyone knew of her new position.' Gunnhild sighed. 'But she was slothful and lazed around all day finding fault with everything and everyone. The thralls were being scolded for doing their work properly. Is it any wonder they lost heart and let things go?'

'What of Sigurd?' she asked with concern. 'Did he not put things right?'

Gunnhild snorted. 'What does a man know of these things? It's woman's work. Now that you're here things will change for the better, I know. Your enthusiasm and caring nature has already won many over.'

She had never thought to hear those words and her heart lifted. She was going to fit in, after all.

Gunnhild began to lightly whip her body with some twigs and Rowena shuddered. She could not bring herself to join in, and when they tired of the steam and douched themselves with cold water, the shock made Rowena squeal.

Gunnhild laughed. 'If you think that's cold, just wait until the winter when people leave the bathhouse to roll in the snow.

'I will never, ever do that,' Rowena vowed with a shiver.

'It can be a very pleasing experience, especially if you've been accompanied by a male companion who has indulged himself by making love to you.' Gunnhild winked playfully, and Rowena blushed.

Little did she know that just a few days ago she had spent a goodly time in the bathhouse being spanked and pleasured by many hands. Just thinking about it made her excited.

'What's a volva?' she asked curiously.

'They are women of great wisdom who often go from farm to farm to undertake various magical and divinatory rites. I've seen one go into a trance in order to summon the spirits.'

'What happened?' Rowena hoped Gunnhild was unable to sense more than a natural curiosity on her part.

'There was a lot of chanting while she worked her spells. Then she issued prophecies of good fortune and everyone was happy and celebrated.'

By the end of the first week everyone who lived in the shieling were used to the chieftain's lady popping up anywhere and everywhere, ready and willing to turn her hand to any task. Rowena went to her bed at night too tired to fret about Sigurd and Maeve, and though she still missed Leif, her spirits had lifted. She had made many friends and learned the intricacies of life in the shieling the best way possible – by joining in. And if not quite proficient at everything, she knew she soon would be.

But Rowena's joy was not to last, for at the end of the second week Sigurd returned, bringing guests. She was busy lifting oatcakes from the flat stone slab across the end of the open hearth in the kitchen when a breathless Algitha rushed in.

'Mistress, the chieftain is come.'

Rowena dropped the oatcakes in her shock. 'Where is he, Algitha? Have you seen Leif? How does he look?'

Algitha was taken aback by the flurry of questions. 'I've not seen Leif as yet. But Sigurd is already in the fire-hall, and he has brought guests.'

Rowena instructed Algitha to remove the rest of the oatcakes from the hearth and, feeling unreasonably flustered, put her hand up to her dishevelled hair with a groan. Algitha had plaited it neatly for her that morning, but what with the heat of the kitchen much had escaped and was curling untidily over her neck and forehead. There was nothing to be done about it now, but she had wanted to be looking her best for Leif.

She took a deep breath and rubbed flour from her hands, then squaring her shoulders she went to the fire-hall.

Sigurd greeted her indifferently, and she smarted at Maeve's triumphant smile as she passed her, no doubt to sneak off somewhere so she could sleep off her journey.

She went forward to welcome her visitors, a man and a woman. The woman was a voluptuous blonde beauty, who was far from friendly. Her pale eyes scanned Rowena with animosity, and Rowena sighed inwardly; was this another of Sigurd's conquests? She was fast tiring of the game.

Sigurd introduced his guests as Gunnar Egilsson and his sister, Freyjr, and when he introduced Rowena, Gunnar, who was a large man like most of the Norse, with a ruddy face, gasped his horror.

'You have a wife, Sigurd!'

Rowena stepped back a pace, shocked at the rage in his face. She had been conversing in mainly Norse since Sigurd's absence, and although not fluent in the language, she understood far more than he knew. She looked at Sigurd for an explanation, but he merely gave her a sardonic smile. Algitha had quietly moved beside her, alerted by the noise in the hall, and she ordered her to translate that which she was unable to understand.

'As you see, Gunnar, I do indeed have a wife. I had thought to keep her a surprise until you met.'

Gunnar looked from his sister, whose skin had turned waxen, back to Sigurd. 'What folly is this?' he asked angrily. 'You court my sister and then dishonour her by wedding another?'

Sigurd raised an insolent eyebrow. 'The woman was ripe and willing for a dalliance. Who am I to refuse such an offer?'

Gunnar's countenance suffused with red and his mouth moved without words. The shock had rendered him momentarily incoherent. Freyjr rushed to his side, gazing up at him with concern, her face still waxy.

'Are you well, brother?'

Gunnar was exasperated. He bent and spoke softly in her ear; too many people knew their business as it was. 'Well? With a slut for a sister? What are you thinking of letting the man between your legs before you are wed?'

Freyjr scowled. ''Tis your own fault. I got the taste for it when you went a-viking and left me with the boring women of the hall and a few guards for company.'

'What are you talking about, woman?'

Freyjr batted her lashes; a few feminine wiles never went amiss. 'Why brother, dear, I had to do something when you were not around, and so did the guards.'

Gunnar grabbed at his chest. 'You mean...' He couldn't bring himself to say it.

'They often found their way beneath my skirts,' she said, her eyes guileless. 'And I decided that as I liked it so much when they played with my pussy, it was pointless pretending otherwise.'

Gunnar seemed to be fighting for breath. 'You mean there was more than one?'

Freyjr smiled. 'Oh yes. My own brother had forsaken me, what else could I do? I needed to have a man inside me as often as I could. It was the only thing that kept me sane during the long lonely months.'

'And Sigurd?' he spluttered, wishing he had stayed at his farm and looked to his sister instead of leaving her so much.

'He was so nice,' she cooed. 'I'm quite unable to resist him, especially when his cock is so big and so satisfying.

Gunnar glared from her to Sigurd, and then to Rowena. 'Family honour is at stake here,' he snarled.

'No man dictates to me in my own house,' Sigurd returned, his voice low and menacing.

'I had thought you an honourable man,' spat Gunnar, his hand resting on the hilt of his sword.

Sigurd smiled cynically. 'A grave misconception on your part, Gunnar.'

'Then you are a snake, Sigurd Thorkelsson, and I demand satisfaction!'

Chapter Nine

Sigurd's men and Gunnar's men eyed one another warily, and some of Sigurd's men stepped forward in order to protect their chieftain.

Rowena, annoyed at her husband's perfidy that heaped more embarrassment on her, and longing to see her sweetheart, peered anxiously at the warriors in the firehall. Where was Leif?

Sigurd sighed and, taking a frothing horn of ale from a thrall, quenched his thirst. Wiping his mouth on his sleeve, his expression bored, he nodded. 'As you wish. Name the time and place.'

'What better time than the present? I have need to settle the matter before I can rest another night in my bed.'

Sigurd nodded his agreement. 'So be it. But we have journeyed far and need to freshen ourselves beforehand.'

'This is true,' said Gunner solemnly, and at Rowena's beckoning thralls brought water and towels.

Rowena was insulted. Her husband should be fighting over her, not another woman, but if only Leif was there she would not mind so much.

Sigurd threw some water over his face and neck before scrubbing himself dry again. A little way away Gunnar was doing the same. The tension in the hall was fearful, but Sigurd seemed completely unaware of it.

Rowena went up to him. 'Is this wise, husband?'

He smirked. 'What troubles you, wife? Don't tell me you're bleating in fear over me.'

'I don't like bloodshed,' she averred swiftly, not wanting him to think she cared what he did. 'Especially when it is over a trollop who should have known better.'

''Tis not her fault. After all, am I not irresistible?'

'Some might think so,' she said tartly, about to walk away when he grabbed her hand. He dragged her close and she was able to feel his erection through his breeches, as strong and upright as an oak. Her sex throbbed. She loved Leif, but her husband was mighty hard to resist sometimes.

She decided to encourage him for once. She had to put him in a good mood in order to find out Leif's whereabouts, so smiling into his eyes, she said, 'You tempt me, Sigurd.' He looked pleased and she patted his damp beard with a towel, hoping to seem wifely and caring.

He made a growling sound in his throat. 'Carry on like that and I'll pierce your cunny right here in front of everyone.'

Rowena hastily withdrew. 'What of Leif?' she asked, as casually as she could. 'I have not seen him since you arrived.'

He quaffed his ale thirstily. 'He's been called home. His father is very ill.'

Rowena felt as though she'd been struck; Leif was the only good thing that had happened to her since her marriage, and even he had been taken from her.

She took a quick sip of mead, fighting to regain her equilibrium. Freyjr continued to glower at her and she longed to tell her she was more than welcome to her husband, she was not the only one who thought she had prior claim to him. However, the situation was dire and did not need any encouragement.

The hall began to empty as people gathered outside, and soon the principals of the drama followed. Rowena saw that a cloak with loops at the corners was being laid down on the ground, and she wondered at its purpose.

'There are specific rules laid down for duelling,' said Gunnhild over her shoulder, Maeve having been sucked into the crowd. 'The cloak has to be five ells square, and as you can see, the men are now fastening it with pegs through the loops. The law says that three borders, or furrows, each a foot in breadth, must surround the cloak, and at the edge they will soon hammer four poles of hazel wood.

'Will thy fight to the death?' Rowena's eyes wandered fearfully to the sharp blades the men would use.

Gunnhild shrugged her shoulders. 'Who can say? There's nothing usual about this duel. They almost always take place on an islet in the River Oxara. But as you saw, Gunnar is eager for blood.'

'What do you think will happen?'

Gunnhild took a deep, sobering breath. 'Satisfaction is usually gained by the drawing of first blood, but I fear tempers are running high.'

'Sigurd doesn't look upset.'

'He rarely shows his feelings. He's a brave and proud man.'

It seemed to be a common fault among the Norse, for although Gunnhild tried to act calm for Rowena's sake, the tremor in her voice gave her away.

Each contestant chose a second. Rig was Sigurd's, and just before he entered the four poles Sigurd gave her a cheeky wink, and she marvelled at his composure.

The fight commenced, and Rowena wondered what would become of her if her husband were killed. Would she be allowed to return to her family? The thought of being reunited with her mother brought tears to her eyes.

The fight was more interesting to her now, and Gunnhild began to explain the rest of the rules to her. 'See, each contestant has three shields,' she said, pointing. 'If these are destroyed the man must defend himself with his sword alone. Sigurd was the one challenged so he had first blow.'

Rowena was only half-listening; Sigurd's bravery was a great aphrodisiac and she was ashamed when her baser instincts began to intervene. 'If one is wounded will they stop the fight?' she muttered.

'If one is wounded, so that blood pours onto the cloak, the fight should be stopped. But who knows what the outcome will be?'

Rowena wrapped her arms around her waist, wishing for once that they were Sigurd's arms. She craved him at that moment, and wondered at the complexity of her nature that had brought this about.

The fighting was fierce and demanding. Their shields parried each blow and Rowena considered how tiring it must be to wield such heavy weapons. She surmised the men to be of similar age, but it was obvious that Sigurd was far more agile despite his size. The crowd gasped as Gunnar aimed a blow to Sigurd's legs, but they need not have feared for Sigurd leapt back and the sword swiped harmlessly at the air.

'He's a fine swordsman.' Algitha had sidled up to Rowena. 'You can see why he's much sought after by the women of Iceland.' She giggled softly. 'Your eyes are fair eating him up. Is your cunny pounding as fast as your husband's feet? And look, Gunnar is beginning to tire.'

Rowena nodded. 'I'm a disgrace, but I can't help it.'

Algitha's eyes slanted knowingly. 'Most of these so-called ladies, watching Sigurd, are thinking along similar lines. They're dreaming of him whipping their pussies with that gleaming sword. And when they are wet enough they imagine him plunging into their feminine folds with his own thick weapon.'

Rowena's hands flew to her private place, crushing her kirtle beneath her fingers. 'Hush, Algitha, you are making me wet myself with desire.'

Sigurd snapped Gunnar's shield with a mighty blow from his sword, and Freyjr screamed. Gunnar was given another and the battle commenced.

Rowena was battling within herself; if Sigurd lost she would be free, but memories of his muscular body, his masterful lust, made her tremble with wanting him.

When it looked as though Sigurd would easily be the victor his own shield was knocked from his hand, and the ladies of the shieling cried out in horror when he refused another. Instead he wiped the sweat from his brow and took his sword in both hands, a sly grin on his face.

Rowena was full of admiration. 'He's taking a chance.'

Gunnhild threw a worried glance at Rig, who had

stationed himself opposite, but he was watching his chieftain so closely she failed to get any reassurance from that quarter. She patted Rowena's arm. 'He knows what he's about, never fear. Without his shield he can deal heavier blows. Sometimes it's just an encumbrance.'

The crowd was more excited now, but Rowena was still undecided about the outcome of the battle. At least Gunnar had the protection of his shield, if Sigurd should become a little sluggish in his actions Gunnar could well deal him a deathblow. She happened to glance at Rig and, judging by the tightness of his jaw, she guessed that their thoughts were running along the same lines.

The crowd gasped when Gunnar's sword sliced into Sigurd's mail coat, but they let out a cry of relief to see he was unharmed. Gunnar had only managed to get near enough to nick his mail. Sigurd attacked swiftly. Gunnar was slow to react and Sigurd's sword sliced into his arm.

For a moment Rowena felt faint, thinking the arm to be severed. Then with great relief she saw it was not. Gunnar was on his knees holding his badly injured arm and Sigurd stood over him, his face grim. The crowd was hushed and his voice rose clearly above it.

'You gave me a good fight, Gunnar. But be sure if there is a next time I will not pull back. It will be a fight to the death.'

His men, who Rowena knew would tend to his wound, surrounded Gunnar. Sigurd stalked out of the area and made for the fire-hall, and Rowena was actually full of admiration for the brave warrior she'd been forced to wed, and was about to follow in his wake when Freyjr confronted her.

'Do not think this the end of the matter, Saxon,' she spat in a heavily accented voice. 'We Norse have long memories.' Then turning, and not bothering to go to her brother's aid, she marched off in the direction of the stables.

There was much rejoicing in the fire-hall, but when Rowena sat next to her husband he viewed her with scepticism. 'Are you disappointed, wife? Did you think to see me carried off the cloak like dead meat?'

'Of course not.'

He laughed mirthlessly. 'You are very predictable, Rowena.'

She changed the subject. 'How was your journey?'

He waved airily at the varied pile of goods his men had placed in the fire-hall. 'As you can see, I traded well with visiting ships. There are good wines from Norway, and from Russia fine furs, wax and honey. You are unused to our winters and will be grateful for the furs come the cold spell.'

'I'm sure I shall.' She nodded her thanks, aware that he would have traded woollens, seal oil, ivory and fats in return.

Much praise came his way on all sides, but in his own inimitable way he was quite unmoved by any of it. He nibbled on some oatcakes and drank from his horn as if it was any other day in the shieling.

Rowena wondered if she should not give Maeve and Freyjr a run for their money, after all, if she flattered him instead of showing her hatred she might receive a little kindness in return, which would make her life easier until Leif returned for her, which she prayed he would.

Tentatively she put a hand on his thigh, trembling at the muscles that played beneath the skin. 'You're the object of every woman's fantasy this day.'

His eyes slanted playfully. 'I take it you include yourself in that scenario.'

She nodded slyly. 'Aye, husband. You are a fine figure of a man. I must admit my heart beat fast when I watched you fight Gunnar.'

For a moment she thought she spied a touch of something akin to tenderness in his eyes, but almost as soon as it came, it vanished. 'Your heart is of no interest to me,' he said with a nasty smirk. 'I am more interested in what lies between your legs.'

She longed to slap his haughty face, but she would not

give in so easily. Her hand wandered up his thigh to the hard proof of his words. 'I have been dying with want of you, husband.'

His warrior's hand slid beneath her skirts and into her cleft. 'Have you missed me, Rowena?'

He began to part her labia and to delve into the warm core of her. She caught her breath and massaged his erection through his breeches. 'Aye, sire,' she said, realising that she had indeed missed the calloused pressure of his hands on her skin, the pleasure of his perverse lovemaking.

'Then you will be ready to do my bidding, will you not?'

Thinking it was what he wanted, she reached inside his breeches and took out his hard weapon, running her fingers down the strong length of it. 'I am ready to do anything that will please you,' she replied, closing her eyes as his thumb made whorls around her clitoris and two of his fingers made like a cock inside her vagina. She reached her crisis quickly and smiled to herself; she was right after all, the Eagle appeared to enjoy her flattery.

But his next words sent any notions of taming him up in flames. 'Enough of this foolish play. On your knees, bitch, where you belong.'

Not caring who saw, he spread a hand on her head and forced her beneath the table and between his thighs. 'Feed on that, wife. I have neglected you and wish to make amends.'

His words echoed around the fire-hall and Rowena's face flamed as she took him between her lips. Though she longed to stab him with the knife that lay on her trencher, she forced herself to nuzzle him gently, inhaling the mix of sweat and man. She eased her tongue against the tip of that salty shaft, pretending she was pleasuring Leif, knowing that if she were this would be better than any delicacy she had ever tasted before. She cupped his balls with both hands and scratched the taught skin of his scrotum. A sigh escaped his lips and she smiled triumphantly; so she did have a little power over him.

She used her hands to slide up the slippery shaft, working the tip with her tongue. It grew even harder, so large and silky smooth; it was a joy on her palate. She sucked and caressed until he shot his seed into her mouth, and still in her fantasy she swallowed, enjoying the sensuality of the act.

Sigurd grunted his satisfaction and she was able to slip back into her seat, embarrassed and ashamed at the way she had been treated in front of all and sundry. The only way she could reconcile herself to sit next to him was to begin another fantasy, one where she plunged her knife deep into his heart.

He raised his horn and drank deeply. 'Come, wench, I am inclined to give you a little present.'

She eyed him cynically. 'A present, husband? How kind you are.'

He laughed loud and long and many turned to see what had amused their chieftain. 'You enjoy discipline more than any other woman I have ever met. Admit it, Rowena. You enjoy being mastered, don't you?'

She looked up at him from beneath the red-gold of her lashes, her green eyes clear. 'I enjoy nothing you have or ever will do to me.'

Sigurd smiled. 'One day you will admit that you are not happy until your bottom cheeks are as red as your hair.'

Rowena snorted. 'You have a long wait.'

Nothing seemed to faze him after his defeat. He hauled her to her feet. 'Deny it as much as you like. I know your cunny's hot and ready for me any time I wish to take you. Now I must make up for the time we were separated.'

Leaving the table he bid her follow, and it was an extremely nervous Rowena who traipsed behind the warrior and away from the turf-covered shieling, and the goats that grazed on the roof.

He led her to a locked building just over the rise, guarded by one of the ferocious looking berserks. Taking a large key from his belt, Sigurd opened the door and went inside, and Rowena's eyes took a little time to acclimatise to the strange contours of the room after the bright sunshine that bathed the fields.

Many sweet smelling candles illuminated two dusky women, seated on some of the silk cushions that ran around the sides of the room, attending to their embroidery. Their reflections were thrown back at them from highly polished metal mirrors that decorated the walls at intervals, rather like shiny shields. They smiled their pleasure at Sigurd's entry, and one found a drinking horn and filled it with mead.

He took the horn readily, throwing a sly glance at Rowena. 'These two wonderful species of womankind are another of my acquisitions from my journey to the coast. They were taken from a faraway country where women are taught how to please their men and each other. Jasmine, Usta, this is Rowena. I have brought her here to learn the art of Sapphic sex, so that I may take pleasure from the performance.'

Rowena backed away from her husband. What she did with Algitha in the privacy of her bedchamber was one thing, having two strange women touch her with her husband watching was another – one she did not relish one little bit! She shook her head violently. 'Do not make me do this thing, Sigurd.'

He chuckled. ''Tis too late, wife. My lust is up and I'll not be disappointed. I bought these beauties for my men to enjoy. And their knowledge and wisdom of sensuality will help you understand and learn all they have to impart.'

Rowena shrank back against the wall, horrified by his words. The woman called Jasmine got to her feet and Rowena gasped. The woman's dark skin was so unusual to her she was unable to take her eyes away. She was tall and majestic in her dignity, her slim curves a foil for her companion's riper ones. Raven hair waved all the way down to her tiny waist, and her body was clothed in a green gauzy fabric that fluttered around her naked curves as though she had nothing on.

Sigurd fondled her body through the thin fabric and Rowena was both jealous and turned on at the same time. 'Do you like what you see, wife?'

'She is very beautiful.'

The other woman rose from her cushion and Rowena took a swift breath, for she was every bit as lovely as her companion, though far more curvaceous. She was clad in bright red, and the translucent garment showed every generous inch of her, including her shaven mound. Her red-brown hair waved to her shoulders, cascaded over her breasts. Sigurd pushed the tresses from them so he was able to view her better. She leaned into him and he kissed her upraised lips and cupped a lovely breast.

'See, Rowena, Jasmine has shaved her mound and so has Usta. Don't you think their cunnies look pretty, their plump labia lips like ripe plums?'

His teasing tone repelled her and she felt her face heat. She didn't want to look at the gorgeous creatures; their nakedness embarrassed her. But she couldn't help taking a peep. She had never seen anything like them before, and a jolt of desire churned her stomach.

'I wish to leave,' she snapped coldly, turning her back on the nymphs her husband displayed so brazenly. But Sigurd was not to be crossed. He grabbed her cruelly and tore every stitch she wore from her body. As she stared down in horror at her nudity he called out some orders in a language she was unable to understand. One of the women took a metal collar and some rope from a chest and gave it to him, and before Rowena was able to protest the collar was snapped around her throat and her hands were tied behind her back.

'Will you never learn obedience?' he asked in mock sorrow.

'I would sooner die than offer obedience to you, Norse dog!' she snarled, struggling against her bonds, appalled at the weight of the collar on her neck.

'Do not tempt me, bitch!' His eyes were bright with his

ire, his lips wet from the spittle of his angry words. He grappled with a chain that hung from a hook in the roof, clipping it to a link in the collar. The chain allowed her a little movement only, and tears formed in her eyes. Her husband had chained her like an animal while the dark-skinned women watched.

Casting her a satisfied grin, Sigurd kissed Jasmine, and caressed her breasts and stomach. Then his head dipped and he sucked a breast through her gauzy covering. His fingers worked lower and he was soon tickling her sex, grinning at his wife. 'Do you like what I'm doing to Jasmine, Rowena?'

Rowena swallowed hard. 'Of course not.' But she was lying. It turned her on watching her husband touch another woman.

'You're not telling the truth,' he chastised. 'Admit it, wouldn't you like to touch Jasmine too?'

Rowena took a deep breath, straining against the cruel metal that encircled her throat. 'Go to hell!'

Ignoring her ire he said, 'Tell me what you'd like to do to her.' He wore a smug smile as he caressed both women, who clung to him like limpets.

Rowena closed her eyes against the sensual scene. 'I'm bored by your sport.'

Sigurd's reply was to slap her hard across her cheek. 'I suggest you open your eyes, lest I think you're tired of having the gift of sight.'

Rowena obeyed, but tried to avert her gaze from the women's breasts, but their compelling sensuality was far too powerful to resist. To her shame she was bathed in their beauty and longed to weigh those lovely breasts in her palms, and suck their rosy nipples.

As if he were able to read her thoughts, Sigurd released both women and relaxed on the pile of silk cushions. The two women immediately followed suit, draping themselves seductively beside him. 'Feast your eyes on my beauteous slaves, Rowena, for you and I both know how much you enjoy a challenge.'

She recalled what Algitha had done to her in her bedchamber, and secretly itched to do the same with these lovely creatures. Unfortunately Sigurd was able to read the naked desire on her face. 'Usta,' he commanded the curvaceous woman, 'introduce my wife to the fine wine from Russia.'

Usta swayed seductively to the corner of the room, where a table was set with rich food and wines, her reflection in the metal mirrors on all sides, her gauzy dress clinging suggestively to every nuance of flesh. She poured a gourd of wine into a ruby goblet and, as Jasmine untied Rowena, so she handed her the wine.

Rowena was forced to walk forward a few steps, which was as far as the chain would reach, in order to take the wine from her. As she moved closer to the enchantress her perfume wafted around her like a flowery summer's day. Their eyes caught and Rowena looked away, quickly sipping the wine that slid down her throat like nectar.

Usta put out a soft hand and touched Rowena's hair. She wordlessly described what she felt inside by putting her hands to her heart and inclining them at Rowena. Then she spoke in a sultry voice that awakened every sensory nerve in Rowena's body, even though she was unable to know what she said. She took some more wine into her mouth, swallowing gratefully.

Sigurd clapped his hands and thralls brought in a hot bath floating with rose petals. Rowena's eyebrows rose and Sigurd smiled. 'They will bathe me in rose petals. It is a custom in their country that you'll find very interesting.'

Sigurd allowed the women to disrobe him. Then Jasmine tested the water in the bath and satisfied, bade him enter with a flourish of her graceful arm.

Sigurd stepped into the deep tub with a smile. The rose petals smelled wonderful, and Rowena inhaled deeply. How she wished she were in that scented water, while the soft hands of the dusky women pampered her skin, anointing her with vials of aromatic scents that pleased her senses, their clever fingers easing the tension from her body with each stroke.

Sigurd lay back, a relaxed smile playing on his lips, his blue eyes taking in every curve of the women as they bathed him. His contentment was obvious and Rowena longed to slap his obnoxious face.

Soon the gentle hands were drying, patting and soothing his body with the utmost care. Sigurd basked in the warmth of their beautiful smiles, of the knowledge in those dark eyes. Then he was dried carefully and draped in a soft, silken robe before resuming his seat on the cushions. He clapped his hands once more and the bath was taken away.

'I hope you are taking note of all this, Rowena. You have the appearance of a goddess, and I've never had the least trouble finding you easy on the eye. But your knowledge of sensuality is sadly lacking. Therefore teaching of this important art will begin, and if you're a willing and capable pupil I might well find myself happy with the results.'

She bit back a sarcastic reply and turned her gaze on the finely carved chest the woman had taken the collar and rope from. She hardly dared to believe her eyes, for the scene on the wood was of sensuality, but whereas at first she'd thought it consisted of males and females in different sexual poses, she found it was nothing but females indulging themselves and each other.

She blushed, and with a sign from Sigurd the women smiled slyly and spirited themselves towards her. To her distress soft lips found hers, lips that were tender and dangerous, leading her spiralling downward into a world of Sapphic passion. When one pair of lips left hers so another replaced them, kissing her until she thought she could reach the stars with one outstretched hand and bring one back to earth to light her way forever.

The candles gave out the aroma of flowers, and Rowena sighed as she was massaged all over. She even forgot the discomfort of the collar as delicate fingers found their way to her intimate places, and she sighed her pleasure as they deftly caressed until she was in a frenzy of need.

Her hands were untied and she reached out in her delirium and found a soft breast, a curving hip, and she weighed the one in her hand while feeling the silky sheen of the other. Rowena was hypnotised by the wonderful creatures and their exotic perfumes, tantalised by their touch.

Jasmine was licking a wooden phallus, slipping it against Rowena's juicy sex lips. Rowena wasn't sure, so she shook her head at Jasmine, but the woman was not to be swayed. Usta quickly grabbed her arms and retied them. Rowena's legs flailed, she'd been drugged by their delightful perfume and saturated with gentleness, but she would not allow them to feed that unnatural object inside her.

Jasmine was deft, and held her still with her superior strength while Usta slid the dildo in her juices and began to burrow it into her vagina. She cooed some soft words to her, which Rowena was unable to understand.

Sigurd translated them with a hoarse voice, so turned on was he by the three gorgeous women. 'She says you are lovely, Rowena,' he explained, 'and that you must be taught to enjoy a dildo. It's exciting for her to pleasure you like a man. She says that in her country sex between women is to be enjoyed, it's natural.'

Rowena realised Sigurd was as aroused as she, and gave herself wholly to the ministrations of the exotic women. As the phallus was applied to her vagina by Jasmine, so Usta began to caress and kiss her breasts. Jasmine licked her clitoris and Rowena writhed in delight, being pampered with great precision.

Then a sturdy finger ploughed roughly into her bottom, and as she looked down it was her husband she saw gazing at her bottom hole in the candlelight, her husband's finger she felt prod inside. But soon he wasn't satisfied with that, and began to slide his tongue inside the tiny rear passage instead.

Rowena shuddered; despite herself she was enjoying her bottom being plundered. The entire situation defied explanation. She was tethered like an animal, her body being shared by her husband and two of the most beautiful women she had ever seen.

Her crisis rolled through her body like a thunderstorm through the ether and she hung from the chain, exhausted and exhilarated at the same time. Then to her relief she was unclipped from the chain and lowered to the silk cushions. Jasmine stepped delicately either side of her head, and Rowena stared up at her vulva. It reminded her of the picture Sigurd had brought back from the coast of an exotic orchid.

When the woman knelt down over her face, Rowena smelled the heady perfume that came from her glistening sex and was completely lost. She stuck her tongue out experimentally and lapped at the lips, delighted by the honeyed taste. The girl moaned her pleasure and Rowena was immediately pleased with her power.

Rowena began to pleasure her and worked frantically with her tongue and lips as her hands took in the fullness of her beautiful breasts. She licked her vagina and clitoris, neglecting her breasts in order to steady her shuddering hips as her climax began to take hold, and when the woman slumped to the floor Rowena smiled triumphantly.

But her euphoria was brief, for Sigurd suddenly appeared to be enraged. He hauled the chain down from the hook in the roof and clipped it back on her collar. 'Me thinks you enjoyed that far too much, wife.' He smote her with the Nordic blue of his eyes. 'You need to be punished.'

Without a word to Jasmine or Usta, he released her and slipped back into his clothes before telling the women to dress Rowena in one of their garments. Then he stomped to the door and, dragging Rowena by the chain, exited the building. He marched her over the green sward, leading her by the chain linked to her collar, taking little notice as she stumbled and sobbed as the cruel metal dug into her throat, uncaring that she was all but naked in the diaphanous dress.

'You will not make me an heir by fucking other woman, bitch!' he snarled.

To Rowena's humiliation the grounds around the firehall and its outbuildings were busy, and many stopped to stare as their chieftain led his chained wife into their bedchamber.

Once inside he locked the door, threw her on the bed and fell on top of her. He quickly released his cock, and dragging the dress out of the way, plunged inside her without a word.

When he was done he rolled over and began snoring loudly, and Rowena's sobs went unheard as she turned her face into the pillow.

Chapter Ten

Rowena lay on her bed, glad there was no window for people to peer in, for the nights were light. She missed the dark; there was a mystery and romance in a velvet night, lit only by the moon and stars. But Gunnhild told her there were only a few hours of daylight in the winter and she would be glad for the light summers to roll around again.

The door knocked, but not wishing to see anyone Rowena remained still, hoping whoever it was would go away. But the door opened and a soft voice said, ''Tis I, lady, Algitha. I have come to help you disrobe.'

'Even you cannot help me now, Algitha,' she said miserably. 'I am disgraced.'

Algitha had been privy to the scene of her mistress being dragged like a dog by the chieftain. Her breast heaved with hate for him and she pinned a bright smile on her face. 'You, disgraced? Never.'

'But everyone saw, how can I ever live that down?'

'You will hold your head high as you always do and they will know who is at fault, for though Sigurd is a great warrior everyone knows he has a dark side. Close your eyes and sleep, Rowena. You need the rest and things will seem brighter come morning.'

Rowena tucked her knife beneath her pillow. 'If he comes near me again I'll skin him alive,' she vowed.

Algitha patted her arm. 'Not a wise threat, dear lady, for although you have won his people around with your beauty and good character, he's still their chieftain. And though he's twisted in many ways he'll always be like a god to them. Their golden chieftain will live on in their hearts forever, his bravery legendary. And they will tear you to pieces without a second thought.'

Rowena shuddered. 'So I'm to put up with his cruelty without any complaint?'

Algitha smoothed the red-gold head tenderly. 'I'm afraid so. You're of noble birth and his wife, but for all intent and purpose you are no more than a foreigner and slave, just as the lowest thrall.'

Sigurd slept beside her that night, taking her like an animal, and though she hated him for the way she was treated, her wayward flesh yielded to him as soon as it was touched, her weapon and dire promise long forgotten.

Although the morning came quicker than she wanted, Rowena rose and went about her business as usual. Sigurd acted as though nothing had happened and that was fine by her. The rest of the Norse gave her sympathetic smiles, but she didn't want their sympathy, and her bright eyes and determination brought even more respect. She threw herself into her work; it was her only panacea.

For the next week the weather took a turn for the worse and those that could kept indoors, tending their weaving, spinning and the many other tasks that were part of life in the shieling.

When the sun returned it brought with it an unwelcome visitor. Freyjr sashayed into the hall one bright afternoon and it was obvious she had spent a goodly time readying herself for the visit. Her golden hair was drawn away from her face and hung down her back in a glistening cascade, interwoven with bright ribbons. A red band encircled her forehead and she wore a gold collar and many silver and gold bangles. The sleeves of her robe were long and greatly embroidered.

Though Rowena longed to smack the smug face that met hers with what looked like a triumphant smile, she had to remember her manners and offer her hospitality. The woman, regal as a queen, acted as though there had been no disagreement between their families, and Rowena decided to follow suit. She began to talk in Rowena's tongue, it was obvious she had learnt it from the many Saxon thralls Gunnar had brought back from his voyages, but her words were so broken and hard to understand Rowena said, 'We shall speak in Norse, Freyjr. I thought you had journeyed back to the coast.'

'I've been enjoying the hospitality of Svein Asleifsson and his family,' she replied haughtily. 'When Gunnar decided to return home Svein persuaded me to stay a little longer.'

'I hope you'll not find us lax in our duties to a visitor,' Rowena said dryly. 'But as you know, it's haymaking time and Sigurd and most of the others are out in the fields.'

'I saw him on the way here,' she said without missing a beat, her beautiful face guileless. 'It was you I came to see, Rowena. We started out on the wrong foot and I'd like to put things right between us.'

This was the last thing Rowena expected, and for a moment she was at a loss for words, but eventually she said, 'There's no need.'

'Oh, but I would like to be your friend. I didn't know Sigurd was married and feel the need to apologise for my behaviour.'

Rowena tried to ward her off, but she held up a heavily ringed hand. 'Please, I insist. The weather is clement and I'm sure it will be the same on the morrow. I wondered if you would do me the honour of having a picnic with me.'

'I'm very busy at the moment.' Rowena wasn't sure she wanted to be friends with Freyjr; there was something about her she didn't like.

The lovely face crumpled, tears formed in her eyes. 'You are unable to forgive me for going with your husband. I quite understand. My shame is never to be forgiven.'

Rowena suddenly felt sorry for the other woman. 'Mayhap I can manage an hour. Where is the picnic?'

Freyjr took her hands and smiled into her eyes. 'Thank you, Rowena, it means so much to me. Will you meet me tomorrow on the hill overlooking the waterfall? Come alone and we shall have a wonderful time. I shall prepare the greatest delicacies and afterwards we will surprise Sigurd with our new friendship.'

She set a time, and was so hard to deny Rowena complied with her wishes. Then satisfied that her mission was a success, Freyjr left and Rowena spent the rest of the day cooking and working in the fields, for every pair of hands was needed. Just before it was time to prepare the evening meal she sat down by the stream that wound its way down the hillside, so exhausted she instantly fell asleep.

She was woken by deep voices. She wasn't sure how long she'd been asleep beside the stream, how long the men had been standing so near, but their voices came to her clearly in the mountain air. She rubbed her eyes and called to them, but her throat was dry and neither heard. She dipped a hand in the stream and drank deeply of the cold water.

'Your wife makes a charming picture beside the stream, Sigurd.'

Sigurd glanced her way, a strange expression on his face. 'Speak freely, Rig. She can't know what we say. You have received news of the Serpent?'

Rig nodded. 'Godmund the Red has done well. It is said the silver he collected from his Saxon raids have made him a rich man.'

Rowena had begun to call out again, but Sigurd's name died on her lips. Godmund the Red – it was a name she'd heard before, but where and when? She shook her woozy head, and scooping up some more of the clear water, rinsed her face in order to wake herself properly.

Sigurd's voice hardened. 'Let the jackal have his day, for mine is to come.'

'What of your conscience?' Rig demanded.

'Don't preach to me, old warrior. Does the Serpent have a conscience?'

Rig shook his head miserably. 'But none of this is the girl's fault. Leave the past where it should be left – in the past. Start afresh.'

Sigurd clenched his jaw stubbornly. 'We've had this conversation before. I want revenge, and she is his seed.'

'But her mother…'

'The Irish woman was his greatest love,' Sigurd interrupted. 'Her daughter is my pawn.'

'The Serpent's rage will be awesome.'

Sigurd flexed his muscles, a smile on his lips. 'And when he comes looking for revenge, I shall be ready.'

Rowena dried her face on the hem of her kirtle, wishing she had not overheard the conversation. It made her uneasy. She was still trying to understand the implications involved when her husband sat beside her.

'You are enjoying the air, Rowena?' His gaze swept over the stream that trickled over the emerald hillside, wild flowers growing in luxuriant splendour along on its banks. She nodded. He noted her untidy appearance, the hair that strayed from its restraining plait, the sleepy beauty of her green eyes. Her breasts swelled against the red material of her kirtle and his cock thickened in his breeches.

'I'm sorry to be so lax, Sigurd,' she replied. 'I was so tired I just fell asleep.'

'You've worked hard this day,' he said, reaching into his breeches and bringing out his cock. 'Now let's see how hard you can work on this.'

'You want me to do that now?' Rowena sighed her reluctance.

'Do not question my motives, woman,' he spat, dragged her head down to his burgeoning stem and forced her to take it in her mouth.

She was tired and she had a lesson with Gunnhild before supervising the evening meal, but knowing she would be beaten sorely if she dared refuse, she took the full length of him into her mouth and pleasured him. He gasped as she worked on the rim of his penis, her head bobbing in his lap, her hair bright in the sunshine. Her tongue lapped like waves against the shore and her mouth was like a velvet purse, and soon his seed spilled into her mouth and throat.

She swallowed the creamy emissions, wiping the excess from her lips and chin. 'Who is Godmund the Red?' she asked without preamble.

He jerked back as though she had physically attacked him. 'What do you know of him?' he growled.

'I overheard you mention the name to Rig, that's all. It's just that I'm sure I've heard it somewhere before.'

He looked visibly relieved. 'Can you recall where?'

Rowena shook her head. 'No, but I will try.'

He gave her a tight smile. 'If it should come to you, I would be interested to hear about it.'

'Aye, but you still haven't answered my question,' she persisted. 'Who is he?'

'No one of consequence.' He got to his feet, ignoring her frown.

She studied his face; it gave nothing away. She had not mentioned her language lessons with Gunnhild, and something prevented her from revealing any more. She dropped her lashes to shield herself from the Eagle's gaze.

'You will tell me as soon as you are with child, won't you?'

The blood rushed to her face and she fanned herself, hoping he would merely think she was hot from pleasuring him. 'Of course.'

He marched off and she lifted her hands to her burning cheeks. She had almost laughed in his face. If he knew what she did after their mating he would no doubt kill her.

As he made his way to the shieling, Sigurd thought of Rig's earlier analysis of his wife, his eyes tender as he watched her sleep.

'She is the daughter of an Irish princess with all the charm and beauty of her breeding, but she has the heart of a Norse warrior.'

His general's words irked him. His wife had wormed her way into his household and was far too comfortable there; he would have to teach her a lesson.

No matter how she tried, Rowena was unable to forget the conversation she had overheard between Rig and her husband. She mulled it over and over in her head. 'She is his seed,' he'd said. He must mean the Serpent's daughter, and the Serpent must be Godmund the Red. Rig had mentioned that the daughter's mother was Irish, but there were lots of Irish thralls in the shieling, it could be any of them. She would like to broach the subject with Sigurd, but he had made it obvious he did not wish her to be privy to anything. She muttered an oath under her breath and Gunnhild scolded her for not paying attention.

After her lesson, which they held sitting on a rock on a hill overlooking the homestead, in order to take advantage of the clement weather, she returned to the shieling. When she neared the storeroom a voice called out to her and she opened the door and went inside. A figure was bent over the ice packed gunnel. 'Did you call me?'

He got to his full height and threw off the cloth that encompassed his head and shoulders. 'Aye, wife,' he sneered. 'I thought we should have some fun together this day.'

'Sigurd!' Rowena's stomach sank; her husband had the mad look on him again. 'I can't imagine what you mean,' she said meekly.

'Oh, but I think you can, bitch,' he snapped. 'Such a sweet-faced bitch, too. But I know differently.'

She didn't know what she was supposed to have done, but she turned to run from him all the same. But he was far too quick for her and caught her by her hair.

'Do not think to escape me, Rowena,' he snarled, snapping metal bands on her wrists and clipping them to chains that hung from huge hooks in the wall. She was hauled up high, her legs dangling and kicking out in vain as she fought for purchase, her arms almost pulled from their sockets.

Her eyes pleaded with him. 'Please, Sigurd, release me. You cannot be happy to see me so.'

'Oh, but I am,' he laughed. Taking a whip from another hook set in the wall, he snapped it in the air and she cringed as it made a wide arc before cracking down in the small of her back. Though she wore a smock and kirtle the whip cut right through them to her skin and she screamed. But he was not satisfied with that and delivered another blow.

Sigurd glared at the beautiful woman he had married, he hated her with such a vengeance he could barely control himself. That he loved her in a strange way, also, he would admit to no one, least of all himself. He was only annoyed that no one else could see the evil in her; no one else could see that she was the Serpent's seed, but soon they would all know and he would have his victory. The whip rose again and found its mark.

'Enough, please husband desist,' she cried as the pain seemed to reach right through her.

'I cannot, wife,' he replied, 'for you are a whore and need to be reminded of who is master here.'

'You are, Sigurd,' she sobbed, 'you are. Now please let me down.'

'But that's impossible. I need to see the dew on your sex lips first.' He shoved a hand between her thighs and inserted his fingers into her sex. The heel of his thumb dug into her clitoris and Rowena sighed as her libido sparked into life. Her body was singing with pleasure, even the pain in her arms and bottom seemed to add to that hedonistic surge.

Sigurd grinned. 'Your cunny's sopping, Rowena. Do you have anything you wish to say to me?' She viewed him blankly. 'Go on,' he urged, 'tell me again who your master is and always will be until I choose differently.'

'You are my master, husband,' she said as his fingers played in her sex. 'And you always will be.'

The following day she worked harder than ever, feeling guilty at having to slip away from the shieling in order to meet Freyjr. She was sorry she had agreed to, for there was so much to be done. The fodder for the coming winter depended upon the success of haymaking, so every pair of hands was needed. Not only were the homefield and the walled meadows mown, but much of the open countryside too. The grass was scythed and raked into swathes, tossed and turned at intervals in order to dry, and dragged to the farm on carts and sledges. As much as was possible was stored in barns, and the rest was built into haystacks.

She saddled Syn herself and made her way along the bridle path through the wood. When she had ridden a little way she spotted some wild flowers and couldn't resist sliding from Syn's back and picking some. There was so little opportunity for enjoyment in her life; this time away from Sigurd was precious. She slipped some flowers into her hair and some she knotted into Syn's mane.

She wondered how many more beatings she would have to suffer, and how much longer she could rely on Algitha's douches. More to the point, how much longer would Sigurd wait for an heir before realising she was preventing nature from taking its course?

She mounted Syn once more, talking softly to her as she rode. Syn seemed to prick up her ears and listen and Rowena told her what good company she was. The buttery sun seemed to play with them as they passed through the wood, now in shade, now in bright light. The leaves on the trees made patterns on her clothing and the air was heavy with the scent of crowberry and bearberry.

It was so lovely she didn't want to go back, but she knew she would have to cut short her picnic with Freyjr in order to return to her work. It was a steep climb up to the meeting place, and she heard the loud roar of water long before she reached the crown of the hill that overlooked the fall. It was her first visit, but Gunnhild had often spoken of the waterfall and its whereabouts, though nothing could have prepared her for the breathless reality.

She reined in Syn and slid from her back. Beneath her was a wide ribbon of sparkling water that thundered down into the river in the valley below. The valley itself was alive with green vegetation, and in the distance were the peaks of the glaciers. She closed her eyes for a split second, it was a mirage, nothing could be so beautiful, but when she opened them again the panoramic view was still set out in front of her.

Now she knew why Freyjr had insisted upon the spot, it was heavenly. When the spell of the falls was broken she glanced around her, there was no sight of Freyjr and she could not wait long. Dragging her rein, Syn nibbled on the succulent grass, flicking her tail over her back.

Rowena waited and waited, then knowing she would be in trouble if she didn't return, she remounted and made her way back down the steep, stony path. As she did a flash of light, like the flash of a mirror, blinded her, frightening Syn. Rowena cried out as she reared, sending her flying through the air to land in a motionless heap on the ground.

She was unconscious for only seconds, and when she came to her head ached. She sat up unsteadily and felt wetness seep down her sleeve, and touching it with her fingers she saw it was blood. Her hair was matted with blood too, and her leg and hip hurt and would, she knew, be badly bruised, if not worse. But she tentatively tested her limbs and was relieved to find she had nothing too seriously wrong with her.

Syn was nibbling calmly at some grass nearby, and she slowly managed to get to her feet and walk over to the horse to check her over. She sighed her relief; Syn didn't have any outward signs of being hurt and she said a silent prayer. They had both been saved. But she would give all she had to find out the identity of the fiend who shone a mirror in their eyes causing their accident.

She found it difficult to climb onto Syn's back again, every part of her throbbed and ached and her return journey was far from comfortable. When she arrived back at the shieling it was to find a worried Gunnhild preparing to send out a search party.

'What happened?' she gasped, when the bruised and bloodied young woman rode into the shieling.

Two of the men helped her down from Syn's back and she was helped into the fire-hall. When she was tended to she explained to Gunnhild about Freyjr and the picnic, the woman's failure to show and her own subsequent fall. She didn't mention the mirror, for she didn't think she would be believed. Even to her own ears it sounded farfetched, though she was fast coming to the conclusion that Freyjr had lured her to that place in order to cause the accident. She had wanted to kill her, but the Lord had been with her and although the hill was steep and dangerous she had survived.

'Oh, by the way,' Gunnhild said, flapping her hands, obviously upset by the accident, 'one of Svein Asleifsson's thralls came by with a message for you, to say Freyjr was unable to meet you after all and sends her apologies.'

'I see.' Rowena bit her bottom lip, trying not to show how troubled she was. How clever of Freyjr to cover herself!

'You had us worried half to death, Rowena. Next time you decide to go riding let someone know,' Gunnhild scolded gently.

Rowena bowed her head. She was ashamed to have caused so much trouble, especially when they were so busy with haymaking. When she apologised Gunnhild patted her arm. 'You've come back safely, that's all that matters.' She gave a little wink. 'Sigurd's still out in the fields, so we'll keep this little matter to ourselves.'

Rowena smiled her thanks, and she and Gunnhild put their heads together to come up with a mythical accident in the pastures to explain her injuries. Rowena breathed a little easier, for if Sigurd knew of the trouble she had put everyone to she would surely be treated to another beating.

She retired early that night. Safely back in the shieling she persuaded herself that she had imagined the incident with the mirror. Perhaps the bright sunlight had momentarily blinded them and caused the accident. She smiled to herself; that was the answer. She was far too ready to jump to the wrong conclusion these days.

Rowena awoke in a tangle of bedclothes, gasping for air. Her skin was wet with perspiration and her throat felt as though it was clogged. An awful foreboding stole over her. The acrid smell of smoke filled her lungs and she thought she would surely choke. Freeing herself from the clothes she shivered, slightly disorientated. At first she assumed the smoke from the fire in the hall was drifting into the bedchamber, but then she realised it was not the case at all. The smoke was coming from the foot of the opposite wall! The shieling was on fire!

A solitary candle burned low beside her, but there was enough light to see the curling spirals of smoke seep in through the wall. She scrambled from the bed, catching her foot in the sheet before tripping over her shoes. Regaining her balance she reached the door and tried to pull it open, but it would not budge. She couldn't understand it; it was not locked from the inside and should open easily. She tried again without success. It was as though something was jammed on the other side preventing it from opening.

Her throat burned, the smoke was swiftly filling the room, curling in the air like grey snakes. Her eyes smarted, tears streaming down her cheeks. She cried out and banged on the door with her fists. Small croaks were all she managed before the smoke started her coughing again. A cold fear engulfed her; was this planned? Had the same person who caused her fall from Syn set the fire and barricaded the door of the bedchamber so she would be asphyxiated or burnt to death?

She became angry; she wouldn't give in without a fight! Besides, if the fire took hold it would soon burn through to the hall, the thought of her friends in danger motivated her, and she fought her way through the bedchamber, with great difficulty, as sooty fumes found their way into her lungs.

Wiping at her eyes, battling to keep them open, she finally found what she was looking for, the large candlestick by her bed. The candle had burnt lower still, but it still allowed her some light. With a silent prayer on her lips she found her way once more to the door, swung the candlestick and hammered on the wood. The heavy object made more noise than her fists and she knew someone was bound to hear. Though she didn't know if they would be in time to save her, for she could hear the fire eating through the wall, could see the flames licking at the floor.

Just as the candlestick fell from her hands the door burst open and Rig caught her in his arms. He carried her out into the air and urged her to breathe deeply. The cold air on her face revived her, and she inhaled gratefully, coughing as the black smoke cleared from her lungs. When Rig was satisfied she was all right he wrapped her in his own mantle and relinquished her into Gunnhild's tender care, before going off to help fight the fire.

She heard Sigurd shouting orders, and thankfully it was under control in a surprisingly short time. She was taken back inside and given a drink to ease her parched throat. Then she bedded down in the fire-hall, and when her husband appeared later, followed by some of his warriors, he viewed her worriedly, his eyes weary from the long night. 'Are you all right, Rowena?' he asked.

'Yes, thanks to Rig,' she said, smiling gratefully at Gunnhild's husband. 'What happened?'

'I couldn't sleep,' he explained as he was served some ale. 'I went riding and spotted the fire from the hill.'

'The door,' she croaked. 'It wouldn't open.'

'There was a heavy trunk blocking it.' Sigurd's mouth was set in a thin line.

'I think someone's trying to kill me,' she whispered a little desperately, telling him what had happened when she fell off Syn.

'And you didn't have the sense to tell me?' he said coldly.

'I didn't think you would believe me,' she reasoned. 'Then I began to doubt myself.'

He sighed impatiently. 'Your lack of faith could have been the end of you.'

Rig saw the little shiver that ran through her and put his body between her and his chieftain. 'Easy, Sigurd,' he warned. 'Your wife has been through a nasty ordeal this night.

'Who do you think it is?' she asked, peering anxiously around.

'I'm not sure,' he admitted. 'But someone set a fire, using the chickweed that grows outside for kindling. And they made sure you wouldn't be able to get out of the bedchamber by barricading the door. We scoured the countryside, but could find no one skulking around.'

Rowena couldn't bear to think what would have happened if Sigurd hadn't seen the fire from the hillside and rescued her. She had a bad feeling, and it frightened her to know someone out there planned her death.

'Whoever it was won't find it so easy again,' Sigurd vowed. 'You'll be guarded at all times.' She was about to protest but he held up a hand to silence her. 'The matter is settled. Now I have to see about the damage to the shieling.'

She was able to feel the extent of his anger, almost palpable, and he was appalled at what had happened. But the facts could not be ignored – someone wanted her dead.

Chapter Eleven

Rowena could not have chosen between the shieling and the homefarm if her life depended on it. It was as large as Gunnhild had said, the beautiful ocean was but a beat away and the hillsides were covered with trees. The sloping beaches were ideal for Sigurd's ships and a nearby valley protected natural hot springs.

She thought of it now as she stirred the large pot over the fire in the shieling. There was still much work to be done before they moved to the homefarm but, when she viewed it with Gunnhild a few days before, she found it very much to her taste. Sigurd was true to his word; wherever Rowena went she was accompanied by one of the Berserks. She was amused at first, but then she fast tired of being followed everywhere. Thorolf, the Berserk assigned to her, sat a little way away from her in the fire-hall whittling as she attended to the meal. He looked so miserable she felt sorry for him.

'I won't be straying far from the fire-hall today, Thorolf,' she said with a smile. 'Why don't you get some air?' He looked dubious and she persuaded him some more. 'I have far too much to do indoors, so feel free.'

That seemed to do the trick, and she sighed with relief when he went about his business. An hour or so later she was outside the fire-hall herself, shaking out some linen, when she saw Sigurd in the distance. She immediately went looking for Thorolf, for if Sigurd knew he'd left her, no matter what the excuse, the warrior would be severely punished.

She looked everywhere she could think of, until the only place she hadn't searched was the stable, so lifting her skirts she scurried towards them as though her life depended on it. When she arrived at the entrance Syn perked up and whinnied at her. Rowena patted her fondly, but she didn't have the time for Sigurd would be upon them all too soon.

Turning her nose up at the malodorous, hay-strewn building, she cast her eyes about but was unable to see any signs of human occupation; even the stable man was missing. She put her hands on her hips, wondering what to do next. It was all her fault! Why hadn't she left well alone? Thorolf would be with her now if she hadn't persuaded him to go off.

Suddenly she heard scraping noises and heavy breathing coming from one of the stalls at the far end. She stood rooted to the spot, wondering what it was. There were no horses in that stall. The noise came again and she scolded herself for being such a coward. Stiffening her back she marched over to the end stall, and almost fainted at what she saw.

Two men were fellating each other, their hungry mouths swallowing their lover's cock! Rowena was lost for words, and quite unable to move or speak. While she watched they altered their position, and she was able to recognise them as Thorolf and the stable man Njal. They were lost in their own little world, quite oblivious to the knowledge that they were being observed.

They began kissing passionately and Rowena was shocked at the male on male display of affection, until she realised it was no different to what she'd shared with Algitha, immediately ashamed of her hypocrisy, though she was at a loss as to what to do next.

Thorolf caressed the other man's stiff cock, feeling between his legs for his hairy balls, which he gently squeezed. Njal sighed his pleasure and allowed the much larger man to turn him over onto his front. He lifted his bottom in the air and Thorolf spat on a finger and wormed it into his bottom hole. Njal wiggled, gasping at the delightful invasion of his rectum. Thorolf fingered him for a while, and then took his large staff and mounted him. Rowena didn't want to watch them but she was completely lost in the moment. As Thorolf fucked his lover well, so Njal grabbed his own cock and masturbated.

The air was filled with the odour of sex and horse. Thorolf was like a bull and Rowena watched in awe as his cock drove in and out of Njal, his balls dancing against his bottom. They reached a climax together, Thorolf roaring like the bull he favoured, Njal exclaiming his pleasure more quietly. They kissed tenderly and Rowena knew she had to make them aware of her presence.

She coughed delicately and the men broke apart. 'Sigurd is on the way, Thorolf,' she warned, then while she turned her back they quickly dressed, their faces red with embarrassment. Thorolf, head down and shoulders bent, then followed her from the stable.

'Thorolf,' she began gently, 'please don't feel embarrassed. I am a married woman and know all about love.'

'I don't think so,' he replied gruffly. 'Not my kind of loving, anyway.'

Rowena touched his arm kindly. 'We females have varied appetites too, you know.' Thorolf stared at her, disbelief in his eyes, and Rowena blushed. 'You'd be surprised.'

Thorolf blushed too, and Rowena hid a smile.

'Thank you, mistress,' he said, his eyes saying a thousand words. 'Anyone else would have reported me to the chieftain, and his wrath would have been mighty.'

'Your secret is safe with me,' she said with a warm smile, which made him her willing slave forever.

Leif was in the hall when she walked in, laughing and talking with another. Rowena saw the tall, broad-shouldered man in a red mantle, his golden hair and dark-blue eyes making him by far the handsomest there, and she wanted to run into his arms and tell him how much she'd missed him. But although her husband was able to parade his affairs in front of her, she had to pretend to be a faithful wife. She was suddenly very angry. He was a cruel man and an adulterer, but she had to toe the line when all she wanted was to let the world know she loved Leif.

He saw her then, and she knew by the emotions that shone from those blue eyes that he felt the same as she did. They made polite conversation, but when the evening meal was over and her husband sought Maeve, she took him to the barn where they found a quiet corner.

'I've missed you so much,' she cried, as he took her into his arms.

'And I you,' he said, kissing her passionately. 'But as you probably know my father died and I had urgent matters to attend to.'

She nodded. 'I am sorry for your loss, Leif.'

He took her hands in his and kissed her fingertips one by one. 'He was a wonderful man and there will never be another like him,' he said sadly. 'But we all have to die, and do I have some good news. I am the oldest son, and my father's demise means that I am now a jarl with a large inheritance.'

'A jarl?' She looked at him blankly, wondering what that had to do with her.

'Don't you see, Rowena?' he said excitedly. 'It means I have plenty to offer you now. A beautiful home and anything your heart desires.'

'Have you not forgotten that I am married to your cousin?' she reminded him sadly, thinking of the wonderful life he was offering her, the life she could never have. The dreams she'd woven around being with him permanently and having children with him were nothing but fantasy. It was time to face reality.

'He doesn't treat you like a wife should be treated. If you divorce him for his cruelty and adultery you will be free to marry me.'

'Marry you?' Her eyes lit up, it sounded so good. If only it were possible.

'Say yes, my love,' he urged, 'and I will seek Sigurd out and tell him about us. It is time he learned of our love and my commitment to you.'

Rowena felt as though she'd been slapped. Sigurd would never let her go, he was far too twisted and hateful to allow that. And he would make Leif pay for loving her. He might even kill him. Her heart thumped in her chest. She had to stop Leif speaking to him; if anything happened to him she would want to die herself.

She got to her feet and brushed the hay from her skirt, forcing a light laugh to leave her lips. 'I can't possibly marry you, Leif. What we had was fun, but I love Sigurd. He has his dalliances, but he always comes back to me in the end.'

As soon as the words were spoken she wanted to rush back into his arms and tell him it was all lies, but she couldn't. She had to let him go to keep him safe.

His eyes dulled with pain, a tic played at the side of his jaw. 'Is that the truth, Rowena?' he asked raggedly. 'Or is this some sick game you're playing?'

Her heart wasn't in it but she had to persuade him that she was no better than his cousin. 'My husband won me the minute he dragged me across the floor of the burh and beat me.'

'This isn't you talking,' he insisted, taking her hand. 'There is something wrong here. Tell me what it is.'

She shook him off, tossing her flowing hair back from her face. 'Yes,' she admitted coldly, 'there is something wrong. The day we married Sigurd did treat me as I said. He dragged me by my hair, and beat me sorely, and then he dumped me in the filth near the byre.' She watched the blood drain from his face, but she wasn't finished. He had to be convinced by her act. 'Then he took me in a barn very much like this one.' She paused for effect. 'But his loving wasn't gentle. He ripped off my clothes and took me like an animal. And when my virgin blood soaked the hay he laughed and called me a whore.'

His eyes pleaded with her. 'Rowena, please…'

He was taking the bait but she had to go further, to make him hate her. 'And he took me with his men watching. We rutted like wild bores, his cock boring into me so hard I thought I would die.' She laughed. 'There is much more I could relate, filth and depravity like you've never heard, and I loved every minute. You see, Leif, you are not man enough for me. I love the excitement my husband gives me. He is the only one who can truly satisfy the whore in me.'

His brave warrior eyes were brimming with tears. 'You are not the woman I thought you were. I will not come to this place again.'

Then he was gone. She had convinced the only good and decent man in her life that she was a depraved creature whom he now despised, and she cried until she thought her heart would break.

Sigurd brought Sleipner to a halt in the valley of the hot springs, and jumping lightly from the stallion he lifted Rowena down beside him. She was so nervous her mouth was dry, and when she asked him what they were doing there it came out as a croak. He appeared to be larger than ever as he stood looking down at her, his mouth twisted in a secretive smile.

'Why are we here?' she demanded. Sigurd never did anything without a reason and she did not trust him.

'Relax, wife.' He smiled again, but it never quite reached his eyes. 'Gunnhild has chastised me for failing in my duty to you, so I've decided something must be done about it.'

Rowena trembled beneath his regard. She hadn't been eating or sleeping well since her confrontation with Leif, and Gunnhild was worried about her. 'Gunnhild's not happy unless she's worrying about someone,' she said flippantly. 'I do not feel neglected.' She gazed around at the rich green valley. The slopes were covered with birch trees, and plumes of vapour from the hot springs wafted around her feet. Sigurd was in a strange mood, and one she did not appreciate.

He tethered Sleipner and led her to a strange pool,

constructed of hewn blocks of stone. 'This is my private place,' he said whimsically.

'What's it for?' she asked cautiously.

'To bathe in, of course, or did you have other ideas for its use?'

There was the usual edge to his voice and she swallowed uncomfortably. 'Nay, Sigurd.'

'See, it is filled with hot water from the springs through an underground conduit. The temperature of the water can be altered by the addition of cold water from the brook.' He pointed to a stone slotted into the conduit.

Her eyes widened. ''Tis a wonderful thing!'

A brow rose in derision. 'Flattery, Rowena?'

She ignored his sarcasm, noting that the low hillocks sheltered the pool from the northerly winds. 'Do you use the pool often?'

'Aye. It's my favourite place. I find it very relaxing.'

The blue eyes held a hint of mirth and she knew why; it was his favourite place, but one he used with Maeve. She could almost see them frolicking in the steaming water, Maeve's full breasts bolstered by the liquid, floating invitingly on the surface. She could see Sigurd in her mind's eye reaching out for her, enjoying the feel of her satin skin in the sensual environment. Yes, she imagined it was a good place for them both to be.

'It must be an interesting experience,' she said hurriedly, realising he was waiting for her to speak.

Their conversation was innocuous enough, but the tension was building between them, and when Sigurd began to unwind her hair from its confining braid she jumped. 'What are you doing?'

'The action speaks for itself,' he said calmly. 'I am merely loosening your braid. You have beautiful hair I prefer to see worn loose.'

'You... you do?' What was he up to? He had never sought her out before, or offered to take her anywhere of interest. It worried her. 'What are you doing?'

'Helping you disrobe,' he said calmly.

'I'm cold,' she lied.

'The pool is hot,' he reminded her. 'When you're in the water you will not be cold.'

He sounded a little terse now and she knew better than to cross him. She disrobed completely and dipped a toe in the pool. 'Ooh, it's too hot,' she complained.

Sigurd had stripped naked too. 'That's easily remedied.' He strode to the conduit and lifted the stone to let in some cold water. 'Try that.'

Shivering, she stepped gratefully into the steaming water and sank into its silken depths. Sigurd was right, it lapped around her body making her forget the cold. She longed to relax, to let herself float freely, but it was something she could never allow herself to do when her husband was near.

He stepped in beside her. 'I tend to agree with Gunnhild; you haven't been yourself.' He viewed her suspiciously. 'You've not been eating properly, and your sleep is often restless.'

She splashed about in the water, trying to think of an answer that would satisfy him. 'I have had a slight malaise,' she admitted. 'A woman's complaint, but I am over it now.'

'Can it have anything to do with my cousin's absence?' His face was blank but his eyes spoke of his mood.

Rowena coloured and a dart of fear shot through her. 'I can't imagine what you mean.'

Sigurd swam from one side of the pool to the other, his strokes strong and purposeful. Water splashed off his wide shoulders, his muscular arms, and Rowena had a nasty feeling of foreboding. Worse was to come, but he had to set the scene first, make her wait until he was ready to tell her the rest.

He swam close to her, while she tried to appear nonchalant. She wasn't a strong swimmer but she was able to do a few strokes. 'You've been deceiving me with my own kin,' he accused.

The hate in his face was all too apparent now and she

trembled, even the hot water unable to thaw the ice from her bones. 'Nay, husband,' she lied. She had managed to save Leif from his wrath, but would she be able to save herself?

'Like all woman you are nothing but a trull and a liar,' he snapped. 'Leif was happy when he journeyed here, but when I saw him after your tryst he was dejected.'

'Tryst?' Things weren't looking good. She should have known Sigurd would have her followed.

'Do you think I don't know what goes on in my own farm?' He had the mad look in his eyes and she longed to flee. 'What happened, Rowena?' he taunted. 'Did he not satisfy you as much as I do?'

She turned away from him. 'It's no good trying to talk to you when you're in this mood.' She could hear the uneven sound of her heart thudding in her chest and she shook all over, but she knew it was no use arguing, it would only inflame him.

As she began to swim away, her hair drifting out on the water like red seaweed, Sigurd caught it and wound it around his fist, hauling her to him. 'Do not try to escape me, bitch. I know you've been fucking him. I just wonder how many more you've been allowing access to your cunt.'

Rowena struggled, almost choking as water splashed into her eyes and mouth. 'No,' she managed to spit out, 'you've got it all wrong!' She didn't care what he thought of her but she must protect Leif at all costs. 'Leif is innocent!'

'Innocent? How sweet.' He laughed. 'You've just condemned the both of you by your pathetic attempts to save your lover.' He ducked her head beneath the water and she expected to drown, but just as her lungs expelled the last of her breath he wrenched her back to the surface. 'I will not be cuckolded in my own household, bitch!'

As she spluttered and fought for air he dragged her to the side of the pool, and for the first time she noticed the chains attached to a ring set in one of the huge stones at its edge. Then with a cruel tug of her arms he pinned them behind her back and chained her wrists to the stone.

As she watched fearfully he climbed out of the pool, water dripping from his massive physique, and moved the stone in the conduit so that more water poured in. 'That would be too quick a death,' he said with an evil grin. 'I want you to suffer.' He adjusted the stone so that the water just trickled in. 'That's better. Now, whore, you will have longer to contemplate your fate, and that of your lover. He will feel the chill of my sword soon enough.'

Shrugging into his clothes he jumped onto Sleipner and rode off without a backward glance, as Rowena watched the water slowly trickle into the pool, wondering how long it would take to cover her head. She struggled against her restraints; she had to free herself somehow, for if she were to die it must be in trying to protect her love. She had to escape, to try to warn Leif that Sigurd was after him.

A little later it was a desperate Rowena who feared she would never escape the steaming waters of the pool in the valley of the hot springs. Her wrists were bruised and bleeding from her efforts but she was unable to release herself, and the deeper water was now lapping at her chin.

Thoughts of her brief romance with Leif flooded her mind. It had been a short acquaintance but they both knew it was instant love. How she wished she had never met him – never put him in such peril.

Thoughts of Leif doubled her efforts, and she was still fighting to release herself when the rising water reached her lips... when she heard the thunder of hooves, as though from a long way off. Such was her poor state of mind the nearby shouts didn't register, but when Thorolf released her from the cruel chains and hauled her, coughing and spluttering from the pool, she looked up into his kind grey eyes, and fainted.

Rowena came round to find him rubbing her arms, praying to Odin for her safe delivery. She smiled weakly up at him. 'Thank you, my good friend. I was suffering from shock but thanks to you everything is fine now.' She knew she should be embarrassed by her nakedness, but she was sure Thorolf wasn't troubled by it. He took off his mantle and dried her, as gently as any handmaiden, before helping her dress. She knew no one would believe that this dear man was one of the fiery Berserks.

She hugged him affectionately. 'What of Sigurd?' she asked.

'He bade me come for you,' he said grimly, his voice telling of his disapproval at his chieftain's actions. 'I don't understand him, doing this to you. He's always been a bit mad, but he's gone too far this time.'

'At least he had the good sense to send you to me,' she said gratefully.

Thorolf smiled. 'I won't ask you why you were being punished, but I will always be around if you ever need me. You did me a good turn, and I will never forget that.'

'You have more than paid your dues,' she replied. 'But I must admit it is nice to have a friend.'

Thunder rumbled menacingly and Thorolf helped her onto his horse, Gymir. 'Thor is riding his chariot across the sky. It will rain soon, so we'd better make haste to return.'

'Do you fear the storm?' Thorolf asked, as they rode for the shieling.

Rowena clung to him tightly. 'When I was a child I would hide beneath my mother's skirts.'

His laughter rumbled through his chest, and Rowena closed her eyes and nestled into him for warmth, but Gymir had barely reached full stride when she heard blood-curdling shrieks and howls. Her eyes flew open and she heard Thorolf curse as five men converged on them from all sides, their expressions terrifying. Before she had time to think, Thorolf gave her the reins and leapt from Gymir's back, then unleashing his sword smacked the horse smartly on the rump.

'Get out of here!' he shouted as Gymir darted forward and Rowena held on grimly. But she'd been practically bred on a horse and she soon brought the animal under control. Wheeling him around she saw Thorolf fighting for his life, obviously outnumbered. Feeling no fear for her own safety, and not stopping to think twice, she nudged Gymir into a gallop.

The man she aimed the horse at screamed in horror, but she knew she couldn't allow herself to waver; it was his life against Thorolf's. But just before she reached him the man managed to throw himself aside, cracking his head on a nearby rock. Fighting back her nausea she saw the sword he'd dropped, and swinging from the saddle, but keeping one foot in the stirrup, she managed to sweep it from the ground. Gaining her seat once more she silently thanked Ethelwulf for teaching her that trick many years before. Having brothers was a blessing after all!

She ploughed into the fighting, and swinging the heavy sword with great difficulty, she managed to bring the flat of the blade down on one man's neck. His eyes rolled and he slumped to the ground. Rowena let out a shriek of triumph that was short lived, for without turning from his fighting Thorolf castigated her. 'Get out of here, you damn fool girl!'

Taken aback by his words, considering she had taken care of two of their attackers, she glowered at him, but the glower soon turned to admiration as he fought the three remaining men with a precision and ferocity that left her breathless.

Then, believing she had idled long enough she swung her sword again, but the man nearest anticipated her action. He swiftly parried the blow, knocking the weapon from her hand. He faced her with a leer and she knew she was at a disadvantage. She heard a groan and glanced quickly at Thorolf, finding him on the ground, blood oozing from his arm.

His eyes were closed and she gave a small cry, thinking her dear friend dead. Then losing any thought of self-preservation, her anger at boiling point, she lashed out with her foot and kicked the stranger in the groin. 'Bastard's all!' she cried, bending over Thorolf.

The one she'd kicked was on his knees, his face full of belligerence. The one wounded by Thorolf was groaning loudly. The one who'd hit his head on the rock was conscious and glaring at her with evil intent, as was the one still standing.

The three healthiest checked their cohorts, and seeming satisfied by their condition, began to converge on Rowena. She knew enough Norse to understand what they were saying, and her stomach sank at their words.

'So, what do we have here?' said a fat fellow with a salacious grin. 'A hellcat with flame-coloured hair.'

'I suppose we haven't lucked out completely,' said a lanky man with a spiteful mouth. 'We had thought to kill Sigurd and caught his wife and escort instead.'

'Aye,' said the third, 'and I mean to have some sport before decapitating her. Her husband will not be pleased to find her served up on his trencher, I'll be bound.'

They looked at each other and sniggered. Rowena, satisfied that Thorolf was still breathing, got to her feet and began to backtrack, out of breath and wondering what to do next. She was alone and unarmed, what could she do to defend herself against three rogues? She desperately searched for ideas, and seeing the sword that had been knocked from her hand on the ground, decided to grab for it, but as she did one of them kicked it aside and she lost her footing and fell awkwardly. A sharp pain spasmed through her foot and she cried out pitifully, grasping her ankle, rubbing the injured limb.

'So, the little cat is downed,' the fat one said, leering at her, his breeches tenting with his burgeoning cock. 'Open your legs, bitch. Let's see what Sigurd rides when he tires of his mistress.'

Rowena desperately cast around for another weapon, and seeing a stone nearby reached out for it. If she could down one of them perhaps she'd be able to fight off the other two, but as before she was thwarted as the fat man kicked it away.

She gazed up at him in frustration and fear and he bore down on her, lifting her skirts, exposing the red-gold hair that covered her mound. She hit out at him, tried to crawl away, but the other two intervened, pushing her down, holding her arms so she was pinned helplessly before him.

He laughed cruelly and kicked her legs apart, making her cry out as her sore ankle was skewered with pain. 'Her mouth makes too much noise,' he remarked with a smirk. 'Can you not find some occupation to keep it quiet?'

'I don't think I'll have any trouble doing that,' the lanky one drooled. 'Though she might scream when I show her what she's to eat.'

The other two sniggered at his vulgarity. 'Maybe she'll faint at the size of it,' chortled the one who still held her in a vicelike grip.

'She'll think it's a worm,' the fat one mocked, pushing his way between her thighs, prodding between her legs with fat fingers.

He took his cock out of his breeches and began to stroke it until it grew larger. Rowena recoiled in horror as his fetid breath wafted over her, and his erect cock shunted into her wilting body. Though it was over in seconds it seemed like an eternity, his cohorts jeering and goading him on as he fucked her, his fat frame heavy and stinking with sweat.

'Move, damn you!' he snarled as she lay limp beneath him. He slapped her face and she managed to bite a fat finger, causing him to scream like a woman. 'You slut! I'd have more pleasure sticking it in a dead horse!'

'I bet you've done that a few times,' the lanky one

wheezed. 'You've never been too fussy when it comes to pleasing yourself.'

The fat man's cock became flaccid and slipped out of Rowena. He rolled off her with a sly kick that brought tears to her eyes, tears she refused to shed. They would never break her. They could abuse her but her spirit would never be broken.

The lanky one leered down at her, his cock engorged with excitement. 'Watch and learn, my friend,' he taunted the fat one. 'Watch and learn. Mayhap women would be more willing to open their legs if you had something more exciting to offer.'

Rowena's eyes glazed over purposefully. If she thought of other things he would not be able to touch her, not the part of her that mattered, anyway. But to her dismay his cock had steel and he knew how to wield it to pleasure them both.

'Come,' he said, panting into her ear, 'let's have a good fuck, you and I.' He rolled her onto her stomach and fed his cock home so well that she could only whimper with shameful pleasure. A finger found and stroked her clitoris as he pumped into her, and she met him strength for strength, her mouth rounded in delight.

Rowena was ashamed that the tardy sex had roused her so, sent her traitorous body into such ecstasy she could barely restrain her cries of joy. The others watched, and to her chagrin it only served to add to her enjoyment. His finger was every bit as masterful as his cock and she came with a loud cry that shuddered through her body. He managed two more lunges before he ejaculated deep inside her, and then collapsed at her side, panting and sweating heavily.

The fat one was jealous of his comrade's prowess, and as his own cock had stiffened again watching the display, he grabbed Rowena roughly by her hair, his grin wide and spiteful. 'I wonder if your husband will be happy when he hears how you squealed with enjoyment at my brother's cock. You fine-mannered women are all the same, pretending innocence while opening your legs willingly for all and sundry.'

Rowena winced as his fist twisted in her hair, but her eyes flashed bravely. 'I can't imagine any woman being with you willingly,' she spat. 'You're nothing but a fat piece of slime.'

The other two laughed, and he caught her a glancing blow across her face. 'Let's see just how smart you are when you eat my cock,' he growled, pulling her into a kneeling position, his sagging belly and sour smell making her want to gag.

'You'll gain no satisfaction from me, you—'

Before she was able to finish her sentence he stuffed his engorged cock into her mouth. 'Shut your caterwauling and do the only thing you're fit for, bitch,' he snarled.

Rowena tried to pull away, but the more she struggled the more hair he twisted around his fist. Tears welled in her eyes and she feared her hair would be torn out by the roots if she didn't comply with his demands. So she reluctantly worked on him with her lips and tongue and the grip relaxed in her hair, which in turn helped ease the pain in her scalp. The other two were bawdily singing her praises, slapping the cheeks of her bottom so they quivered enticingly.

'Did you ever see such a pretty purse?' the lanky one said throatily, his fingers delving into the slippery folds, squeezing her sex lips together.

'I've never seen a finer arse.' The third, bearded one, slapped her again, his laughter rumbling in his chest. His finger joined his associate's in her wetness from behind, and then began pushing into her bottom hole. Rowena tried to cry out but it emerged as a muffled groan around the fat man's stalk, and when she tried to pull away the fat man grumbled because his sport was disturbed.

'Pay attention, bitch,' he said gruffly, grabbing a hank of hair and tugging it cruelly. The pain brought her into line, but when the bearded one manhandled her, in order to change her position a little, and decided to replace his finger with his cock, tears of shameful delight dripped from her eyes, wetting the fat man's expansive belly and groin. The sensation of having her mouth and bottom fucked in unison was mortifying and wonderful at the same time.

The fat man climaxed first, groaning loudly as he came, flooding her mouth with semen that she swallowed hastily. The other one was still ploughing into her and she whimpered dreamily as her own climax began to build. The fat man began mauling her breasts, spitefully pinching her nipples, the pain increasing her pleasure, her body at war with her psyche.

The one with the beard orgasmed too, his strong fingers clamping her hips as he erupted deep inside her rear passage, grunting his pleasure.

Just then the earth seemed to tremble as Thor rode his chariot across the heavens and rain poured on them in a torrent. Thorolf stirred and let out a loud growl, so Rowena didn't mind the rain that soaked her through in moments, or the cold that chilled her to the bone – Thorolf was alive!

But the fat man regarded him warily, and foraging for his weapon he was about to plunge it into the Berserk when Thorolf rolled out of the way, and finding his own sword stuck him in the belly. Seeing his cohort downed the bearded one swung his weapon, but Thorolf was quicker and pulling his sword from the fat man's belly, parried the blow before spearing him in the leg. As the lanky one tried to flee Thorolf threw himself and tackled him to the ground with a bone-crunching thud. He was winded, his eyes rolling, and Thorolf cursed him in Norse and struck him a blow on the chin that knocked him unconscious.

Rowena grinned at his handiwork, but Thorolf was furious when he saw her nudity and the bruises on her body. 'What have they done to you?' He found his sword and was about to decapitate the men one by one when

Rowena restrained him.

'Don't do this, Thorolf,' she pleaded. 'Let Sigurd deal with them. I'm not harmed and Sigurd will enjoy sentencing the scum. Besides, there are things we need to know. Our attackers may well have information about the fire at the shieling and my accident on Syn.'

Thorolf reluctantly sheathed his sword and began heaving the senseless bodies over the horses that were grazing nearby, his grim face telling her of his misery.

Rowena limped to her wet clothes and struggled into them, shivering as the icy rain continued to fall. 'There is blood on your arm, are you hurt?' she asked, concerned for her loyal friend.

He shrugged dismissively. 'It's no more than a flesh wound.'

'Don't look so unhappy,' she said, with a cajoling smile. 'You captured them single-handed. I'm so proud of you.'

'Don't be,' he replied, lashing the bodies securely to the waiting beasts. 'I let you down when you needed me most.'

She went to his side and wrapped her arms around his waist. 'Nonsense. You were unconscious.'

He looked down at her, his eyes tender and filled with shame. 'Yes, I was unable to protect you and those beasts defiled you. I shall never forgive myself.'

She hugged him. 'My friend, you are the bravest warrior I know. None of this was your fault. As for what happened to me, those men treated me less harshly than my own husband.' She looked down at her sodden figure. 'See, I am quite all right. Now let's be on our way before we both catch our deaths.'

Chapter Twelve

Sigurd viewed his wife's attackers, the sons of Svein Asleifsson grimly. The morons had almost robbed him of his means of retribution. One had been killed and the others were injured, though not as badly as he would have hoped had he been there. 'What do you have to say for yourselves?' he demanded.

The three Norse brothers left from the five all looked worse for wear. They hung their heads in shame. They had ambushed a chieftain's wife, not any chieftain, but Sigurd Thorkelsson. No doubt they would soon be as dead as their poor brothers. Sigurd had been questioning them unstintingly for some time and they were weary. The youngest, Harald, offered some information. 'As you know, Gunnar Egilsson's sister resided at our farm for a short while.'

Sigurd nodded impatiently. 'Go on.'

Harald trembled visibly at the great chieftain's anger. 'Our poor dead brother, Hjalti, fell madly in love with this woman, but she didn't return his feelings and he tried desperately to win her, without luck. Eventually he hit upon a plan to gain her respect and admiration.'

Harald paused fearfully, wondering if he was doing the right thing in telling his story, but a nod from his brothers and a fierce bellow from Sigurd forced him to continue. 'To his mind,' he said tremulously, 'Gunnar had failed abysmally as Freyjr's protector and so he appointed himself to champion her cause. He... he persuaded us that we should help him ambush you, to help make you pay for insulting his love. We watched and waited for our chance, and when we saw what we considered to be you and your wife riding together we took our chance.'

Sigurd's mouth drew into a tight line. 'And what of the fire at the shieling and the riding accident my wife had?'

The men shook their heads and mumbled their

innocence, and Sigurd's steely regard soon set another talking. Njal Asleifsson, barely able to stand on his damaged leg, continued for his brother, 'I swear, lord, it was not us. Hjalti could have done it alone. He had been strange for a long time, ever since Freyjr told us her story and he fell for the woman.' He spat into the straw. 'Whore, more like, for she lay with us all. Her pussy was as hot as the geysers and she couldn't get enough.'

Sigurd was quite unsurprised by the revelation. 'The woman's morals are not on trial here. I want to know about your perfidy.'

Njal shuffled his feet uncomfortably. 'Hjalti changed completely after the Egilsson woman bewitched him.' His siblings nodded their agreement and he went on. 'There were long silences and he would go off on his own for hours at a time. He was quite mad in his desire to please Freyjr, and he knew she despised your wife, but he would not have told us what happened. He abhorred failure. It is quite possible he caused your wife to have a riding accident. In his state of mind anything was possible. As for the fire in the shieling, he would have found it quite easy to conceal himself in the hills; we have played there since we were children and know the area better than most. No doubt he hid when he started the fire and remained hidden until all was quiet again.'

Harald was loud in his agreement. 'We were fools to listen to his ravings,' he bemoaned. 'We are disgraced and feel deep remorse for our wrongdoings.'

Sigurd's stern features did not soften one iota. 'You will find no forgiveness here,' he vowed. 'You will be tried at the next Thing. In the meantime your father can deal with you. If he were not one of my greatest friends you would all be minus your heads. I am just sorry you've brought disgrace to his name. He is a good man and undeserving of such prodigy.'

Harald proceeded to blame his dead brother for corrupting him, and they began to squabble between themselves. Sigurd looked as if he would explode.

'Enough! You are like squabbling babes. Bah, get them out of my sight!'

Rowena watched the proceedings uneasily; she had sworn Thorolf to silence regarding the men abusing her. She knew, had Sigurd been aware of the facts, he would soon decide she had asked for their attentions and punish her too.

Maeve slid into the shadows at the back of the hall; she needed to speak with Rowena. It was merely a matter of days since the attack by the Asleifsson brothers, but she was unable to wait any longer to confront the chieftain's wife. She knew she'd be heading for the bathhouse soon, and she'd have her chance.

Her mind went back to the time she and Sigurd stayed with Gunnar Egilsson and his sister. She was convinced they'd never been closer until the day she walked to the shore in search of him, and found him and Freyjr fucking like wild beasts. Her hackles rose and she thought she would choke with fury. They hadn't even had the decency to find cover, unless one considered a rock to be concealment enough. Which of course it wasn't, for hadn't they had quite an audience when she saw them?

Not that it bothered either of them. Sigurd was beyond caring and the blonde bitch was no more than a trollop. She probably enjoyed being watched. After all, she'd had practically every man on her brother's farm. She was well known for her low morals, and every man from the lowest thrall up knew he only had to wink her way and she would willingly open her legs for him, and for two or three at a time, also.

Sigurd had broken her heart, but he would be sorry for all the pain he caused. Her mouth tightened; she was the one who knew of the indignities heaped upon him when a boy. She was the one who understood his problems, who loved him so much she even cleaned him up when he soiled himself. But he had severed that bond and there would never be another who understood him like she did.

Let him find out the hard way.

Rowena was limping her way to the bathhouse, thinking that at least Sigurd seemed to have given up on his plan to harm Leif. Since the incident at the hot springs he hadn't mentioned him once, and she was still deep in thought when Maeve attracted her attention. She faced her coldly. What was the Irish woman thinking? If she was about to boast about her conquest of her husband she was wasting her time. Rowena cared nothing for him or the women whose beds he sought.

Thorolf's eyes were watchful of the Irish woman, his brow furrowed in concern. Rowena put a comforting arm on his sleeve, noting to her surprise that the dark-haired girl had the appearance of sadness, not spite, on her pretty features. 'What is it, Maeve?' she asked, when the young woman urged her to walk with her to the bathhouse.

Once they were closeted inside Maeve studied her lover's wife with tearful eyes. 'I have to apologise to you, lady.' Rowena was about to tell her that she had no interest in any apology from her when she put up a restraining hand. 'Please, listen to me,' she pleaded, 'for I have done you wrong and need to make amends.'

Rowena shrugged impatiently. 'Why, when your whoring never bothered you before?'

Maeve dropped her eyes in shame. 'I need to make my peace with my God. And as I know you are a Christian too, I was sure you would understand.'

Rowena sighed; she supposed it would do little harm to listen to what she had to say. 'Very well, but make it quick. I have the evening meal to attend to.'

Maeve sat down on one of the slatted benches and Rowena sat opposite. She pushed a lustrous dark curl behind one ear. 'Sigurd took me from my land as he did you. I fell madly in love with the golden warrior and I thought he felt the same for me. I always knew he would not take a lowly thrall to wife, but it was still a shock when he came back from his travels with you.'

Rowena was beginning to feel sorry for the girl.

'Please, continue.'

'I am ashamed to say that I hated you for having claimed my man, but when we visited the coast I saw him with Freyjr and realised how you must have felt all the nights he shared my bed.' She paused in order to wipe her eyes. 'I was sick with misery and jealousy when I saw them together, but I could do nothing but flirt with Phelim, one of Gunnar's thralls, to try to make Sigurd jealous. But a wonderful thing happened.' Her face broke into a wondrous smile. 'Phelim and I fell in love and I am carrying his child.'

Rowena's head was reeling with all the information Maeve had imparted. So even his mistress had become sickened by his infidelity! Then she realised that the name of Maeve's beloved was familiar. 'Phelim,' she repeated. 'Was he not among the servants who conducted Freyjr to our farm? A tall man with sad eyes and a haunted smile.'

Maeve nodded, her eyes dreamy. 'That's Phelim. He is haunted by the thought that he will never see his beloved Ireland again. You see, unlike me he was not a willing captive. He's never settled here. He yearns for his homeland so much he can think of nothing else.'

'Does Sigurd know about this?' Rowena asked cautiously.

Maeve shook her head. 'He cares little for anyone or anything, apart from that which serves his own ends.'

Rowena knew better than anyone how true this was, but she kept her own council. 'What will you do?' she asked sympathetically.

Maeve fiddled with her tunic, pleating and re-pleating the garment nervously. 'Can I trust you?' she asked shakily. 'For what I tell you now will mean the success or downfall of three lives.'

Realising the seriousness of the situation, Rowena patted the other's unsteady hands. 'I have never been known to break a trust, and we are sisters beneath the skin, are we not? Sigurd has done us both a great injustice.'

Maeve looked relieved. 'That is true. Then I will share the secret that is so near to my heart.' Her eyes filled. 'We are going to escape from Sigurd's land of fire and ice. We intend stealing a ship and sailing to Ireland.'

Rowena was stunned. 'You will never survive! What is Phelim thinking?'

It was the Irish girl's turn to pacify. 'Don't fret, lady. There are others with the same fire in their bellies as Phelim, men of the sea before they were taken as slaves.' While Rowena mulled this over Maeve looked uneasily towards the door, where Thorolf stood guard, and lowered her voice. 'If it is convenient Phelim would meet with you. He has some news to impart.'

'What is it?' Rowena couldn't imagine what the Irishman would have to say to her.

'I cannot say. Phelim wishes to tell you himself. After Freyjr left Svein Asleifsson's farm she moved on to take advantage of Snorri Tryggvason's hospitality. No doubt she lingers in the area in order to save herself from her brother's wrath.'

'No doubt,' Rowena agreed coldly.

'Phelim is part of her entourage and he hopes to slip away later this day. If you are willing, you must plead a slight malaise and meet us here when the evening meal is served.'

She was greatly puzzled; what news could Phelim possibly have that would interest her? However, she nodded her agreement. 'That should be easy enough.'

Happy that Rowena had complied with her wishes, she smiled. 'Thank you. You will not regret your decision.'

Maeve took her leave, elated by her success with Rowena, and the fact that she would see Phelim the same day. She barely acknowledged the presence of Thorolf as he stood guard at the door, her thoughts all of Phelim. Before she'd met her countryman she had thought Sigurd to be the most wonderful man she had ever known, particularly in bed, but then she fluttered her eyelashes at

Phelim and was quickly disabused of her ideas.

She found him to be flattered by her attentions, eager to please. Their first mating had taken place behind the same rock Sigurd and Freyjr had used. To her it was a way of wiping out the incident, of making peace within herself. She hadn't expected to find a new lover with the prowess of ten men. He wore her out that night on the shore, and she climaxed many times before he was done with her.

The following day they met again, but this time he seemed in a strange mood, though he kissed her just as passionately as before, then led her to the pagan temple of the Norse. She put her hand over his when he attempted to enter that strange heathen place, but he merely gave a sly chuckle and pushed the portal open and led her inside.

Lighting the candles either side of the altar he smiled at her. 'This, my sweet Irish maid, is where we show their so called gods what we think of them, where we have fun with the idols of the heathens.'

Although she had seen inside other temples, there was an eeriness here that sent shivers down her spine. The odour of blood pervaded the place, and dark stains spread over the floor, telling of the cattle and horses that had been sacrificed. She'd heard that during the ceremonies their blood was sprinkled all over the temple and the people gathered there.

'Before we can start a proper relationship,' he began, his face becoming a saturnine mask that made her uneasy, 'I want to purge you of the bastard Sigurd Thorkelsson. Thinking of you with him tears my insides apart.'

She stared at him blankly, and with one swift movement he picked her up and carried her to the idol of Thor, and then stood her on her feet. 'I need to punish you for your misdemeanours, Maeve, here in his temple. Only then will I be satisfied that you really want to be with me.'

'Punished? I don't know about that, Phelim.' She had begun to feel wary, there in the temple of the Norse where anything could happen.

'Take your clothes off,' he demanded suddenly, his voice rising with his ire. She shook her head and turned towards the door, meaning to escape, but he forestalled her, holding her firmly, roughly stripping her of her garments.

Maeve shook with fear. She had thrown over one beast for another. 'You'll be sorry you did this,' she vowed. 'I thought you loved me.'

'I do,' he swore, 'but I have to beat the bastard out of you first. It's for your own good,' he assured.

Before she had time to plead with him he flung her over one of the goats that drew Thor's silver chariot. Her stomach recoiled as the cold silver slammed against her. 'You call Sigurd a beast and treat me so,' she cried, hoping he would be more reasonable. She had never felt more vulnerable.

'Quiet woman!'

Tears stung her eyes, he was suddenly so angry she feared for her life. 'You are not the man I thought you to be.'

He undid the belt from his waist and wrapped it round his fist. 'Brace yourself!' he advised gruffly, bringing the harsh leather down sharply on her buttocks.

Maeve screamed. He was not as large as Sigurd but he used a belt with the same effect. He brought it down a second time and she howled in pain, her bottom stinging as the leather scoured her skin. Before she could scream again at her cruel treatment Phelim stuffed a cloth into her mouth, stifling any sound she might make.

'You will soon be free of your sins,' he soothed, wielding the belt harder so that she almost choked on the rag. Her tears came as the unbearable pain shot through her rear, then with one last stroke he sighed deeply, 'There, now you are mine completely.'

Lifting her down from the goat he removed the cloth from her mouth and kissed her eyes and lips tenderly. 'There, brave girl, don't cry. Now that's done we can have fun here where the Norse pigs worship.

She glowered at him, but when he began kissing her breasts, dipping his fingers into her wetness, stroking her nubbin, her knees became weak and her juices flowed, as the longing for possession welled inside her. 'Oh, Phelim,' she whispered huskily.

Phelim, still whispering sweet nothings in her ear, rubbed her emissions over the large carved phallus of the idol Frey. Then he positioned her over it.

'Gently, my love,' he said. 'Take it inside you until you are full of him, then I want you to pleasure yourself until you are satiated.'

She was about to protest, but the wickedness and excitement of what they were doing appealed to her. She imagined how horrified and distressed Sigurd would be to see their mockery of his gods. She giggled. 'You are a devil, Phelim, but I am beginning to appreciate you more by the second.'

He watched fascinated as the huge phallus slowly disappeared inside her body. 'Ride him, Maeve,' he bade throatily. 'Ride the pagan filth.'

She began to move, tentatively at first for it filled her to capacity, stretching her more than she had been stretched before. Then she found it was a good feeling, a fine feeling to be fornicating with Sigurd's god. She strained against the phallus, pumping and grinding, wishing Sigurd could see her now, loving the feel of it inside her. The only sound in the temple was of her exertions and mews of pleasure. Candlelight flickered eerily, the smell of dripping wax mingling with that of stale blood.

Phelim's eyes lit with fire as he watched the dark-haired beauty, breasts bobbing, fucking Frey. He found her soft mouth and anointed it with his lips, took her bouncing breasts in his hands and kissed and teased them with tongue and lips. When her eyes were closed with delight he took her from the seat of her pleasure and laid her on the altar that sat in the middle of the temple.

'Now, my sweet one, we will make love on their most

sacred of places, defile that which we know to be the root of their evil.'

But he did not enter her straight away; he let his cock rub her tender channel, teasing her clitoris and vulva until she was shaking with her orgasm. Only then did he penetrate her, leaving her sobbing and writhing with ecstasy.

Rowena pleaded a headache and sought her bedchamber, glad that no one thought her behaviour remiss. When all, including the brave Thorolf, were busy with their meal, she crept away from the shieling and hurried to the bathhouse. Maeve and Phelim were already inside. Maeve smiled and the sad eyed Irishman gave a polite nod.

'What can be so important as to drag me away from my evening repast?' she asked a little more sharply than she meant, as a sudden foreboding stole over her.

'I ask forgiveness if you have been inconvenienced,' he began in his low, attractive brogue, 'but I fear this news is of more import than sustenance.'

'Then you must tell me at once.' A nagging pain began in her head and she massaged her temples.

Maeve sat on one of the slatted benches and Rowena sat also. 'When Phelim related his story, lady, I decided you must know. Its telling might go a little way to erasing my sins against you.'

Rowena looked to Phelim, who nervously peered through the door to check that they were indeed alone, before taking a seat next to his beloved. He took a deep breath. 'One of Gunnar's captives passed away last autumn, she was an old woman he had taken from Wessex. She was a friendly soul, and before she died often boasted about her sister who was midwife in the household of an Irish princess.'

He paused dramatically and Rowena, her face as white as driven snow, bade him continue. 'I would be from this place soon, before my absence is discovered and pondered upon.'

'The princess's name was Grainne,' he said softly. 'Her husband would have nothing to do with the babe, which was not surprising since the child had been conceived before the princess reached Wessex.'

Rowena clung to the edge of the bench, as fumes from the peat fire beneath the stones seemed to clog her throat. 'Before?'

Phelim nodded. 'The old woman's sister told her Grainne had been taken from her land by a Norse pirate – Godmund the Red, known as the Serpent. The princess had managed to escape him but she already carried his seed.'

'Godmund the Red...' Rowena murmured, suddenly transported back to the day in the burh. She was agitatedly awaiting news of Sigurd's health when the voices of her mother and aunt had come to her through the unglazed window of the bower – Elfrida urging Grainne to tell her about Godmund the Red, her mother swearing she never would. It explained a lot, especially Athelwine's treatment of her. She looked at Phelim wordlessly.

'The woman told and retold her story until it came to the ears of a certain great Norse chieftain.'

'Sigurd,' Maeve said, almost apologetically.

'He became very excited,' Phelim said. 'He went to the old woman and questioned her repeatedly. I was taken with his interest and overheard him discussing her story with his general. "So that is the woman he mourns", he says. "The one his pride stopped him going after". He spat out Godmund's name like snake venom, almost shaking with rage. "So he has a daughter", he says. I hid and listened to his dastardly plans for the Serpent's child, because she is the daughter of a princess from my land also.'

His haunted eyes settled on Rowena. 'He planned to get you with child and then return you to the Serpent. From what I could understand it is his way of revenging

Godmund for some past ills.'

As the tears coursed silently down Rowena's face Maeve tried to console her. But Rowena was inconsolable. No wonder Athelwine hated her. And she had heard aright, at the stream near the shieling, when Sigurd discussed his evil intentions with Rig. 'I... I am the seed of the Serpent. The pawn in Sigurd's game.'

Maeve looked at her sorrowfully. 'I am so sorry, mistress, but you had to know.'

Rowena nodded. 'You did right.' She was suddenly very calm, surprisingly so. 'When do you sail from this place?'

'Soon, very soon,' Phelim replied sombrely. 'Before the winter sets in.'

'Then take me with you.'

'We will take you home,' Maeve said quickly.

Rowena laughed harshly. 'Home? I have no home.'

'Then come with us to Ireland,' Maeve said excitedly. 'It should not be too hard to find your mother's kin.'

Rowena was thinking of her poor mother and how she had suffered. 'Aye,' she said, making her decision, 'let it be so.'

Chapter Thirteen

Rowena huddled miserably into her mantle, almost wishing she were back in the big bed in the shieling. She tried to breathe some warmth into her hands, wishing she'd had the nerve to slit Sigurd's throat before she left. She shuddered, thinking of her lot had Maeve and Phelim not saved her, and she thanked the Lord for Algitha's douches, or she would surely have been large with Sigurd's child by now. No doubt, during the long dark winter, he would have managed to impregnate her and then his plans for her would have taken off.

She looked up at the giant oak beneath which she sheltered, listening to the wind whistling eerily through its branches. Her companions were sleeping nearby, exhausted as she was by the sea voyage. But there was to be no sleep for her, her mind far too active for that.

Algitha had helped drug Sigurd into a deep sleep, appalled at Rowena's story. Maeve had used some of the potion to drug the men who Sigurd kept on guard during the night, and it was easy after that to sneak away from the farm and steal one of the longboats from its berth and cast off on their adventure. But they had not taken into account the rough weather that set in shortly after their escape.

The men suffered the most on the journey, as they'd had to put up with all the elements threw at them, while she and Maeve were closeted in a small tent on deck for most of the journey. She watched the men nervously as they steered by the sun and stars, taken note of cloud formation, the colour of the seawater, used a line to search the ocean's bottom. They had even noted the sea creatures and birds and searched for pieces of driftwood to give them some idea of their whereabouts.

And here they were in that green, verdant land her mother loved. She dashed away a tear, shivering in her thin clothes. She surmised that dawn would be upon them soon, and with a yawn drifted into a dreamless sleep.

She was rudely awakened by a sharp kick to her left foot. Having had little sleep she was disorientated, and opened her eyes wondering where she was. But seeing Maeve and Phelim and the other Irishmen talking to some rough looking strangers soon brought her to her senses.

'Who are you? What do you think you're doing?' she demanded, as one particularly hairy individual hauled her to her feet and dragged her none too gently towards her companions.

Maeve was smiling and Phelim seemed to be doing some sort of deal. Rowena saw money pass hands and Maeve turned to her. 'There, we are done. Phelim, our friends and I will make our way to civilisation. You, Rowena, are to go with these gentlemen.'

Rowena pushed her damp hair out of her eyes, fighting to understand what the Irish girl was saying to her. 'But, I don't understand.'

Maeve gave a cheerful laugh. 'It is not so hard, lady,' she said sarcastically, sketching a bow. 'You took my man, thinking nothing of what it meant to me. From the first day I saw your simpering face I swore to get even, and guess what, I have. We have sold you to merchants who will barter you in foreign lands, where women are bought and sold and treated like dogs.' She flicked a tress of fiery damp hair from Rowena's shoulders. 'You are not shabby looking and will no doubt adorn someone's bed until he tires of you and sells you on. Or you could be sold to a brothel; I have heard there are many in the east.'

Rowena's head swam. She'd been tricked! Maeve and Phelim had sold her to some traders who would use her as they saw fit. She had been saved from Sigurd only to find herself in more danger!

One of her captor's tied her hands behind her back with some rough rope, and then he dug his spear into her side to move her on. With Maeve and Phelim's laughter ringing in her ears she stumbled over the rugged ground as the merchants made for their destination. After being aboard the longboat for so long she was stiff and she knew it would take time for her land-legs to return, but these savages had little pity for her as they poked her with their spears, kicking her when she fell after being unable to keep up with their fast pace.

They were in a thickly wooded area when loud whooping noises made her blood run cold. Then to her shock many tiny beings dropped from the trees onto the merchants, who were wrestled to the ground and their throats cut where they lay.

Rowena cowered behind a tree in terror as the blood of her captives ran into the earth, mingling with leaves and mud. The pageant before her was so unreal her mind cast around for something peaceful to cling to. She suddenly thought of her mother's bower, where she would sit with her family and attend to her needlework. But the gentle scene could not compete with the reality of the grotesque little men who had attacked them.

They were laughing, their knives making arcs in the air triumphantly as they surveyed their prey, stealing all they were able to lay their hands on. Rowena's stomach rebelled at the stench of blood and she vomited. Trembling with fear she tried to flee that awful place but her legs froze and she lent against the tree weakly, her bonds chaffing her wrists. The small men moved clumsily on bandy little legs, their awkward gait as ugly as their large heads and hideous features. She had heard Sigurd and his men speak often of similar creatures they'd met on their travels, and they called them dwarves.

She took deep breaths, trying to suppress her nausea, and then with a swimming head and trembling limbs she turned and staggered through the trees. But before she'd gone far they were on her, pinning her to the ground, their bloodied hands all over her.

'Have pity,' she cried as they tore at her clothes, but

they took little notice until their leader, a little taller than the rest, shouted an order.

They immediately retreated and Rowena scrabbled to her feet, her bonds making her almost as awkward as the dwarves. They were chattering in Irish and her heart dropped when she heard them proclaim that they would take her with them. But then she realised she should perhaps be relieved, for at least she was saved for the moment.

Their voices became quieter and the group broke apart, some of the men running off into the trees, while the others dragged her along with them. They only came up to her waist, and she wished her hands were free so she could fight them and escape. But the thought did not linger, for the awful memory of the merchants' deaths at the hands of the tiny devils made her shudder, and she knew she would not stand a chance against them. Small though they were, they were strong.

At the edge of the wood was a clearing dotted with small huts, and as the sound of their approach reached the occupiers of the huts, so they came out to greet them. Rowena was astonished to see several tiny women emerge, each one as grotesque in shape and features as their men.

She was dragged into the middle of the clearing and thrown to the ground. As the damp earth seeped through her torn clothes she saw the men and women embrace, their excitement at their spoils almost palpable. The tiny women danced around her, tugging at her hair, exclaiming at its brightness, prodding her body, amazed at her perfection and beauty despite the cruelty she'd suffered at their hands. The women gathered into a group and chattered slyly, turning occasionally to look upon the stranger in their midst.

Rowena hoped they would take pity on her, after all, were they not sisters in the flesh? 'Please,' she began in their language, 'release me. I need a drink and my bonds hurt so.'

The women, amazed at her use of their language, pointed at her and laughed. One slightly more forward than the rest came to her, her bony fingers poking her ribs. 'Do not ask us for help. You're the finest slave we've seen in an age, and we'll make sure you serve us well.'

The other women sniggered, and overhearing their words two of the men came over to see what was going on. 'Aye, you'll serve us well, bitch,' one sniped. 'And I think you can start right now.'

The women watched in delight as the men dragged her to her feet, lifting what was left of her clothes in order to expose her legs and most of her pale flesh from the waist down. They sighed at her beauty and stroked her thighs. She cried out at the roughness to which she was bring subjected, but uncaring of her distress the men took out bulging penises that were huge in proportion to their body size.

The man they called Aed stroked the length of his cock, and Rowena suddenly wanted to laugh; he was not as threatening as he thought, he barely came up to her waist! But as though he could read her mind he punched her right in her middle and she doubled over with pain. 'Stay like that, bitch,' he snarled. 'That's exactly how we want you.'

Before the pain had time to dissipate Aed jumped on the back of his friend, and standing on his shoulders, stuck a stubby finger in her sex, forcing first one then two inside her. Rowena winced, and her flesh cringed as the evil stranger plundered her core. The women saw her discomfort and laughed.

One called Mageen cocked her head to one side, remarking, 'Aed has lovely fingers that make a woman tingle, does he not?' Rowena remained silent and the Irish female tossed her head. 'Perhaps she is enjoying it too much, Aed. And if she is happy we are not.'

The other women muttered their agreement and Aed smirked. 'I cannot help the magic in my hands. And if she's pleased by them just think how highly she will prize the magic of my cock.'

The women sniggered and Mageen viewed him with disdain. 'Then you shall not have all the fun.' So saying she dived beneath Rowena's legs and nipped at her thighs with sharp teeth, and even before her cries had died away the teeth found her juicy sex lips and bit them too.

Mageen chuckled evilly as Rowena cried and begged her to stop, but she was more interested in what was going on above her head to care much about anything else. For Aed, still balanced on his friend's shoulders, had inserted a wet finger into Rowena's anus, and Mageen was incensed to see that even that private place was as pretty as a flower that opens its petals to the sun.

She was able to see his magnificent member throbbing to be allowed entrance to that haven, and as she watched, her tongue between those juicy lips, he removed his finger and vigorously fed his cock into the tight fissure. Mageen gasped and so did Rowena as the dwarf's obscene phallus ploughed relentlessly in and out of her.

He was a tiny creature, but when it came to his sex he was all male, and to her disgust, although the first few thrusts were uncomfortable, even painful, Rowena soon began to enjoy every thrust of that tumescent cock.

The women babbled their excitement and Mageen's eyes were on the magnificent stalk that burrowed in and out of the new slave's arse. Her own sex began to throb and she grabbed another of the men, exclaiming, 'Come, my fine Fennen, let us see how your cock can compete with that fine specimen.'

She flung herself to the ground between Rowena's thighs, loathe to deprive herself of the appealing sight of Aed fucking the slave, and lifting her skirts, opened her legs to Fennen. Obligingly he fell on Mageen and began fucking her valiantly.

Rowena grunted as loudly as Aed and wished she were able to be free of her bonds so she could rub that demanding little nub that throbbed unerringly between her thighs. It was strange to see the dwarves called Mageen and Fennen copulating between her legs, but she had to admit it was a distinct turn on.

Aed's crisis was upon him, and within seconds he removed himself from her. He jumped down from his perch and she heard him call out to another dwarf. 'Take a ride on her, Gregory. Your cock will fair fly in that heaven between her legs.'

'Me first,' shouted the man called Bard, who had acted as his platform. 'I think I should be next.'

A fight arose and there were many flying fists. Rowena dared to straighten up, rubbing her aching back with the knuckles of her bound hands. Mageen and Fennen reached their goals in noisy unison, and while some of the men were fighting over who would have sex with Rowena next, she was commanded to bend over again and was roughly taken from behind by another dwarf, who adopted Aed's method of jumping on the shoulders of a friend.

It seemed that all the dwarves were well hung, and Rowena railed at the indignity of her position as she was taken again and again by one dwarf after another. They were only interested in their own pleasure, but their stamina was great and she was worn out and quite sore before they finished with her.

When she was finally thrust into a hut and left to lie in a heap on the damp ground, her insidious position instilled itself in her brain. Tears flowed, but they were tears of shame as well as despair when she thought of how she'd thrilled to the abuse she'd suffered. Her marriage to Sigurd had opened her up to a world of perversion; would she ever be satisfied with a normal life?

She laughed mirthlessly – yes she would, given the chance. But she was slave to this community of ruthless dwarves, and they would no doubt use her until she was too weak to serve them any more. But her mind would not go beyond that point, for the horror of what would happen then was far too terrible to contemplate.

'Get up!'

Rowena had fallen into an uneasy sleep only to been awoken by a cruel kick in the ribs. She looked up to see Mageen glaring down at her. 'W-what time is it?' she asked, letting out a small cry at the cramp in her arms from being bound in one place for far too long.

'Time you got up off your lazy arse and attended to our meal,' Mageen replied, spitting into the dirt at her feet. 'Then when you've cleared away you can entertain us again. We are looking forward to it. Get up, slut!'

Wearily Rowena was dragged into the clearing between the huts. She looked around her fearfully. The fire that had smouldered earlier was giving off bright flames, and over it hung a cooking pot. A woman was stirring it with disinterest, and Rowena was stunned to realise it was Maeve.

Mageen pushed her towards the fire. 'There is much to be done. Fetch some water. Then you can peel the vegetables and put them in the pot.'

Maeve saw her with much surprise, but there was no time to talk for Rowena was untied and a rope was bound around her waist instead. One of the men supervised her as she was made to fetch water from a stream nearby, and as she bent to retrieve the water he lifted her ragged kirtle with the stick he held, chuckling lasciviously at her nakedness.

'Get your hands off me, you filthy snake!' Rowena hissed, throwing the water she'd gathered into his face.

His eyes narrowed to aggressive slits, and he angrily swept the stick in an arc and brought it down on her legs. At the same time he jerked on the rope wound around her waist, and Rowena cried out in pain and found herself laying half in the stream and half in the mud, her legs throbbing from his attack.

'Spread your legs, bitch!' the dwarf growled, beating her once more so she was swift to do his bidding, and without further ado he began fucking her with violent gusto. Mageen came to see what was keeping them and her laughter blended with the dwarf's loud breathing. Then they were joined by more of the community, who laughingly egged him on, and when he finished she was made to refill her jug and retrace her steps to the fire.

Maeve surveyed her with interest. The lovely girl who had stolen her lover was covered in mud, her clothes hanging from her like rags. Her beautiful red-gold hair drooped over her shoulders thick with dirt, dripping filthy water over her body. Maeve's eyes glowed with spite, but not for long for Mageen, alerted to her new slave's inattention to duty, slapped her arm.

'If you can't summon the energy to cook, maybe I should beat some into you.'

Maeve apologised and returned to stirring the pot, and shivering in the crisp air, Rowena joined her at the fire. She was tethered to a ring in the ground, as was Maeve, and gathering up a knife she began to scrape at the vegetables.

'It seems as though your fine plans have come to naught,' Rowena remarked, glad of the warmth of the flames that licked at the peat in front of her.

Maeve began to cry softly. 'They took us off guard, killed the men and brought me here.'

Rowena bowed her head over her task. 'I am sorry for your loss, though you thought nothing of my plight.'

Maeve's green gaze took in the sight of the dwarves around them. 'Your plight, but not mine for long. I aim to escape from these deformed pigs as soon as I can.'

Rowena raised her eyebrows. 'You must be careful of your child.'

'There is no child.'

Rowena seethed silently. 'I see. All the same, mark me well; these people are far more ruthless than you can imagine.'

Maeve tossed her head. 'I know about ruthless and cunning, as you know to your detriment. They are no match for me.'

Rowena said no more. She would not waste her breath, but she was every bit as desperate as Maeve to escape.

The weeks went by and nothing varied. Rowena and Maeve were made to wait on the little community and were treated cruelly in return. They were often whipped for small offences and used regularly for the pleasure of their perverse captives.

One day Rowena lay in the cold, comfortless hut, her body and her beautiful hair filthy for she was not even allowed to wash, when she was awoken by the usual kick in the ribs from Mageen.

'Rouse yourself. We need to go into town and you will be required to help. Go down to the stream and wash the filth from your face.'

Rowena did not need to be told twice, so with one of the dwarves as her guard she plunged into the stream fully dressed, scrubbing the dirt from her body and tattered clothes, plunging her grimy hair beneath the icy, sparkling waters. The heavy-eyed dwarf took little notice of her, his eyes more intent on closing. When she emerged from the water she felt fresher than she had in a long time, and much brighter too. It was an autumn day but the sun was shining, allowing a little warmth to her bones.

She dried off by the fire as she cooked the breakfast, wondering what the town would be like, excited that she would be able to see something other than the drab encampment. Her heart soared; mayhap she would be able to escape from her servitude, from the cruel people who held her captive.

When she set off in the little cart that was drawn by a donkey, Maeve watched dejectedly, her heart filled with as much hate for Rowena as ever.

Dubh Linn lay at the point where the rivers Poddle and Liffey met, and Rowena gazed with pride at the place of her ancestors. The town was busy, teeming with life, now that the Vikings had returned years earlier, settling as merchants. Market stalls were heaped with all sorts of goodies and Mageen fingered some sweetmeats greedily. Aed smilingly bought her some, for they had been out on a raid the night before and returned to the camp loaded down with booty.

Rowena followed in their footsteps, the hood of her mantle pulled up over her bright hair, the sack she was carrying filling swiftly with Mageen and Aed's purchases. The shouts of the traders were a boon to her ears, their bright smiles a panacea for her bruised heart. Even the whores, who plied their trade well on the streets of the town, wiggling their bottoms, lifting nearly bare breasts and promising each man they saw a good fucking for a few coins, could not upset her today.

Aed tugged impatiently on the rope around her waist when she lingered for too long at a fish stall, and her happiness faded, for it reminded her that she was no more than a slave, and that she would be hard pushed to escape the two.

The sights of Dubh Linn ceased to thrill her and she followed dejectedly behind Aed and Mageen, dragging the sack that was becoming heavier by the moment. A huge red-haired man with drawn brows blocked her path and Rowena looked up at him fearfully. If he delayed her Aed would pull on the rope and she would surely be punished on their return to the settlement. But he gave such a loud exclamation of surprise she was momentarily shaken out of her ill humour.

'Grainne!' The man shook with emotion and his complexion drained of all colour. 'Grainne, you have come back to me.' He ran his fingers through locks every bit as fiery as her own, and Rowena stared at him in confusion.

He started towards her and she took a swift step back, trying to ward him off with her arm. As she did the hood of her mantle fell back and the man came to a halt, his arms stopping in midair as he began to reach out for her.

He took in the flame tresses that curled about her shoulders, and gave a loud cry like a huge beast in deep anguish.

'Who are you?' he demanded. 'Why have you come to haunt me?'

Rowena was as shaken as he. Why would a stranger call out her mother's name in such a way? She glanced around to see that Mageen and Aed were busy sorting through some bright cloth, quite oblivious to what was happening to her. 'Who am I?' she cried. 'You call out my mother's name and ask who I am.'

The huge stranger fingered a stray curl tenderly. 'Mother? Grainne is your mother?' Tears ran unbidden down the well-weathered face. 'Then she was with child when she fled from me. The gods have brought my daughter to me.'

Rowena's bloodless lips moved, but there was no sound. He suddenly embraced her and she clung to him. This was her father, but far from the heathen she had expected he was warm and tender. 'Godmund the Red... father,' she whispered.

They were not to be in each other's arms overlong, for Aed, having found what he wanted on the stall, took up the slack in the rope, tugging Rowena away from her father. But when Godmund realised what was happening he roared, stopping Aed and Mageen in their tracks.

'What is this infamy? Who are you to treat my daughter so?' Before Aed and Mageen were able to give any explanations they were surrounded by Godmund's men and borne away. It was all too much for Rowena and she fainted clean away in his arms.

When she awoke it was to find that she was in a huge bed, swaddled with furs. A woman moving around the bedchamber immediately came to her and gave her some water before asking after her health. Then she went and brought Godmund to her, and they spent the next few hours catching up on each other's lives and adventures.

Rowena looked at the thick red fringe tinged with grey on his forehead. He swept it aside to reveal the serpent-shaped blemish that matched the one on her wrist. She smiled. 'No one could dispute our kinship.'

But Godmund was sombre. After learning what had been happening to her he was stiff with anger. 'The dwarves will be punished,' he promised. 'There have been many tales of their thievery and murders, but they have been clever at averting discovery, moving around frequently. And the Irish woman will be sent away so she will be unable to hurt you again. A life of hard servitude is no more than she deserves.' He paused. 'As for Sigurd, I have another punishment in mind for him.'

'What happened between you and my mother?' she asked curiously, for he had hardly mentioned Grainne since their meeting.

His expression was grim. 'I was a stranger, an interloper in her land. I saw her and wanted her, so I took her. It is not the way gentle bred maidens imagine they will be treated, so she ran away from me.' He sighed. 'I am older now and the world has worn off some rough edges, but I loved her more than I have loved anyone since.'

'I know what it is to love like that.' Her eyes filled and Godmund's sad gaze fell on her agonised face with pity, for she had told him about Leif. But feeling his strength she shook off her self-pity; she would be strong like her father. 'And what of Sigurd?' She asked guardedly, wondering why he hated her father so.

Godmund ground his teeth angrily. 'I suppose he had reason to hate me, but he should have sought me out like a man, not used my daughter so.'

He paced around the room and Rowena took in the kindly features, the huge shoulders, with delight. He was hers and no one could part them now. 'Father,' she said quietly, breaking into his thoughts, 'will you not tell me what happened?'

Godmund paced some more before stopping at the foot

of her bed. 'I fell in love with Sigurd's mother. She was unhappy and Thorkel treated her worse than the lowest thrall. She was a good woman but she was ripe for love, and I gave it to her.'

'I see.' Rowena strove to take in the news. 'But she died?'

He gave a small groan. 'Aye, we decided to run away together, taking the child. But we were captured by Estonian pirates.' He swallowed hard and his eyes misted as cruel memories were forced to the surface. 'Helgi's heart gave out. All I had left was the boy. I swore to protect him with my last breath, but we were separated and I never saw him again until years later when he was almost a man.' His eyes were haunted. 'He recognised me and came at me with much anger. I refused to fight him, but what can a man do when faced with a battleaxe but defend himself? Unfortunately I disfigured him, you know the rest.'

He was at her side and she took his hand in hers, pressing it to give him her support. 'Oh, father.'

'I have loved but two women in my life and brought naught but death or sorrow to them both. And so I live here now, in your mother's land, converted to her faith, hoping her God will forgive me.'

Rowena soothed him with gentle words. They held each other until the door knocked and Godmund went to see who it was. When he returned it was with a mysterious smile. 'If you are feeling better, daughter, I suggest you repair to the hall. I shall await you there.'

He left her in the capable hands of a kindly maidservant, who gowned her like a queen. Her hair was braided and upon her head was placed a gold circlet. Her shift was neatly pleated, her tunic of the finest wool in a rich blue that fell in folds around her, accentuating every curve and detail of her lovely body. The jewels she wore were the richest she had ever seen. Thus attired, she made her way to the hall, intrigued by her father's sudden change of mood.

Godmund's hall thronged with his people, who nodded gleefully to see their beloved chieftain reunited with his lovely daughter. It was full of the treasures he had brought from abroad and Rowena admired them as she glided up to him, the perfumes of the east wafting around her.

He held his hand out and greeted her with a kiss. 'Rowena,' he began, a frisson of excitement in his voice, 'there is someone here to see you.'

Rowena frowned slightly, wondering who it could be, for no one knew where she was. But when the golden-haired man with the bluest eyes she had ever seen, walked up the aisle of the hall towards her, a broad smile on his face, she went to him on feet as light as angel's wings. 'Leif,' she breathed, as he embraced her in powerful arms, 'I don't understand.'

'I thought over what had happened between us,' he replied, hugging her close, 'and I decided I acted too hastily, so I returned to Iceland only to find you gone and Sigurd set off after you.' He looked to her father, who nodded and he went on. 'Only Sigurd's boat was caught in bad weather and he was lost at sea.'

Rowena's head was spinning with all this new information, and seeing her dilemma Godmund whispered something to Leif, who led her from the hall and back to her bedchamber.

Standing in the beautiful chamber Godmund had given over to his daughter Leif kissed her fingers. 'Forgive me, my darling, I should have known better than to believe any of those things you told me in the barn. I should have realised you were only thinking of saving me from Sigurd's wrath.'

'But how did you locate me?' she asked, afraid she would wake up and find herself back in the camp of the dwarves.

'Algitha told me of your plans. And as I knew Godmund I decided to stop off at his hall first.' He smiled and her stomach seemed to somersault. 'But I never suspected to find you so quickly.'

She led him to her bed. 'It was fated,' she whispered, slipping out of her blue smock and kirtle, reclining on the large bed, welcoming her lover.

'And will you miss Sigurd?' he asked uneasily, shedding his clothes to reveal the corded strength she was unable to resist.

Rowena shook her head, a wicked smile lighting her face. 'No, but I do like a man to conquer me. A little rough with the smooth is good for the soul.'

She giggled as Leif's cock reared and he lifted her from the bed, flipping her over his lap. 'Then, shall we see just how pink we can make this naughty little bottom?'

Backlist titles available from Chimera

1903931614	BloodLust Chronicles – Charity	*Ashton*
1901388492	Rectory of Correction	*Virosa*
1901388751	Lucy	*Culber*
1903931649	Jennifer Rising	*Del Monico*
1901388751	Out of Control	*Miller*
1903931657	Dream Captive	*Gabriel*
1901388190	Destroying Angel	*Hastings*
1903931665	Suffering the Consequences	*Stern*
1901388131	All for her Master	*O'Connor*
1903931703	Flesh & Blood	*Argus*
1901388204	The Instruction of Olivia	*Allen*
190393169X	Fate's Victim	*Beaufort*
1901388115	Space Captive	*Hughes*
1903931711	The Bottom Line	*Savage*
190138800X	Sweet Punishment	*Jameson*
1903931754	Alice – Lost Soul	*Surreal*
1901388123	Sold into Service	*Tanner*
1901388018	Olivia and the Dulcinites	*Allen*
1903931746	Planet of Pain	*Bradbury*
1901388298	Betty Serves the Master	*Tanner*
1901388425	Sophie and the Circle of Slavery	*Culber*
190393172X	Saxon Slave	*Benedict*
1901388344	Shadows of Torment	*McLachlan*
1901388263	Selina's Submission	*Lewis*
1903931762	Devil's Paradise	*Beaufort*
1901388077	Under Orders	*Asquith*
1903931789	Bad Girls	*Stern*
1901388042	Thunder's Slaves	*Leather*
1903931797	Notebooks of the Young Wife	*Black*
1901388247	Total Abandon	*Anderssen*
1903931770	Bondmaiden	*Bradbury*
1901388409	Domination Inc.	*Leather*
1903931800	Painful Consequences	*North*
1901388735	Managing Mrs Burton	*Aspen*
1903931819	Bound for the Top	*Dean*
1901388603	Sister Murdock's House of Correction	*Angelo*
1901388026	Belinda – Cruel Passage West	*Anonymous*

All **Chimera** titles are available from your local bookshop or newsagent, or direct from our mail order department. Please send your order with your credit card details, a cheque or postal order (made payable to *Chimera Publishing Ltd*) to: **Chimera Publishing Ltd., Readers' Services, PO Box 152, Waterlooville, Hants, PO8 9FS**. Or call our **24 hour telephone/fax credit card hotline: +44 (0)23 92 646062** (Visa, Mastercard, Switch, JCB and Solo only).

UK & BFPO - Aimed delivery within three working days.
- A delivery charge of £3.00.
- An item charge of £0.20 per item, up to a maximum of five items.

For example, a customer ordering two items for delivery within the UK will be charged £3.00 delivery + £0.40 items charge, totalling a delivery charge of £3.40. The maximum delivery cost for a UK customer is £4.00. Therefore if you order more than five items for delivery within the UK you will not be charged more than a total of £4.00 for delivery.

Western Europe - Aimed delivery within five to ten working days.
- A delivery charge of £3.00.
- An item charge of £1.25 per item.

For example, a customer ordering two items for delivery to W. Europe, will be charged £3.00 delivery + £2.50 items charge, totalling a delivery charge of £5.50.

USA - Aimed delivery within twelve to fifteen working days.
- A delivery charge of £3.00.
- An item charge of £2.00 per item.

For example, a customer ordering two items for delivery to the USA, will be charged £3.00 delivery + £4.00 item charge, totalling a delivery charge of £7.00.

Rest of the World - Aimed delivery within fifteen to twenty-two working days.
- A delivery charge of £3.00.
- An item charge of £2.75 per item.

For example, a customer ordering two items for delivery to the ROW, will be charged £3.00 delivery + £5.50 item charge, totalling a delivery charge of £8.50.

For a copy of our free catalogue please write to

**Chimera Publishing Ltd
Readers' Services
PO Box 152
Waterlooville
Hants
PO8 9FS**

or e-mail us at
info@chimera-online.co.uk

or purchase from our range of superbly erotic titles at
www.chimera-online.co.uk

All titles £6.99

The full range of our titles are also available as downloadable e-books at our website

www.chimera-online.co.uk

Chimera Publishing Ltd
PO Box 152
Waterlooville
Hants
PO8 9FS

www.chimera-online.co.uk
www.chimerabooks.co.uk
www.chimerasextoys.co.uk
www.chimeralingerie.co.uk

***

Sales and Distribution in the USA and Canada

Client Distribution Services, Inc
193 Edwards Drive
Jackson
TN 38301
USA

***

Sales and Distribution in Australia

Dennis Jones & Associates Pty Ltd
19a Michellan Ct
Bayswater
Victoria
Australia 3153